ACCLAIM FOR

"Both a thrilling romance an   ıl
tour de force is for anyone v

—Foreword Reviews

BEST FIRST BOOK SILVER MEDAL
—Independent Book Publishers Association
Benjamin Franklin Awards (Fiction)

BOOK OF THE YEAR FINALIST
—Foreword Reviews INDIEFAB Awards (Romance)

"A thought-provoking blend of romance, poetry and adventure, *The Poet's Secret* satisfies on many levels. Elegant prose explores the infinite promise of art, while a quickening pace unveils the story of star-crossed lovers, whose union feels timeless and exceptional at the same time. More than just a good read. This is a book to savor."

—Kim Fay, Edgar Award Finalist
author of *The Map of Lost Memories*

"Golden Heart® Finalist"
—Romance Writers of America (Romantic Suspense)

"A beautifully crafted gem of a story."
—Dirk Cussler, best selling co-author of *Dirk Pitt*
adventure novels, with Clive Cussler

"A richly detailed novel suffused with exotic mystery and romance."

—Judy Reeves, writing provocateur
and author of *Wild Women, Wild Voices*

THE POET'S
SECRET

THE POET'S SECRET

KENNETH ZAK

PUBLISHING

THE POET'S SECRET © 2015 by Kenneth Zak
Second Edition © 2016 Kenneth Zak
All Rights Reserved, Penju Publishing.

 First trade paperback published in the United States of America by Penju Publishing.
Penju Publishing and Penju logo are trademarks of Penju Publishing.

Please visit the author's website: www.kennethzak.com

Cover design by Randy Gibbs
Book layout by Golden Ratio Design: goldenratio.anthonybonds.com
Author & Diver Photographs by Bill Livingston

ISBN 978-0-9903200-0-5

Printed in the United States of America

 Penju Publishing is proud to be a member of 1% for the Planet. Members donate one percent of their sales to one or more of the over 1,500 environmental and sustainability charities across the globe who participate in this program.

The Poet's Secret is also available as an eBook

For Kyona

Let me hold this breath
Forever

CHAPTER 1

A flicker lost beyond myth
danced in those eyes
like a nascent sea
of rippled reflection.

Silence.

Elia stood behind the mahogany lectern. Her sweaty palms gripped into worn grooves left behind by the hundreds who had stood there before. She huddled over the words she had just read aloud, as if trying to protect a faint flame from a threatening wind.

A tear welled up. She cherished the imagery of that final stanza, savoring it like a wine's lingering finish. She pondered over the meaning behind "a flicker lost beyond myth." What flicker? Why lost? And beyond what myth was it lost? What did the poet intend? What did it mean to her? Was it the same? Could it be? Five simple words, yet for her a tantalizing puzzle.

She pictured a fresh sea of rippled reflection. This was certainly a familiar, more concrete image, yet it still beckoned another question. What was being reflected? But most of all Elia wondered what those eyes looked like, what kind of eyes could elicit such poetry. All this she imagined. All this she craved. Her grip loosened. But even after the slight echo of her voice faded, she remained transported.

Words could do this to her.

Falling strands of auburn hair framed her face, serving as blinders to everything but that page. At a bar, a drunken art student had once whispered into her ear that she was an island princess worthy of Gauguin's gaze. But she didn't believe him because it wasn't written down anywhere.

Her slender fingers caressed the wrinkled paper from which she had read. She handled the page like a hallowed manuscript. But other than the handwritten words on the yellow sheet, nothing about it appeared unique.

"And?" said a man's voice.

"It moves me," she said.

She barely raised her voice a decibel. There seemed too much to say, but all of it speculation. Her measured cadence and monotone commanded attention.

"We see that, but how?"

"A loss of hope, but more, a loss of memory of what hope and love and desire ever felt like. All of it, perished beyond myth, the final frontier, allegory, gone. The author is not just apathetic, but hollow to the core, emptied of imagination. And then, something—no, someone—resurrects him. Something in those eyes revives the majesty of hope, and thus a newborn sea of rippled reflection."

"Yet so quickly?" he asked.

"Simple flicks of the brush. Seemingly random, and then—"

"An infinite seascape," offered a fellow grad student from a nearby chair.

Elia knew his voice well, having heard it before in this class and several others. He was the one who always sat near her. He was the one who listened to her. She never looked him directly in the eye. Yet she could sketch his every feature from memory.

Deep set hazel eyes. Pale skin. She even noticed on those days he forgot to shave.

Something in his voice bolstered her.

"Exactly," she said.

Her eyes lifted from the page, but still she didn't look at him. Instead, she stared toward the back of the sparse classroom, toward Professor Weitzel.

"The author?" the professor asked.

"Beck."

Professor Weitzel leaned forward in his rickety armchair. The old wooden frame groaned. He pushed his bifocals over the notch on his crooked nose and folded his arms across his bland, faded blue oxford button-down. Afternoon sun streaked through a bank of windows to his left, casting his pallid face with a sort of chiaroscuro, all light and shade with barely any hint of color.

"Excuse me?" the professor asked.

"Cameron Beck," she said.

"I don't think so," he replied.

"Yes."

Her answer filled with confidence.

"And where did you unearth the reticent boy wonder?" he asked.

"The Village Poet," she said.

The professor nodded.

She frequented the offbeat campus pub, as did most other grad students cloistered in their tight literary community. Every now and then an author showed up and read something, usually as part of some book junket. But Professor Weitzel's skepticism didn't surprise her. She knew the professor, or anyone for that matter, had good reason to doubt her claim. The poem, if truly written by Beck, would be the first to surface in ten years.

Professor Weitzel snapped his fingers.

"Back to life again, just like that?"

"I don't think he ever left," she said.

"Just fallen mute this last decade?" he asked.

She wobbled. A knot twisted in her stomach. Her grip on the lectern tightened again. There are defining moments in life, moments when fear and doubt fall aside to clarity and purpose. She had read about it plenty of times. But this was different. This moment felt like hers.

Only days earlier, upon hearing the poem recited by the bearded man on that otherwise mundane Tuesday night, had the notion first occurred to her. Could that really be Beck? He looked so different than the outdated book jacket photo, different than she imagined.

The dim light inside the Village Poet hadn't helped. The pub as always was a web of shadows. Flickering candles within honeycombed orbs dotted the tables huddled around the podium. She had been sitting at the bar, nursing a tepid glass of Torrontes, a cheap Argentine white wine, when the man had begun to read. Anybody could get up and read almost any night. But Cameron Beck wasn't just anybody. Ever since that night, she had become consumed by the idea. Was that Beck? That question had swelled into a storm she could no longer ignore. Three days later, she thought of nothing else.

"I'm going to find him," she said.

The knot in her stomach loosened.

It was the final hours of spring semester. She had all summer to roam the globe in search of her human thesis. But peering over his bifocals, Professor Weitzel still looked cynical.

"An interview with a ghost poet? What next, the holy grail?" he asked.

She felt him studying her. Elia was one of only a dozen master's candidates completing the first year of Professor Weitzel's advanced lit seminar. She wasn't one to just blaze through titles or pontificate about prose. She drilled deep to enter the page like few of her peers. But she had also heard the whispers. She knew she was considered an odd bird.

And she did little to dissuade such beliefs. Each time she read in the cramped seminar room tucked at the end of the desolate wing of the redbrick university hall, in every selection she made, and with every word that parted her lips, she soared within the essence of the piece. And at the tender age of twenty-one, Elia had a feeling that she had already become one of the professor's favorites. In the world of literature she was wise well beyond her years. It was off the page she felt hapless.

"He's out there still," she said.

"No Keats, Browning or Wordsworth for you. Too obvious, I suppose. Not even Neruda this go around. Instead, Cameron Beck, local prodigy, the romantic revivalist's poster child after just one dog-eared volume," said the professor.

"And soon in a theater near you," quipped a classmate like a carnival barker.

Stifled laughter filtered through the room.

"Ahh yes, *Secrets of Odysseus*. Ninety-nine odes to one anonymous muse," the professor said.

Elia straightened. Her shoulders rolled back.

"The arc of love," she said.

"And the ever-burning question, who was she?" the professor said, echoing the decade of speculation over Beck's muse's identity.

"I'd bet that she's married, that's for sure," said the boy from the nearby chair.

Elia had long suspected the same.

"Shall I compare thee to Petrarch?" said a blond, freckle-faced classmate with hands clasped over her heart.

"Wait just a minute. Solitary allegiance to one lover still sells, even five hundred years later," said another guy sporting a goatee.

"In search of the reclusive poet, the Howard Hughes of modern American verse," said the jester.

"Perhaps he just died of a broken heart," said the girl.

"Gay," offered another.

"Playing checkers with Salinger," said the beatnik.

It had been over a decade now, but a kaleidoscope of mystery still surrounded Beck's sole published work, with only his languishing words to serve as a guide. Only words. But his words had sustained scrutiny. They survived. Even amidst the fading controversy, *Secrets of Odysseus* still flared through many reading groups, which was how Elia had come upon the work.

"So where do you think he is?" asked the familiar voice, the one she felt so drawn to. He stroked the damp hair behind his ear. It was a habit she secretly adored.

"Words of love, words in love. Jazzy splatterings. Pollock kneeling over the page," said the carnival barker.

"I always thought his poetry almost Mondrianesque, sharp contrasts in imagery," said the freckled girl.

"No, no, no. Renoir's gardens," said the beatnik, "Beck's an Impressionist."

Their playful riffing relaxed her.

Even the professor couldn't refrain. "A palette filled with obsession to one and one alone, but the name forever unknown."

While Elia couldn't blame them, she refused to bend. Like a phoenix, Beck had risen again into the public eye. Just months earlier she had read about a South American director buying the film rights to *Secrets of Odysseus,* outbidding several independent studios. Film rights to a book of poetry, unheard of.

She was astounded, yet it pleased her. The film rights to Beck's collection of poems sold at auction for two hundred and fifty thousand dollars. She had counted the zeros twice to be sure. The article reported that Beck's agent had confirmed only that the money had been wired to an overseas bank. A quarter of a million dollars paid for a book of poems written by a ghost poet lauding an unknown lover. And to that highest bidder passed creative license to flesh out a story, reveal an identity and divine a resolution.

That was the one part Elia didn't like: a fictionalized closure now within the control of someone other than the author. That part didn't feel right.

Yet Beck remained cloaked in silence.

She knew that was what made her claim so startling. Why would he finally reappear, and do so incognito?

"If it's his verse, when was it written?" asked the carnival barker, who now feigned a terrible German accent.

"Maybe this is part of *Secrets*? Or a prologue?" said the fair-haired girl.

"Perhaps even a budding interest in another," said the beatnik, stroking his wispy beard.

"Only Beck knows for sure," Elia said.

She held her own views about the final poems in *Secrets*. She believed that, like all great romances, the author and his muse were destined for doom, at least on earth. But she also believed there could be no *other*. Not like the one Beck had written about.

"What did they say at the Village Poet? Beck just dropped this by one day?" asked the professor.

"Well—" she began.

But he pressed.

"This man has any medium to air his words."

"And he chooses the simplest, just like he chooses the efficiency of a sound when that will do, a word when just a word will supplant a phrase, and a phrase that will speak volumes," she said.

She felt Professor Weitzel studying her as he combed his lanky fingers through his thinning gray hair. The class silenced, awaiting his verdict. He let out a long sigh.

"Touché. If you're serious, you'll need to speak to Dean Baltutis."

"Baltutis? Why?" she asked.

"Tell him what you've found. He'll explain."

As if on cue, century-old bells rang three times from the nearby campus tower in Orton Hall. A fog of baritone echoes rolled across the grassy oval, crept up the old brick building's skeleton and rippled through her. Her classmates began to stuff notebooks into backpacks.

But Elia remained poised at the lectern.

She stared toward Professor Weitzel and nodded before stepping away to collect her things. Without another word she walked out of the classroom. She looked at no one, not even the favorite boy, whom she felt watching her as she left.

Exiting Page Hall, she crossed a universe of green blades that tickled her toes through the openings on her sandals. She hardly noticed. She climbed the cement steps to Hayes Hall, past pungent geraniums in full bloom, but barely smelled a thing. Her sandals clapped across speckled granite floors. She was nearly deaf to the sound.

The spell broke only when she knocked on the door to the office of Dean Lawrence Baltutis.

CHAPTER 2

You marvel
As if it is some divine blessing
To feel so deeply
To give so freely
To so completely crave another
Lost in time
With just a look
And to know passion.

Alas
It is but a tempestuous curse
To be so filled
Life's brim overflowing
All the while knowing
It shall leave you
Hollow, alone, and naked
Shorn of love's lustrous coat.

One week later, Cameron Beck wrote these words intending them to be his last.

Now he stood alone, perched atop a cliff. Sinewy toes clasped like talons onto the ledge of an ancient lava flow. His calves flexed against a tropical gale that jostled his gray-flecked hair. Island palm fronds swayed in a brooding rhythm.

Cast above him was a celestial audience. The midnight sky filled with every last star attendant for his farewell. Just weeks earlier, he might have seized upon the idea, convinced he mattered somehow in the universal mix of things, that he too had a peculiar place of importance in this cosmos. And he would have challenged himself for days, weeks, and even months to reveal that essence. Sometimes pondering for hours over the slightest of sounds, stringing together words braided by passion, but not tonight.

On this night, hopelessness vanquished inspiration.

Wishless stars fizzled across the horizon.

Below him, waves battered the rocks in a hypnotic cadence as if goading him: *just do it*. Whitecaps lunged over a distant outcropping, their peaks glistening under the moon's glow before retreating into the black opal whirlpool.

The water seemed infinite.

Even the sea seemed to mock his insignificance.

He imagined howls of island gods synchronized to the drumbeat of his heart. Their restless chants grew stronger and stronger. He couldn't discern the language, but he knew what they wanted.

Sacrifice.

Behind him, along the serpentine path he'd trekked to this precipice, lay the last shreds of his earthly existence. Five paces back were his tattered khakis. He'd parted ways with his sandals twenty yards earlier, their balding treads worn through to the sole. And outside the thatched-roof hut just beyond he had tossed his ashen white T-shirt into the clay.

He stood fully revealed and wavering upon the edge of his world.

The night before, he had buried his most-prized possession, the silver watch she had given him, just off to the side of the hut. He marked the grave with three rocks. Culled from a quarry seemingly foreign to the island, the rocks looked to have fallen from the moon. At least that is what he thought as he bedded them into the dirt above the treasure.

Each half the size of a grown man's palm, the stones were as pasty as the skin of his own forearm. The spot that, no matter how hard the man, remains so soft. The same spot that once pillowed her head as she slept. The same spot that, so many years later, still reminded him of her.

Depositing the watch into its earthen grave he glanced one last time at its inscription: *'til the end of time.*

Until tomorrow then, he thought.

A tired grin broke across his lips as he imagined the puzzled look on some native child digging up the watch one day, perhaps cherishing it forever after as a lucky trinket. Only such innocence could wash away the curse it had brought upon him, or so he believed.

Inside the hut, on a small table, rested a half-empty bottle of his favorite red wine brought over in his duffle bag from the States, its dislodged cork embedded in the sandy floor. Next to the wine bottle a squat, maroon-rimmed glass knocked on its side, a pen and some paper.

Blank paper.

He considered if only for an instant leaving a note, but then decided against it. He wanted to disgorge his heart and place it on that paper. Anything less seemed a mockery. And he feared that even attempting to reduce his suffering into words might threaten his resolve.

Words, his chosen tools, now seemed vague, hollow and foreign. He would have none of it. Flickering just left of center on the table, a candle's dancing glow spread the last silent spark of light.

Still life reveals so much.

Cameron spent days nestled away in that hilltop hut, isolated from any hint of the villagers clustered around the island's tiny bay. Only Isabella, the matriarch of the sleepy paradise, had shared words with him upon his recent return, and even then very few. She spotted him late one morning stepping off the puddle-jumper after it splashed like a wayward albatross into the bay. Expecting only the mail and some overdue provisions, she had watched the plane sputter toward the swaying dock.

Seeing Cameron again made her heart race.

Isabella kissed her charm twice. She brushed the talisman across her chest, crossed it left to right and right to left over her heart, then kissed it once more. Shaped like a whisk broom, the charm's jet-black strands, bundled at one end by three emerald beads, tickled her lips.

But Cameron looked different, even from four stone-skips away. His normally square shoulders slanted. His gait was hesitant. His sunglasses were intact, but she sensed him hiding behind the oval shades. And she knew to trust that instinct. The entire island trusted it as well. Isabella knew things. She just did. The islanders called Isabella a *seer*. The gift, if one dared call it that, had passed from her mother, who had died giving birth to her.

While Isabella could often see what might come to others, she could never foretell her own future. She had tried, but nothing ever came. She had long wondered whether her mother had seen her own fate. Eventually, Isabella smothered that wonder with a belief in a mother so filled with love that she gave her life knowing she would never hear her baby's first cry.

For Isabella, it was more important to believe than to *see*.

But she still approached Cameron wanting to see his eyes. He stared at the sky in an awkward pose, as if for the first time considering the enormous cerulean dome overhead. Daylight appeared a stranger.

His dark baseball hat only highlighted the stark paleness of his forehead and cheeks. Compared to the island dwellers, he looked like a vampire caught after sunrise. His faded pants frayed at the cuff. His T-shirt, worn nearly skin-thin, did little to veil the angular, almost emaciated torso underneath. Slung over his shoulder, the green duffle bag looked to be at best only half-full. She knew that he always traveled light. Yet she sensed something simmering within this walking shadow of her friend, something more than even she might divine.

She bustled down the dock toward the plane. Six gold bracelets clamored about her thick right arm jutting out from her tangerine sundress, seven about the left. Like a pumpkin wobbling under a floppy straw hat, she nearly consumed Cameron before his hidden pupils turned from the sky.

She sang out to him in her rich West Indies accent.

"Of all the lost paradises you come back to mine?"

"Bella."

Cameron had always called her Bella, right from their very first meeting so many years ago.

"Come here, Mister Cam."

Her voice purred like a kitten on catnip.

She engulfed him in her thick arms. He even felt different. Pulling back, she looked him in the face. Her eyes reflected in his sunglasses, sparkling like coffee beans in the sun.

"So, this is your triumphant return?"

"What's that?" he asked.

Releasing him, she squinted.

"Darling, we get newspapers here too. Maybe three months late, but we still get 'em."

"Yeah, but you never used to read 'em," he said.

Isabella let out a hearty laugh.

"Well, since you gone, ain't much else to do."

"I bet."

He feigned a smile.

"Come on, we wake Paco and have a drink," she said.

"Not now, Bella, I need to rest a bit."

His smile faded just as fast.

A calypso melody breezed from the village.

"This afternoon?" she asked.

"No, I need some time, couple of days or more," he said.

Isabella bit her plump lower lip.

"Take the star loft. I'll tell Paco leave you be for now, but don't keep us waiting too long."

"I won't," he said.

She squeezed his hand.

"Promise?"

"Sure."

"Tell me one thing."

Isabella never went quietly.

"Watcha gonna do with all that money?" she asked.

"*You* probably already know."

"Nah."

She shook her big head back and forth, smiling the whole time.

"Give it to you," he said.

"No sirree, don't want it, got what I need right here," she said.

She opened her arms to engulf the bay.

Two noddy terns glided by, their dark wings extended upward. Dangling yellow feet skimmed the water before landing.

"Truly, you ain't figured that?" she asked.

"I'm gonna hike before it gets too hot," he said.

"You go on, love. I'll send up some food."

"Thanks, Bella."

He started down the dock toward shore, then stopped. Turning, he stared at her. "I mean it. I don't know what I would—"

"Shush," she said.

She beamed at him. "I know you mean it. You always do."

She shook her head again and watched him walk away.

Isabella turned toward the seaplane. She put her hands on her ample hips. The gold bracelets slid to her wrists, stacking up halfway to her elbows. Her sandaled foot thumped against the dock planks.

The pilot methodically unloaded three wooden crates and stacked them on the dock. Like everything on the island, there appeared no rush.

She knew the pilot by his nickname, Falcon. She didn't know his real name, nor did she ever bother to ask. The constantly shifting winds necessitated his swooping landings, but from the village the plane's final trajectory often looked akin to a meteor plummeting from the sky. Falcon had made these islands hops for nearly a decade, ever since washing out of the commercial airlines courtesy of two failed drug tests. That much he had confessed to Isabella over a half-dozen Red Stripes many years ago.

Isabella didn't always pay on time. But that was okay. Falcon rarely delivered on time. Long ago they had reached a tacit agreement. Falcon plunked his airboat into her bay on a haphazard schedule and they settled things like they always did on the island, over a couple of cold beers at Paco's *cantina*.

Years ago, after several rounds of three-way barter, Falcon ended up the owner of a corner table at Paco's, along with an open tab, a silver spider earring he wore in his left lobe and half-ownership in Chuey, Isabella's pet monkey. Isabella in turn got a credit account for her deliveries, which she regularly drew upon. Paco on his end got stow-away rights to and from the States—a perk he never used. Just as important, Paco also dumped his half-interest in Chuey.

Ever since, Falcon chided Isabella that he boasted stateside, "I got half a monkey on Mataki," while Paco happily denied any interest in the mischievous fur-ball when Chuey went on a banana rampage.

"Not my monkey," became Paco's stock response.

Far from a perfect balance sheet, things on the island just sort of worked themselves out. Isabella hoped that was why Cameron had come back to them, to work something out, but her gut told her otherwise.

Hunched over, Falcon was unloading the last crate of goods when Isabella's shadow eclipsed the sun. Without looking up, he wiped the sweat from his brow.

"That's perfect, don't move 'til I'm done," he drawled.

"What's with our boy?" she asked.

"Dunno."

"Well, what he tell ya?"

Falcon shrugged.

"Nothing," he said.

"The whole flight?" she asked.

Falcon craned up to catch her glare.

"Yeah, the whole damn flight not a word, just stared at the big blue."

Even when excited, Falcon's words still fell in a slow drip, a remnant from his youth amidst the Florida everglades.

"That's not him," she said.

"Damn right."

Isabella looked back over her shoulder. Cameron had already vanished onto the path leading up the hillside.

"You didn't ask nothing?"

"Hell yeah, I asked, but he said he was tired, tired of talking and tired of being talked to, said he needed to float off in himself for awhile."

"Float off in his self?" she asked.

"Something like that, clear enough," he said.

"That's all?"

Falcon straightened up.

"Isabella, just once in a while you gotta respect a man's right to shut the hell up."

"Don't you curse at me," she said. "Well, I'll give him couple of days, but I'm keeping my eye on him."

Falcon chuckled.

"Okay, mama bird."

Paco woke just past lunchtime to open the *cantina*. By then, Isabella had finished stocking the newly arrived provisions in her market. And Falcon, well, he kept no schedule, airborne or otherwise. So, true to form, he sat down at his favorite table, popped the cap off a cold Red Stripe and extended his trip at least for the night. Isabella arrived before his second sip and pulled up a chair. Soon Paco brought over a stool and the island council convened, the three of them stewing over Cameron's return.

Hid away in his mountaintop sanctuary, Cameron had told nobody of his plan. Hell, he never before had even considered the notion. But recent events had snuffed out his last bit of hope, simultaneously spawning the awful idea. It was the last option he could fathom in a suddenly empty existence. It had first appeared as a nightmare. Now the idea crept into his waking thoughts and refused to let go.

He knew the timing would seem ironic.

The clamor of late had resurrected his meager celebrity. His agent hadn't stopped calling. Outdated images had resurfaced in the trade papers. But when he saw those old photos of himself, he didn't even recognize that face.

The window of opportunity to go underground, to hold his breath until it all passed by, had slammed shut. That he knew. The island offered him his only solace. Perhaps only for a moment, but just the same he needed something.

Space.

After a decade of canvassing most of the globe, Cameron craved space for the first time in a long while. Life felt like a python clenched around his chest. He needed to fill his lungs again with familiar air. Maybe if he could find enough space he could just vanish into it, forever. Maybe he could make the thought of her go away.

This island seemed the right place. Their first place together might as well be his last.

CHAPTER 3

Summer streams
Incandescent, ribbons blue
endless swells
celestial, tides anew.

Mirage to my desert
Venus awoke, imbued
a wellspring beyond thirst,
nothing left to do

. . . but drink.

Elia knocked on the faded oak doorframe. With each rap the door's window rattled in its loose casing. Stenciled across the frosted window was the name "Professor L. Baltutis," and just a few inches below that the word "Literature."

Elia loved that word.

She was particularly fond of the third prong from Webster's definition of literature: *writings having excellent form or expression and expressing ideas of permanent or universal interest.* The concept of permanent or universal interest captivated her. Literature captured the quintessence of all humanity. Literature was all-powerful. Elia envisioned herself its humble, fleeting disciple.

A voice shouted, "Come in."

She twisted the worn brass knob. It was cool to her touch even on a warm Ohio spring day. The latch slipped and then clicked open. She walked into the Dean of Literature's third-floor, corner office.

She had visited the office several times before. Each time she had liked it. She liked places with books and there were plenty here. After the three university libraries, Dean Baltutis's office was her favorite place on campus.

The walls were lined with shelves crammed with volumes of all sizes, colors and conditions, some literally falling apart at the seams, others frozen in a deep, pristine hibernation. Hardbacks, paperbacks, manuscripts and screenplays filled the room. A first edition of Jules Verne's *Une ville flottante* was locked behind a glass-enclosed bookshelf. Interspersed in the rare cracks between books were stacks of term papers, magazines with yellowed tabs and newspaper clippings. She wondered just how many words, each a precious jewel in an *expression of permanent or universal interest,* lay within this vault.

She liked the idea of walking into a room filled with books, blindly pulling out a volume and being transported into another world, taking flight upon a jet stream of words to travel anywhere and everywhere, including those places within.

She sniffed in a deep breath. Musty leather, parchment and stale binding glue scented the room. That smell comforted her.

The oval ceiling lights were off. Afternoon sunlight filled the office through a double set of grand windows. Infinite dust particles danced in the sunlight. But in Dean Baltutis's office there seemed even more words than dust.

The bottom windows were open. White flecks of paint polka-dotted the window handles. A hint of sweet lilac floated upon a humid breeze that meandered through the room, cutting the smell of stale books. A fly buzzed across the office before escaping out a window.

She approached the weathered cherry desk that anchored the room. Its bear-claw feet rested upon uneven oak planks. Elia treaded lightly, but the cranky floorboards betrayed her every step. Beyond the desk a dusty credenza pressed flush against the wall. An old desktop computer bulked at its center.

A tight barrel of a man was hunched in front of that computer with his back to her.

"Dean Baltutis," she said.

Graying yellow hair fell over the back collar of his checkered, short-sleeve shirt. Black glasses propped atop his head. She waited for him to turn, but he appeared oblivious to her presence. He continued to tap away at his keyboard.

"Just a second," he said.

He raised a thick forearm as if signaling a right turn. She waited as he flicked a few final keystrokes. He swiveled around in his armchair. He smiled and stood.

"Ms. Aloundra."

Elia felt welcomed by the warmth in his voice, no doubt earned from her having aced one of his classes wherein they had spent an entire semester dissecting Gabriel García Márquez's *Love in the Time of Cholera*. Elia felt that even that was not enough time to study such a masterpiece. To her, Florentino Ariza's closing reply, which he had held ready for over half a century, was one of the most powerful lines of dialog ever written. She had already reread *Cholera* since taking Professor Baltutis's class, probably for the fourth time. Yet each and every time, and even though she knew it was coming, she always cried at Ariza's declaration of invincible love. It seemed perfect, but like all things perfect, unobtainable.

She had enrolled in a graduate course Dean Baltutis would teach in the fall, The Comparative Study of Literary Periods and Movements. He motioned for her to sit down, and waved toward two armchairs across from his desk. She paused. Both chairs were stacked with a disarray of papers that side-by-side looked like an awkward, unbalanced scale.

"Just put those on top of the others," he said.

By the way he said it, she figured he didn't know what was in either stack. She did so, leveling the imbalance when she sat down in the emptied chair. Professor Baltutis plopped back into his seat.

"What can I do for you?"

He clasped his hands in front of his chest. His forefingers pointed toward her, but his thumbs pressed against his sternum. Without fail he did this every time she sat before him. She next expected the head nods. Recognizing the tics of professors had become a bit of a grad school distraction.

"It's my thesis."

He nodded. "Isn't that for you and your advisor to discuss?"

"Yes, but—"

He cut her off and wagged a finger.

"Don't tell me Professor Weitzel's giving you trouble."

"No sir, not in the least."

"Good, because he can get crotchety."

His eyebrows crinkled. He shook his head. He looked pleased to invoke the Dean's privilege to criticize professors. His deviant grin reminded her of the Cheshire Cat. But she noted that grin in her periphery, because she avoided direct eye contact. It was an artifice she had perfected. Yet she could stare at a single page for an hour.

"He actually suggested I come see you," she said.

"All right then."

He perked up a bit. More nods.

"I've found something," she said.

Dean Baltutis tapped his finger on the desk.

"Do tell."

"A poem."

"Splendid, a poem," he said, and his voice trailed off before it rebounded an octave, "And?"

"I think the author is Cameron Beck," she said.

His eyebrows rose higher than mere intrigue warranted.

"Really, do you have it?" he asked.

This time it was Elia who nodded.

He perched forward in his chair. She opened her notebook and took out the yellow paper with the scribbled handwriting. Leaning across his cluttered desktop, she handed him the same scrap from which she had read in Professor Weitzel's seminar.

He pulled his thick glasses down over bloodshot eyes and perused the verse. She watched his face as he read. Then he stood up. He walked over to the window and gazed out toward the college oval. His head dropped down to the paper and he appeared to read it again. She heard him sigh.

He was hunched over the paper, much like she had been at the lectern in Professor Weitzel's class. He lifted his head and stared back out the window. She heard a distinct whisper.

"Cam."

"Excuse me?" she asked.

"Where did you find this?"

The floorboards creaked when he approached her.

"At a Village Poet reading a few days ago," she said.

She felt him examining her. It was the same feeling she had from Professor Weitzel.

"The Village Poet?" he asked.

"On Lane Avenue," she replied.

"Oh, I know the VP," he said.

His questions accelerated.

"Days ago? You said a reading?"

"I did."

"By?" he asked.

"A bearded man. He read this and walked out, leaving it at the podium. I couldn't believe it—I mean everyone saw him leave but nobody else seemed to notice that he left behind the poem. A few people were clapping. He headed toward the bar, I figured to maybe get a drink, but then right out the front door. It was weird. I mean the paper just sitting there. So I grabbed it, ran after him hoping to return it, maybe talk with him, but he was gone."

A hint of that same mischievous grin broke across the professor's face. He leaned toward her like a plant straining for light.

"What did he look like?"

"Late thirties, maybe forties—like I said, bearded, light brown hair, slim but fit, kind of angular."

"And his eyes?" he asked.

"Excuse me?"

"Did you see his eyes?"

"No," she said, "he was wearing tinted oval glasses, even inside. Strange."

He clasped his hands together so quickly they clapped, and then gnawed on a knuckle before he let out a deep exhale.

"Why don't you and I get some fresh air?" he asked.

Elia got up and tried to decipher how much of the leaning tower of term papers to replace in her chair.

"Never mind that," he said and led her out the door.

They walked down three flights of speckled granite, out of that redbrick building and across a grassy oval. The center of campus was crisscrossed with narrow sidewalks in every direction. He remained quiet while they walked and seemed almost somber. She sensed he was mulling over something and didn't dare interrupt his thoughts.

He chose their path, led her down a hill and guided her toward a shallow lake surrounded by old weeping willows.

Drooping branches caressed the stagnant water, kissing their reflections in a liquid mirror. Water lilies hugged the sandstone shoreline, the flat quarry-cut rock stacked in a basket-woven pattern. Moss tinted the creviced joints between stone. A bullfrog plunked into the lake as they walked past.

He again inspected the scrap of paper. Then he handed it back to her.

"Congratulations," he said.

"Excuse me?" she asked.

"Damn, you're right!" he said with a big smile.

The confidence in his voice caught her off guard.

"How are you so sure?"

"The handwriting," he said.

He motioned for her to sit on a bench by the lake's edge. He sat next to her. They huddled in patches of sun-speckled shade, draped beneath a willow branch. Mosquitoes buzzed about the lake's surface in a late spring ballet.

"You know his handwriting?" she asked.

"Yes I do," he said.

"But how?"

"Cam and I were close for a time."

"For a time?"

She felt like she was reading the first page of one of those special books, the kind she could never put down.

"For *the* time," he said.

He grinned.

"When he was writing *Secrets?*"

He laughed.

"That's the time all right. Showing up at the Poet—the bastard didn't even call me," he said.

He shook his head.

"You know he grew up not far from here, just off Chittenden," he said.

His grin faded. He looked over his shoulder toward Chittenden Avenue. "So you knew him," she said.

"You bet I did."

"Well?" she asked.

His face dropped at her question. But now she wanted to know everything.

"I may have been as close to him as almost anybody back then, except for—"

"The muse?"

"Of course," he sighed.

The professor leaned back on the bench. Elia sat upright.

"Go ahead, ask me," he said.

And without missing a beat she asked, "Who was she?"

She stared at his lips while he spoke.

"I didn't know. But I was the first to read what she inspired."

He paused before adding, "And it was me who pushed him to publish."

"Pushed him?" she asked.

"That wasn't Cam's motivation. I mean he damn well knew poetry should be shared. That's the raison d'etre of all writing; otherwise why the hell bother. But he was consumed. He once told me he didn't care if it got published during his lifetime, generations later, or ever. Just as well stash it all away."

"I cannot believe—"

"What? *Secrets* not published? He would have imploded without those words. Those poems kept him going. They sustained him after she left. For him it was survival."

Survival. That wasn't mentioned anywhere in Webster's definition of literature. But maybe it should be.

"So then how—"

"Once he purged, it was over, at least until the next flurry."

He paused. He stared at the lake and then added, "I sometimes regret what I did."

She had never before heard Dean Baltutis speak of Beck, and he certainly had never before been so candid with her.

"But why?" she asked.

"Success didn't drive him. Fame just cloistered him off. And the money simply bankrolled his disappearance. When I heard about the sale of the film rights I was sure I'd never see him again."

She followed his gaze toward the lake. A pocket of tadpoles nipped along the edge of a water lily, creating a palm-sized flutter in the otherwise perfect sheen. Shimmers folded into each other along the glassy surface.

"One man loses himself to a muse, another to regret. Maybe there's no difference," he said.

"But to the world's gain," Elia said.

"Hardly a fair trade," he muttered.

"What do you mean?"

"I never knew someone like Cam. He opened himself up, but he didn't care about approval or acclaim or anything. I couldn't understand it at the time. We were so young, all of us reaching for the brass ring. But he wrote for an audience of one. One lost to him. I could never do that. Instead, I discovered *him* and parlayed that friendship into my own meager entree into the literary world. Eventually I published and became a dean of literature, but I was forever basking in *his* afterglow. I ran in *his* circle. And the allure of *Secrets,* which I helped spawn, only drove my friend underground."

He glanced up at the dreary willow branches. She chased his gaze. A thought occurred to her. *A man filled with regret sits under a tree of sadness.* With those words she somehow had framed that moment.

She reached out and touched his forearm.

"He's still out there," she whispered.

A hesitant smile returned, absent the mischief.

"What the hell has he been doing?"

"I need to find him. I want to ask him these questions," she said.

"I don't know if that's such a good idea," he said.

He shook his head.

She touched his forearm.

"He read these words at the Village Poet, *in public,* for a reason."

"Perhaps," he said.

"I need to find him," she said. "Please, help me."

He glanced at the lake one last time.

She tried to imagine what he might be thinking.

Cardinals began to chirp.

Elia perceived a subtle silence between the staccato notes of their song, a silence filled with anticipation and expectation, a silence distinguishing stillness from action. She looked at the Dean of Literature. She now witnessed such a different man. She imagined him recalling his friend, the poet, drunk with emotion, flowing with creativity. She wondered whether he saw Beck laugh, and whether he felt Beck cry. He must miss him still. He must.

Somewhere in that silence, Dean Baltutis turned to Elia and said, "I'll tell you what I know."

CHAPTER 4

What lily blinks upon inspection?
What grace cringes
With age or dissection?

Impervious
The ultimate fleet
Life
This once
Perfection
Awakened blossom
Delight
Until
Slumbered moon
Petal-cupped droplets
One night
Unfettered
By winds
Of doom.

Once, on a dare, Cameron had leapt from a ledge on that same jagged rock face, just down the crag and skewed off to the right from where he now stood. As he balanced and stared down at that spot, memories flooded back.

§

Hiking along the island path, he was mesmerized by the dimples in her lower back, two precious indentations just above her waist. God's fingerprints, that's what he told himself. He wanted the pads of his thumbs to fit perfectly into those soft grooves. He wanted to take hold of her from behind, grab her above the hips and press his thumbs into those hollows. Those dimples seemed sacred. But he was ready for a bit of sacrilege.

Dangling tie-strings from her orange halter bounced with every step. Beads of sweat trickled down her back. He imagined the taste of her salt upon his tongue. They had yet to touch. They had barely spoken. The tacit silence between them only heightened his anticipation. They climbed up the steep path. She turned and smiled, and then doubled her pace. Higher and higher they scaled until the clouds reflected in the sea below.

He noticed how easily she moved up the slope, like a mountain cat. She seemed lighter with each step. Her springing grace delighted him. Honeysuckle and fan palms gave way to an exposed ledge. She stopped beside him. She teased a glance over the cliff's edge. It was a long drop to the sea below.

"I will," she said.

Her breathy accent made even the simplest words exotic.

Her green eyes challenged him. He still knew nothing of her. But now he felt he knew so little of himself. He gleaned something within her eyes. Not just a challenge. An invitation? Something he couldn't comprehend. The hairs on the back of his neck pricked up. Why didn't she look away? Why couldn't he? He would remember those eyes forever. No matter what happened. He was already certain.

Nothing in his history had prepared him for this. He never jumped tall fences as a boy. He dared not cannonball off the high dive at the summer pool in State Road Park as a teen. Even when his college chums goaded him, he never peeked over the edge of the limestone quarry just off campus. He didn't like high places. They made his stomach flutter, like she did. Just thinking of heights made him feel he was falling. He preferred the security of the soil. He liked being grounded. It was safe. Safety he knew. Leaping made no sense, particularly from high places.

He jumped.

And now he was flying. He couldn't do anything. There was nothing to which he could cling. The wind spliced through his fingertips, taunting any grasp. His voice deserted him. It all happened so fast. He screamed past daggered rock hungry to slice his flesh upon the slightest nick.

He accelerated faster. Senses mutinied. Colors blurred. Sounds hushed. This was too fast. He waited for impact. He waited to splatter into the water or, worse yet, the rocks. He waited for what might be death. Everything was so very fast, except for the waiting. The waiting seemed uncommonly long. Only the waiting dared move in slow motion.

Hurling faster, followed by more waiting. He forgot everything. He forgot why he came to the island. He forgot why he jumped. He was about to hit something too fast. *Shit.* He prayed it was water.

He looked down. The sea was the color of her eyes. All else went blank.

Self-preservation howled. He tucked his arms to his sides. Muscles clenched. He rocketed into the sea. The blast emptied his lungs. His feet burned as if on fire. An electric pulse jacked up his spine.

He torpedoed several body-lengths deep, past a dark mass, narrowly missing a submerged ledge. The water erupted in an explosion of bubbles. He knifed deeper until he raised his arms to slow the descent. A school of sea chubs scattered. The jade nibblers scurried away. Tiny sea plants hugged the outcropping, jiggling like spineless white umbrellas from his impact. A frenzy of bubbles convulsed to the surface.

He floated there motionless, suspended under water, shocked from flight, still stunned by what he had done.

Yet he felt elated, and free.

That was the most remarkable feeling, complete liberation from senses, and reason. In that one spontaneous act he had touched something previously unknown, one part warrior, one part lunatic.

Bubbles dispersed. Dancing swords of sunlight summoned from the surface. His lungs tightened. Pulling his arms to his side he kicked his legs and undulated up like a dolphin. His dulled senses returned. Cool water prickled his skin.

Salt water stung his eyes. He looked up. A sapphire sky arched above. He gulped a breath of salty air and peered toward the cliff. It looked even higher from the water.

And there she stood, like a siren, teetering upon the edge. She had taken off her halter-top. Her copper skin glistened in the sunlight. He felt the urge to scale the side of the cliff to take her. He felt ready to sprout wings and fly to her. He would tear down the mountain face one stone at a time until she crumbled into his arms.

She disappeared.

He swam toward shore.

And then she flew like a seraph from that ledge. In that one instant when her feet left the ledge everything changed. The feeling of freedom he had touched was gone. Instantly displaced with something else, something more.

Leaping from a high place had changed his life. But watching her fly to him trumped everything.

Clearing the rocks she sliced into the water. He ducked underwater. A trail of swirling bubbles percolated to the surface.

She fluttered up. Her tanned face broke the surface. Her skin looked as silky as a newborn seal.

She stroked closer. He was locked within her beaming, emerald stare. Everything blacked out except those eyes. Her eyes danced like fireflies in a night sky. The tide bobbed them up and down. They drifted closer and closer. She touched his shoulder. His arm slid below the surface and clasped her waist. His fingertips searched out the dimples in her lower back. His fingertips fit perfectly within those dimples. And for the first time, he claimed that spot as his own. He pulled her close. Any thought of freedom sunk away.

Her brown hair matted over her shoulders. She tipped her head to the side, but her eyes stayed fixed on him. He felt he already knew her thoughts. He knew what she wanted. He did not know her at all, yet he knew everything, because nothing else seemed to matter but that moment.

Their lips touched. She tasted of the sea, her tongue silky and cool.

He embraced her even tighter. Their bodies touched everywhere, but it was not close enough. To be close enough to her seemed impossible. He needed more.

He propelled them to shore. They clawed up the rocks. She untied his shorts, pulled them off and then slipped off her own. A cushion of moss coated the rock. They lay upon that natural bed smoothed by the sea. Like Nautilus he rose above his mermaid. And when she pulled him inside her he entered a tropical, lush, exquisite kingdom previously unknown. All the while her eyes seared into him, unblinking. Every ounce of him flooded to his core. He thrust into her again and again. He wanted to obliterate anything and everything that dared separate them. She in turn rocked above him. Nothing had prepared him for that. There was nothing so ideal.

Thought and reason vanished. He rolled back on top of her. He became Krakatoa, Vesuvius. He became the Creator and Destroyer entwined with the supreme Goddess. Not just her eyes now, but her entire convulsing body seared into his, fused around him, goaded him, screamed for him, squeezed him, and soaked him until they erupted together. His teeth clamped into her neck just below the ear. Atoms split and two continents shifted into one perfect primal cataclysm. Her aftershocks throbbed through both of them clamped together in a vice-gripped union of life and death and everything in between and before and after.

She was shaking.

So was he.

He loosened his bite on her neck and licked her with the tip of his tongue. She tasted of salt and sweat and paradise. They lay there, decimated, conqueror and conquered, in each other's arms, with the waves pounding against the ancient lava rock.

Climbing the cliff afterward her halter clung to her dripping skin. The sun fell into a tangerine glow. They reached the summit in dazed silence, before walking back toward the village market where they had first seen one another earlier that day. Near the seaside village she turned and kissed him, then tucked her head against his chest.

"I must go alone," she said.

"But why?"

She didn't answer. Her eyes lifted to meet his and she whispered one word.

"Aluna."

Her accent hinted of South America.

"Cameron," he said.

She held his stare as she pulled from his clutch, and then ran off. He watched her turn down the hillside path back toward the village. He sniffed for every last remnant of her scent on his skin.

Now, more than two decades later, as he stood perched on that cliff looking at the sea churning below and contemplating one final leap, he couldn't help but think that it might have been better had that been their only encounter. No complications: she to wander off into obscurity, he to forever live within one euphoric memory.

But that didn't happen.

Later that night so many years ago, tucked away in the mountaintop hut, he scribbled into a leather-bound notebook. Words poured from him like a waterfall. A dam burst, and out a man flowed.

> *Never before had I felt the touch*
> *Never before had I kissed the lips*
> *Never before had I held the heart*
> *Of the one who revealed forever.*
>
> *Never before had everything*
> *Been supplanted*
> *With a smile*
> *A kiss, a passion.*
>
> *Never again need I wonder*
> *Nor wander*
> *Nor worry*
> *For I have found my home,*
>
> *In her arms*
> *The one place*

I am everything, but free,
And will never leave.

While these words tumbled out, Aluna sat at a dressing-room table in a cabin on a yacht just off shore. She stared at a platinum ring on the table before her. Her middle finger caressed its circular edge, round and round, as if trying to cull the hum off the rim of the half-empty glass of chardonnay in front of her. She pressed the ring's edge with her thumb, and flipped it over again and again. She was lost in thoughts of that afternoon. She was lost in thoughts of him inside her. She still felt a faint throbbing within.

A knock rapped at her door. Another man's voice beckoned.

"I'll be right there," she said.

She gulped down the wine, slid the ring on her finger, pulled on a loose-fitting dress and left the cabin. While she picked over a gourmet meal that night, Cameron ate some bread, goat cheese and tomatoes doused in olive oil with a sprinkle of salt. She drank another glass of chardonnay. Cameron drank a glass of a harsh red wine, savoring each sip.

Alone in the hut, Cameron felt surrounded by her, as if she were right there beside him, as if he were still inside her. He could feel her that close.

He looked up through a hole in the palm fronds interlaced with the bamboo of the hut's roof. The night sky seemed on fire. The first streaking stars heralded a meteor shower.

Aluna gazed at those same stars. Perched against the rail of the yacht's deck she fumbled with the diamond ring upon her finger. The yacht listed back and forth. But something had rocked her world from its axis.

Cameron had no control over it then, just as he had no control over anything now, two decades later. His eyes closed.

He leaned beyond any hope of balance. His toes left the cliff without even a push. The butterflies in his stomach vanished, along with the desire to suffer through another breath without her, and he plummeted toward the rocky shore.

CHAPTER 5

Stop the bells from ringing
Hush the infant's cry
Lovers lower your gaze
For one moment of respite
I am among you no more.

Wind be calm
Birds keep your roosts
Clear the sky
If only for an instant
Because I need this.

Quell the tides
Let the sea fall placid
Quiet the ancient whale's song
For there is but one honu now
And he is lost.

Elia huddled beside Dean Baltutis. The two of them were tucked away in a turreted alcove in Orton Hall. Massive blocks of native stone belted the fortress, stacked in the same stratified layers found in the underlying bedrock. It was as if the three-story building had sprouted from the earth's crust. Arched bay windows, a gargoyle bell tower and a steep pitched roof gave the structure the look and feel of a castle. Ashen, columned walls and oak floors dominated its corridors.

The century-old bastion cradled the most rare books at the university, esoteric tomes ignored by most. But Elia found sanctuary within its musty corridors. She often wandered amongst forgotten titles and ran her fingers along crumbly, gold-leafed bindings older than the building itself, and nearly as ornate. She felt safe here. This stock house of words felt like a home.

What had lured them here, however, was the university's extensive collection of maps. An atlas was spread across the table between them. Dean Baltutis scrawled his finger over a section of the map and circled a splash of baby blue, nothing more than a nondescript speck on a grand piece of glossy parchment. But within that imaginary circle lay a very real place.

"There's nothing there," Elia said.

She scooted forward. Her chair's leg stuck in a crack between the floorboards and caused her to jerk forward. She felt herself blush, but the Dean didn't seem to notice, or at least pretended not to.

"Hardly a blip on the radar," he said.

He pointed at a barely legible word. Undeterred by the stubborn chair, she slid forward on the worn seat and squinted at lettering finer than an ant's leg.

"I've never heard of it," she said.

She felt her cheeks flush again. Of course she hadn't. The mapmaker had barely spared it a droplet of ink.

"Few have. It's due east of an old Spanish shipping route from the 1600s," he explained. With his index finger he traced along an imaginary line just south of the West Indies.

She stared at the map. Scaled distances vitiated. She wondered whether squinting might transform time as well, like those nights when her eyelids succumbed and she drifted asleep still transported off within the open pages on her nightstand.

She looked up at Dean Baltutis.

"But you know it?" she asked.

"I spent about a month there," he said and nodded, "twenty years ago."

"With Beck?"

She knew that was why he had brought her here, but she wanted to hear it just the same. She noticed crow's feet creased his temple. Twenty years ago those lines likely weren't there. She had never imagined the Dean in his youth. She brushed her fingertips against the skin alongside her own eyes, still smooth.

"Sort of. He was writing up in this mountain hut. I was pining away over a lost love. Heartbreak—I think that's what finally prompted my island invite. It was the one time Cam shared his getaway with me, but even then he never allowed me up to that hut. That was off limits."

A hazy watercolor of the island started to take form. She envisioned sand and warm, teal-blue water and palms trees. She began to contemplate how she would get there.

Steps approached. The two fell silent. A backpacked co-ed with a black, braided ponytail peeked into the alcove but found the hideaway occupied. The Dean pushed his glasses back up his nose and stared at the intruder. She glanced at Elia and the Dean, sighed and walked away. Elia wondered if their coupling looked odd.

"I never saw him during the day. But every couple of nights or so he came down to the village. We'd plop down in this shed of a seaside bar and thrash out life, love and eventually his writing."

"Eventually?" she asked.

She had always assumed a writer spoke of nothing else.

"Yeah, we talked sometimes 'til dawn, the *cantina* long empty, just me and him and a bottle or two of wine, always red. Like a couple of candles burning into the night."

He flashed a yellowed grin. She lifted her chair over the floor crack and felt the table press into her stomach.

"What is it?" she asked.

"It was strange. I would listen to him ramble, but he just knew."

"What? What did he know?"

She heard a book thud down the corridor. She barely flinched. Instead she stared at the tiny speck on the map while he spoke.

"Everything I was feeling. One night Cam shared with me a few of his poems. I was sitting there, half past drunk, and listening to what became *Secrets*. I still remember the full moon flooding through the window. It lit him up like a spirit."

She'd have to fly through Miami.

"Right then I knew. He was the real deal, a poet dancing naked. The stuff everyone else bullshits about. He had nailed it. And I began to tear up."

She gave him some room to deflate.

"Cam looked at me, like *what the hell is wrong*, but those words hit me like they were my own. He had tapped into something I thought only I felt, but couldn't describe, and had transformed it into something more."

He glanced toward her and sighed.

"That's one humbling awakening."

Ten days later, Dean Baltutis's words rumbled around in her head as she crouched in the backseat of a decrepit twin-prop Cessna. Not a single ticket clerk in Miami had recognized the name of the remote island. But a dreadlocked baggage clerk knew a cargo pilot who might know somebody. The cargo pilot in turn scribbled down directions to a tiny hangar along a dusty airstrip twenty clicks south of Miami. The taxi dropped her off in front of a sunburned man slouched in a lawn chair. The haggard guy had a death grip on a sweaty can of Coke. The dilapidated hangar, barely bigger than a Quonset hut, looked like it would collapse with even the most modest gust. But the guy had a seaplane and knew the island. Indeed, he told her he was the *only* pilot who flew there.

Staring out the window at the ocean below, she imagined Spanish schooners skimming across the water, their tall sails buffeting in the wind. The seaplane's diminutive shadow swept along the rolling waves, not a spot of land anywhere in sight.

Sticky hot, she reached down and fished about her ankles. She could have reached forward and touched the pilot's knee if she wanted, but still Elia felt alone. She often did. Not lonely, but simply alone within the insignificant speck of riveted, flying metal and glass flitting like a water spider above the blue aquatic universe, alone hovering along the great arc of the unknown.

Her fingers caught the top of a water bottle and she lifted it and took a sip.

It was a familiar, unshakable solitude. That feeling that as a youngster fostered entry into a world of books, where she discovered fictional wonders to fill the voids in her life. But the more she lost herself into those stories, the more she was reminded of the infinite plays in which she held no part. A feeling of insignificance branded itself upon her. Elia became a loner, a quiet one.

Thus, not speaking to the pilot was anything but awkward. For Elia, silence brought comfort.

Tucked on that bumpy flight, in chase of a ghost poet, she reflected upon her abbreviated history of boyfriends, each of which was predestined for doom. None could measure up against the great loves of literature. And while Beck's *Secrets* was a far cry from a classic, she had elevated it into a literary continuum that had left her paralyzed within an unreachable ideal of what love required. Seas had to part. Mountains had to move. Nothing short of life and death had to be at stake. She trusted nothing less.

She took another sip, but the water did little to cool her teeming mind.

Finding Beck and resolving the mystery of the muse had hatched as an academic pursuit. But the tentacles of deeper feelings were beginning to unfurl and push toward the light. Maybe it was just the heat.

The safe harbor of university libraries, professors and classmates was hundreds of miles away, but it might as well have been light-years away. She felt like she was stepping through some portal into the world of fiction. Her fingers fanned through her only guidebook, a worn copy of *Secrets of Odysseus* by Cameron Beck.

She flipped through the pages. Some of the poems were variations of traditional verse and others free flowing, but all touched her in a different way than how Dean Baltutis had described. For Elia, Beck described a world she longed for but had never visited, a world perched on a precipice between paradise and peril. She paged to one of the final poems, one of her favorites.

> *What becomes of love?*
> *Where does it go?*
> *Who keeps it?*
> *If any?*
> *Is it not vital?*
> *Almighty?*

Of course it was; she could imagine nothing more vital. But, she had only *imagined*.

> *If so, how can you plod about?*
> *Unknowing what I have lost?*
> *What all have lost?*
> *Does Nature not mourn?*
> *Where are Her tears?*
>
> *Oh you foolish boy*
> *Dare mock us with your pain?*
> *Be encaged for three lifetimes*
> *Perish in a desert tomb*
> *Pondering a single strand of hair*
> *Crucify yourself*
> *Then protest.*
>
> *But you see*
> *I have done all that*
> *In a single instant*
> *Beyond soul-aching forever*

The water bottle slipped from her hand and thumped to the floor beside her foot. She struggled to envision a fullness that could leave behind such a void. She knew nothing of that fullness or that void, at least apart from the page. She peered out the window at the sea below. She imagined an empty desert.

> *So I throw myself before you*
> *Begging*
> *Heal this wound*
> *If not*

Just recognize it matters
Someone must know.

Yet while you danced
Who watched?
Yearning for your place
Delighted by the splendor
All the while tending to the quiet
That is not Love.

You see
The bells have long been silent
The winds serene
The seas tranquil
All the while, bearing witness.

.

Mourn love's passing?
Don't mock us with cries for pity
From where does despair sing?
Listen close to the whale's song
Reigning within you now.

She gazed out the window. A dark mass broke the surface just beyond the flickering shadow of the plane. She pressed her nose against the glass and squinted. The enormous black opal rolled out of the water again and dwarfed the plane's silhouette. The goliath sank back into the water with spectacular grace. Its great tail fanned the surface before disappearing back into the depths of oblivion.

A cool tear ran down her cheek. Her stomach lightened as the plane tapered into a descent. She looked at the pilot and through the front window saw a small speck of land.

"Listen close to the whale's song," she said aloud.

"You okay?" shouted the pilot over the propellers. Rings of sweat marked his shirt.

"I thought I saw a whale," she yelled.

He looked back at her and smiled.

"Oh, you did."

"How often do you come here?" she asked.

"Every month or so, I bring out some provisions, now and then a stowaway like yourself."

"Anybody lately?" she asked and took another sip.

She had to pee soon, but the sight of land allowed her to quench her thirst without worry.

"Why? You lookin' for somebody?" he drawled.

He raised his eyebrows as he peeked again over his shoulder.

"Actually, I am."

"Who's that?" he asked.

"His name's Cameron Beck. He's a writer."

Falcon stared ahead at the island and fiddled with the instrument panel. It was too late to come up with an excuse to abort the landing. He needed to drop the crates and refuel. He kicked himself for not pressing the quiet, owl-eyed girl why she wanted to come to the island, but when she had placed two crisp one-hundred-dollar bills into his palm he figured she had bought her right to silence. He recalled her staring at the money like a gambler pushing in a last bet. It was a look he knew well. Plus he had been all too content to spare the small talk, hoping to belatedly dilute last night's fifth of rum with the Cokes he had sucked down the whole flight.

"Nope, haven't shuttled anybody else in a while," he lied.

He wasn't about to sell out Cameron's arrival ten days earlier.

CHAPTER 6

Imagine.
Intoxicant, so rare
Exotic, extraordinaire
Seductress, surreal
Enchantress, revealed.
Imagine.
All this, yet more
Come hither, explore
All dared, all dreamed
Eclipsed emeralds, this sea.

Cameron awoke alone in the hilltop hut. He had planned to write the entire day. He needed to remember why he had come to the island. He closed his eyes and envisioned sable-trimmed petals, interlaced with patches of coppery gold webbing framing brilliant emerald daggers, the markings of the island's rare *siproeta stelenes*. In full blossom it resembled a Malachite butterfly in flight. A local had told him it blossomed once every ten years, and then only for several days: brief, brilliant, doomed. Until its next bloom it was nothing more than the barest twig.

Cameron had seen the butterfly orchid's blossom once, a few summers before.

He had knelt by the orchid in awe of its wild perfection. Something about that simple, remote, fleeting spectacle had captivated him. He had never seen another since, even though he had returned to the island several times. But the image he now envisioned wasn't that fragile blossom. He couldn't get her out of his mind. He opened his eyes.

Writing could wait.

He jumped up. His feet planted on the cool dirt floor. He pulled his notebook off the table and glanced at the hectic scribbles from the previous night. There she was, staring back from every slashing word. She even filled the spaces in between.

He yanked on a pair of shorts and stretched his torso into a threadbare T-shirt. He grabbed his scratched sunglasses, slid on sandals and ran from the hut, tracking her footsteps down the path to the seaside village. He recalled her pensive look as she turned away to leave.

His sandals clapped against the dirt. By the time he reached the village he was drenched in sweat. The villagers seemed in a hypnotic lull. The sea lazed against the shore. Beneath that calm he knew the sea floor dropped so quickly that yachts often moored barely a spit from the sand. But there wasn't any vessel in sight.

He rambled past a dozen shanties, rickety houses stacked no more than three deep from the water, all lounging in a permanent recline in the unforgiving sun. A steel-haired woman beating a rug outside her window shook her head as he passed. He prowled streets nothing more than alleys, streets so narrow they didn't warrant names.

He scoured the small open-air market. Weary tables clustered under spinnaker tarps overflowed with island bounty. Here he slowed. This was where he first saw her just the day before. He caught his breath and picked up a bunch of green bananas, squeezed several mangos and mulled over some guava, wondering if her fingers might have graced these same fruit. He stood in the same spot she had been when he first noticed her, next to a bushel of pomegranates. He wanted to inhabit the space she had filled. *What the hell am I doing?*

But the island boy had told him the blossom lasted only days.

A bone-skinny, russet-skinned woman offered him a pomegranate. She looked to be one hundred years old, but her eyes tracked him like a hawk.

"No thanks," he said.

She broke into a gummy grin.

"You lookin' all *obzokee*. Maybe you need it. This one's sweet too bad," she said and sucked at her gums.

"Yesterday, the woman?" he asked.

"Gone like a *duppie*?" the old woman asked and chuckled.

"Please," he said.

Her grin dropped away and she shook her head back and forth.

"*Peong*," she said under her breath.

"Where? What's that?" he asked.

She tapped her hand against her chest, pointed the pomegranate at him and smiled.

"Your heart *peong*," she said.

"If you see her, tell her Cameron was here."

She nodded. He ran off to the *cantina*. He peered through a broke-open shutter. The tables were empty. The stale smell of beer wafted through the window.

Why did people come to Mataki? To disappear, or maybe to forget, he thought. Was that why she was here? He had come to find something, to remember. He had come to finish that short story about the butterfly orchid, to resurrect his voice.

His stomach began to knot. His head felt light. He started to feel sick inside. *Man, pull yourself together.*

He asked a fat old man who rented rooms by the day. The bald landlord swatted at sparrow-sized mosquitoes while he shook his head. He hadn't seen her.

Cameron jogged past a young boy fishing along the beach. The boy watched him pass, squinting in the sun to reveal a missing front tooth before turning back toward the bay to eye his line.

Cameron finally collapsed on a bench. He pushed back the sweaty strands of hair matted against his forehead. The sun had nearly reached its late morning peak. The sleepy village would soon deaden even deeper into siesta. Backtracking to the market, he bought a missile of bread, a palm-full of goat cheese and a cheap bottle of wine, all the while obsessing over how she had vanished without a trace, convinced he had blown it. He doubted sleep.

Stinking from the search, he dropped the plastic sack of food on the sand and waded into the bay. The fishing boy had pulled his line and was sitting in the shade of a drooping palm. Cameron glided between two decrepit fishing boats resting after the morning catch. The skiffs reminded him of Hemingway's *The Old Man and the Sea*. With each stroke he stretched further, trying to calm himself into a rhythm, but her face remained right in front of him. He recalled Santiago's battle with the great marlin. He thought of the old man's perseverance. He felt capable of the same. But would he get the chance?

A navy of blue tangs parted beneath him.

It seemed useless. He swam ashore, picked up his sack and hiked back to the hut. The afternoon sun dried him. His sweat soon smelled of brine.

Several miles away a yacht's engine rumbled.

§

By the time Cameron reached the hut, an ivory ship had entered the bay. The fishing boy squinted as it slipped back to its mooring. The boy knew its inhabitants. He waded into the water and set down his pole into a small wooden boat.

Back in the hut, Cameron sliced the goat cheese and sprinkled the fleshy insides of a tomato with salt and olive oil. It was the same thing he had eaten for dinner the day before, and the day before that. But this afternoon he ate more from ritual than hunger. He uncorked the bottle of red wine and poured it into a squat tumbler. He emptied the tumbler and poured another. Only after the second glass did the velvet breeze finally soothe him asleep.

And he dreamed.

Swimming down, he descended beyond an underwater cliff into deep recesses. Daylight dimmed into a marine-blue fog. No longer needing to breathe, he was surrounded by underwater creatures. Schools of fish engulfed him. Dolphins danced in and out of sight. They grinned, chattered and enticed him to swim even farther, leading him toward a distant light, where one figure eclipsed that glow.

A mermaid.

A flicker of recognition.

Aluna.

But he couldn't reach her, no matter how hard he tried. She turned away from him and toward the glow before swimming away. He gasped for breath, and the sudden pressure collapsed his lungs. Gulping for air, he began to drown.

He awoke drenched in sweat. His heart pounded. He opened his eyes. And there she was again. Aluna gazed at him from the doorway.

But this was no dream. Backlit by the sun, a halo framed her, yet he could still make out the green of those eyes.

He sat up. She walked into the hut and sat down by his side. He felt an instant pang in his gut. But instead of offering the kiss he craved, she collapsed and buried her face into his chest. Her hair smelled of gardenia. He hugged her and she began to cry.

"What is it?" he asked.

She didn't answer. Tears laced against his bare chest. The insides of his stomach began to twist. This woman, so filled with life yesterday, now felt so fragile, like she might break apart in his arms and her petals fall to the ground.

She pulled back from his grasp. Her eyes that just yesterday had so unflinchingly locked on him now avoided his own.

It took every ounce of strength to not pull her close for a kiss. But he waited, submitting. He brushed her cheek with the back of his hand to wipe away the tears. He caressed her face and stroked the ridge of her ear, and then around to the nape of her neck where his fingers combed through her auburn hair.

The two sat there in silence, in almost every way still strangers to one another except for yesterday's inexplicable, primal connection. Aluna placed her hands upon Cameron's shoulders and pressed him back down onto the cot. He slid over to one side and she slipped off her sandals. She lay down next to him, still without a word spoken. She kissed his bare chest and nestled her head upon him. Her hair felt like silk. He wrapped one arm around her waist. His fingertips sought out those dimples in her lower back. She clutched one hand and pulled it up to her chest. Her body again seemed perfectly encased in his.

Tucked away from the afternoon swelter, with the sultry breeze slipping across them, he watched her eyelids surrender for the first time. Only then did sleep return for him.

And this time, he slept without dreaming.

Cameron awoke to the scent of gardenia and the sensation of clutching her. Neither had stirred. Both his panicked nightmare sweat and her tears were long dried. He checked to be sure she was in his arms and watched her chest rise and fall. Each sleeping breath coincided with his.

He watched her awaken to find him. She smiled, closed her eyes again and nestled deeper into him. Then she sighed as her eyes reopened.

Still cradled in his arms, she spoke in a hush.

"Promise me something," she said.

He finally placed her accent as Portuguese, but her diction was perfect.

"Anything," he said.

He propped himself on one elbow.

She lifted her head and stared into his eyes.

"I mean it," she said.

He met her gaze without blinking.

"So do I."

"Never speak my name."

"What?" he asked.

"Do not speak my name, to anyone, ever."

He flashed to his frantic search that morning. Had her name already passed his lips?

"But why?" he asked.

They had shared so few words and already she was taking one from him, and one so precious. A myriad of reasons shot to mind, none of them good.

"Just promise me," she said.

She sounded as if her life depended on it. Cameron had a sick feeling that maybe it did.

"If there is some sort of problem, let me—"

"Please," she said and cut him off.

He felt helpless. He wanted to protect her, but from what, he didn't even know. Her request seemed so trivial to the resolve he felt. Take away all his words. Burn his notebooks. He would fall mute.

"As you wish," he whispered.

And hidden away from the world in that mountaintop shanty on a remote island, with the two of them wrapped only in one another, they sealed a lover's pact.

She sat up and slipped her feet into her sandals.

"Don't follow me. Don't try to find me," she said.

The knots in his gut tightened. He could not bear to lose her again, even for an instant.

"But I'll be back."

She leaned into him. He felt her even before their lips met, like the electricity foreshadowing a thunderstorm. He cupped the back of her head with his hand and she kissed him.

"This is real," she said.

She sounded somewhat bewildered, almost as if she were trying to explain it to herself.

"I know," Cameron said, "I know."

And she left.

Aluna peered back toward the island in the late afternoon sun. The gray fishing boat had only two wooden slats for seats. She perched on the front bench while the dark boy with jet-black hair and a missing tooth sat on the rear bench facing her. With calm, even strokes, he guided them toward the yacht.

As the boy steadied the small skiff, she climbed up the rope ladder and stepped onto the deck of the yacht. She looked down at him and nodded, then walked toward the main cabin door and peeked in. Inside the cabin, five men huddled over a nautical map spread across a table.

A dark, tattooed man looked up and nudged another, who turned to her and said, "We can talk at dinner."

Aluna turned from the room, but before she left she heard the same man announce to the others, "Okay then, we'll give it one more week."

She left them studying their maps.

A smile crossed her lips.

Another week.

CHAPTER 7

What is this tragedy that consumes me?

I cannot breathe
Without her whisper
No less crawl
Without return
To the blue
Mystical wellspring
Mirroring her
And her alone.

Morning surf
Crashing hope
Into sun-kissed stone
Yet, golden sand
Snows
Like stars
Below the surface
Each wave
Pleading
Over
And again
Return.

Shimmering minnows
Beckon
Out to sea
Come my love
Once more
To me
And I think
But for her
I would not be here
But for her
I would not be . . .
Alone
But for her.

Like a fool
Words sling
Heads bob
Only to sink
Empty shells
Battered
Against time
The siren
Still elusive
Foaming
Come to me
Come.

Again
And again.
Swimming
Drowning
Swimming
Drowning

Endlessly
Blissfully
Painfully
Alive . . .
Yet forever
Dying
Of her.

The yacht disappeared from the bay just after dawn. Several waves past a nautical mile the engine quit. The anchor groaned into a shoal where the sea floor stepped off, doubling in depth. On deck, three rust-colored men, and a fourth with lighter skin, wriggled into scuba gear and slipped into the sea. They left behind on deck a deflated dive marker next to an orange and white flag, both stashed well out of view of any passersby.

A fifth man stayed on board.

As the divers bobbed at the surface he took out a long fishing pole, weighted the end of the line with a lead sinker and cast into the water. He spooled out a random length of line, letting it go slack. No bait. No hook. He secured the rod into a brass rail mount, took out another rod and followed the same scripted routine. And then he took out another rod. Three poles, three lines and sinkers, no bait or hooks. Unless they flew aboard, he wouldn't be catching any marlin today.

The night before, the five men had plotted their finds from the prior dive to grid out this morning's search. Only these men and Aluna knew the purpose of the expedition. Each was sworn to secrecy. Any breach of their pact risked the threat of competitors or worse, piracy.

Jackson Gray, the only son of a Texas oilman who had parlayed his wealth and connections into a Brazilian ambassadorship, descended first. His lungs filled with enriched nitrox, while his mind filled with images culled from the dog-eared volumes sprawled behind in his cabin. As he kicked beneath the surface, everything seemed to slow down. He envisioned the great island city of Tenochtitlan within Lake Texcoco. He pictured the chiseled monolith Cuauhxicalli, the twenty-five-ton calendar stone depicting a mythological universe. But mostly he imagined a single relic from the notorious sacrificial ceremonies of a lost civilization, the Aztec.

At ten meters, he gripped an underwater ledge, pinched his nose and blew hard to equalize the pressure mounting inside his ears, sinuses and mask. He did so every several meters to release the squeeze to the air pockets within his body. Bubbles erupted around him. He checked over his shoulder to confirm his dive partner, Esteban, trailed by less than a body-length. Behind Esteban, the second team followed their bubbling descent. Above them, the hull of the *Atlaua*, christened after the Aztec "lord of water," disappeared from view.

Jackson's father had plundered land for oil. Jackson in turn squandered his share of the family fortune searching for remnants of an entire culture that centuries ago had been plundered by the Spanish for gold. But this expedition bore a particular significance to him, its import intertwined with the ritualistic ceremonies that dominated his thoughts. He reached down to check his depth gauge. The dial hit twenty meters. He equalized again. Another flurry of bubbles erupted.

The scant record of the treasure bordered upon myth, but fact or fiction he knew its every detail by heart. He filled his small crew with tales of gilded offerings to the Aztec gods. But more than any cache of gold, what intrigued Jackson was a solitary, silver bracelet purportedly worn by virgins sacrificed in the Aztec rituals. Legend had it that the bracelet bore an inscription revealing the secret to life beyond death. The secret to immortality was their quest, he reminded his crew. And he had convinced himself that that was his true destiny.

At twenty-five meters he rested his fin tips upon the ocean floor. The other divers followed, forming a close circle with him. Each in turn flashed deliberate hand signals indicating their respective air supplies. Jackson signaled the final okay and they disbursed along rotted timbers surrounded by a scattering of artifacts buried in a surprisingly shallow grave of sediment. The hull of the lost ship had long collapsed upon itself. Most of it had disintegrated. Only a few skeletal ribs remained distinguishable from the sea floor.

He hovered along the site at a depth roughly four atmospheric pressures denser than sea level. Every tiny pocket of air within his body crushed. He felt a squeeze in his teeth and equalized again. But a different pressure was also mounting. Time, something his family fortune could not buy, was limited. Seasonal storms would soon blow them off the site. All this weighed him down as his hand sifted into the ocean floor.

Earlier that morning, before the *Atlaua* had left the bay, Jackson had hurriedly hugged and kissed his Brazilian bride, ten years his junior, before setting off. Named for the moon, his young wife dutifully hugged him before climbing down the ladder onto a small fishing boat.

But her lips did not return his kiss. In his drowsy haste he didn't even notice. Ferried by a gap-toothed fishing boy, Aluna returned to the island in search of her own treasure.

The boy rowed toward shore, his lazy strokes creasing the surface. Aluna unclipped a small hand purse. She took out several gold coins. The young boy watched her count them but kept rowing. Then she removed two bills from her pocketbook and offered them to the boy. He stopped rowing. As the boat glided in the calm waters she placed the notes into his hand.

The boy studied the green, fine-print paper.

She watched him inspect the portrait of a man with a long, narrow face, gray shock of full, flowing hair and serious eyes, plus some words she figured he couldn't decipher and numbers. Both bills had a "20" in each corner.

"*Quarenta dolares*," she said and placed the coins on top of the banknotes before closing his hand around the money.

His black eyebrows arched.

"*Sí?*" the boy asked.

Aluna nodded.

He whistled through the gap in his front teeth, stuffed the money in his pocket and beamed at her. He spit in his palms, rubbed them together and retook the oars. The boat sliced through the water at a hastened clip.

By the time the *Atlaua* hovered over the dive site, Aluna dawdled along the cobbled promenade that hugged the bay. She wandered until she thought the fishing boy no longer watched, and then meandered past a slumbering open-air market. A stoic old woman with a yellow bandanna around her head sat in a wicker chair and studied a young, copper-skinned boy sweeping a patch of dirt. The display tables and baskets were still bare. Aluna smiled as she hurried past the woman toward the path that led up the mountainside, the path where a day earlier she had left Cameron.

She noticed for the first time how fast her heart was pounding. But it had little to do with the rapid climb. Before she knew it she stood at the clearing at the top of the trail. She untied the cream bikini top beneath her linen sundress and stuffed it into her crocheted day bag, which did little to slow her heartbeat.

A collection of bamboo shoots intertwined with dried palm fronds framed the hilltop shanty. Just to the side of the hut's doorway a fallen palm bridged two low, flat rocks. What looked to be machete hacks had carved it into a rustic bench. She wondered if it might be the work of the man she hoped to find inside.

Slung between two palms at the far edge of the clearing, an empty hammock hung like a crescent moon in the dead calm. Past the hammock, a gap in the tangled tropic underbrush opened into a glistening, blue vista. Her husband scavenged through silt somewhere along the bottom of that marine universe, while she brushed her fingertips through her brown hair and floated toward the hut.

Three tethered bamboo shoots dangled in the doorway like a lethargic wind chime. She peeked through the bamboo. A small round table and wooden chair tilted upon the sandy floor. Atop the table an unlit candle was entrenched in wax. The rustic interior was the antithesis of her husband's yacht. Her life with him was beginning to feel cluttered.

Across from the table, a shirtless Cameron slept upon a cot. She studied him and tried to slow her breath to match his, careful not to brush into the bamboo. Even asleep, his body reminded her of a panther, taut and sleek. His lean muscle made him appear younger than his years. Although suntanned, his skin was still lighter than hers. His sculpted shoulders looked like the spot on a peach where it melds from orange to red. His sun-flecked hair curled into a sandy mop.

And then his eyes opened, and any hope of calming her heartbeat vanished.

Cameron's first waking image of seeing Aluna peeking through the bamboo was beyond any dream. He almost slipped, breathing a barely audible "ah," but as his tongue brushed the back of his front teeth, the place where the second syllable of her name would take flight, he recalled his promise.

He stretched his hand toward her.

She brushed through the bamboo. The bamboo caressed against her, hardening her nipples. The hollow reeds parted, bumping together in a lazy percussion. The swooped neckline of her linen dress revealed the soft, caramel ridge of her collarbone. Hints of each breast dissolved into white linen shadows.

She had kept her word and returned. He had kept his promise.

Two lives began to entwine like creeping shoots of star jasmine.

He stood, engulfed her in his arms and whispered, "Good morning."

"Yes it is," she said and closed her eyes.

Her ear pressed against his bare chest. Her body melted into his. She felt herself getting moist.

"Come on," he said.

"Where?" she asked.

"A swim."

His eyes captivated her. They were the teal of the shallows where the sea meets the sand. Amber moons circled his pupils. She sensed both a calm and a lingering danger. But the danger did not come from him. The danger was from inside. The danger was what she wanted. The danger was why she had come in the first place.

When she met his stare he didn't blink. It unnerved her. It excited her. It captivated her. Her husband never looked at her this way anymore. In that moment she couldn't recall the color of her husband's eyes, only the vagueness of his stare.

"Perfect," she said.

Cameron cleared his throat and motioned for her to turn. She grimaced, feigned surprise and covered her eyes with both hands. He slipped on swim trunks. She peeked the whole time. They were two children playing, but something far from innocence tugged below her navel, like an invisible cord pulling her toward him.

"Let's go," he said.

That magnetic pull grew stronger as they hiked through the violet morning glory, orange-cupped honeysuckle and pink oleander that framed the trail. The circumstances of her life should have undermined such feelings. They didn't. She had no idea where this man came from, who he was or what he did, yet nothing mattered more than to go for a swim with him. It was that basic.

He led her down a steep, switchback trail and grasped the rock to secure the descent. She followed the placement of his hands and feet with precision, trusting his every move. Halfway down, he stopped and sat on a ledge that overlooked the sea. A sheen of sparkling blue satin swept to the horizon. He leaned back, reached behind a large rock and pulled out a black diving mask and two fins.

"You know the way from here," he said with a smile.

Holding the mask and fins, he jumped into the water.

Without hesitation, she plunged in after him.

The fins were too large for her feet, but they shared the mask and took turns diving.

Cameron pointed to a purple starfish. She ducked her head beneath the surface and watched him pry it loose from the rocks and cradle it in his hand while he swam back to the surface. He placed it upon her palm. The spiny arms extended just beyond the tips of her fingers. Hundreds of spongy suction cups clung to her wet skin.

"I've never before touched one," she said.

"There's more," he said.

He sounded like a little boy wanting to share every wonder.

He peeled the sea star from her palm. She noticed how carefully he treated the creature. A pang shot through her. What would he think of her once he knew the truth of her life?

He dove back down with the starfish.

Lightning bolts of silvery green minnows scattered along the surface.

She felt an urge to tell him her secret.

She had to.

But when he resurfaced a sea turtle popped its leathery head into the air and exhaled a muffled "puffff." The cap of its emerald shell, almost as long as Cameron's torso, sparkled in the sunlight before it again submerged. Then another turtle, just a bit smaller, broke the surface with another puff before ducking beneath the water.

"Did you see them?" she yelled.

"Take this," he said and tossed her the mask.

She pulled the mask over her face and started to dip her head above and below the surface in sync with the turtles. Their shells were magnificent patches of jade-ticked emerald. Slight thrusts of long, leather-like front fins propelled them through the water with astonishing ease.

The turtles continued to puff fresh gulps of air between shallow descents, while she and Cameron swam above, below and around them to observe the turtles from every angle. The smaller turtle drifted closer and closer to Aluna until the two came face-to-face. She peered into the creature's eyes and a chill shot through her.

Something in those primitive-looking eyes reminded her of Cameron. But so did the crystal-clear water, the tropic breeze and the sun overhead. She realized everything did. Her cluttered, confused life suddenly felt simple. She felt tears welling up inside as she stretched her arm along the water's surface. The sea turtle craned its neck at her and let out another audible puff, but this time it didn't dive. Instead, it paddled even closer. She touched its front fin.

The turtle submerged and dropped out of sight around a reef.

"Did you see that?" she asked.

By his smile she knew he had.

"I think the big boy swam off," he said.

Treading in the tropic warmth they both waited for the smaller sea turtle to surface again. But it didn't.

"Give it to me a second," he said.

"What is it?" she asked and handed him the mask.

"I'm not sure."

Cameron pulled the mask over his face, sucked in a deep breath and plunged down. He dove about two body-lengths toward the reef, grabbed the edge of the outcropping and peeked beneath. An oblong opening, about twice as broad as his shoulders, tunneled into the rock. But he could see deep into the tunnel, even though it appeared to be surrounded by rock on all sides. His lungs started to tighten and he kicked back to the surface.

"Did you find it?" she asked.

"No. But maybe something else," he said and caught his breath. "Let me take another look."

He dove back down, pulled himself halfway into the reef opening and discerned again that glow from within the tunnel. He kicked back up to Aluna, who was treading above the spot.

"Okay, just one more look, a little longer," he said.

"Be careful."

"Trust me," he said and kissed her on the cheek.

He smiled and swam back down to the ledge.

This time, he pulled himself into the tunnel and fluttered the fins toward the faint glow. He was surrounded on all sides by reef rock, unsure if he could turn around without serious scrapes. But as he thrust closer toward the light, the passageway widened.

His lungs began to tighten, but he stayed calm. He had another minute, maybe two at most, before he would be in real trouble. He recalled diving for silver dollars as a boy, exploring the murky shallows of Lake Erie along Euclid Beach Park. Heights were not his friend, but underwater he was confident. He had tested that crushing feeling seconds before blackout enough times to know he was within his limits. *Relax*, he thought. He still had time.

The glow began to brighten. He could almost touch it. He wasn't going to turn around now. The bottom of the tunnel turned from rock into sand and he clawed his fingers deep into the sand. His lungs depleted. His entire body convulsed forward.

With one final thrust he broke the water's surface and his hand reached into light and air and life. He gasped for air. He rolled onto his back inside a cavernous pocket of stone. Above him sunlight filtered through two vents at the cave's apex. The sand was hot against his back and the stale air, which smelled of brine, felt like a sauna, but he was alive and breathing.

He scanned the cavern.

It was almost as large as the bamboo hut. The ceiling slanted downward and the sandy floor sloped up toward the back. He knew the island well, and he had explored these waters many times. Yet in all of his adventures he had never before found the cave.

But his hunch was right.

He wasn't alone.

Tucked near the back of the cave the smaller of the two sea turtles scuttled into the sand, pushing mounds aside with its front flippers. Speckled grains of sand were caked to its paws and the ridge of its shell. It didn't seem to notice him. The pit it dug was nearly half the size of its massive jade shell. The flurry of digging stopped and the turtle swiveled its spade-like tail along the edge. Sallow, oval-shaped eggs began to tumble into the pit.

He heard Aluna's muffled call, but dared not shout back.

Instead, he slid back into the water, pushed the mask over his face and gulped a deep breath of air before swimming back out the tunnel. His fingers probed along the sides, careful in the dim light to avoid the sea urchins he now noticed were tucked along the reef, until he found the end, pulled himself out and undulated back to Aluna.

"What happened?" she asked.

"How long can you hold your breath?"

"Long enough," she said.

"Good, you've got to see this."

Cameron handed her the mask. She pressed it over her face and pulled the strap over her wet hair.

"On three, okay?" he said.

"Okay," she said.

He counted to three. They took one last breath together and like a pair of ducks dove down. She gripped his hand and they swam into the tunnel side by side, his finned kicks pulling her along. He propelled them inside. He could feel her furious kicks trying to keep up.

But this time he relaxed even more, confident they could make it, and the more he relaxed the stronger his lungs felt. Even without the mask, the water was so clear he was able to guide them past the patch of spiny urchins. He was ready to give her his last breath if needed, but they burst into the cave and together sucked their next breaths.

"You okay?" he asked.

"Yes," she said.

He sensed relief in her voice.

The turtle was right where Cameron had left it, still dropping its cache of eggs into the sandy nest.

She sat up.

"*Ninho*," she whispered and leaned back into him.

"We might be the first to find this, other than her," he whispered.

"*Mae*," she said and pulled his arms around her.

The sea turtle finished depositing eggs and started to sweep sand on top of the nest. She looked exhausted and lingered for several minutes, sitting like a queen on a throne atop the otherwise nondescript mound of sand beneath a vent of sunlight. With deep, wheezing breaths the turtle stared at them before dragging its wedged trail through the sand. At the water's edge, the mother turtle craned her neck to look back at them one last time, and then lumbered off and submerged into the tunnel, leaving the two of them behind with her secret.

The sun streaking through the overhead fissures made the incubated cave feel even warmer. Her shoulders pressed hot against his chest. His arms ran alongside hers. Their fingers intertwined. The small of her back pushed against his stomach. The sweat of his thighs began to stick to her legs. Hot and sweaty they melted into one another. She tugged off the mask and leaned back, her wet hair dripping against his cheek.

And she forgot all about what she had dreaded telling him.

She turned her head.

Her lips were only inches from his.

"This is sacred," she said.

Then she kissed him and within that cave they began their own ancient ritual.

CHAPTER 8

How long mourn the empty sea?

I cannot condition my love
Upon any act or deed
If I do, it is not the love I believe
That one great mystery, even to me
Like the sea.

And the oak
Once barest twig in slumber
Always reaching
Beyond sun and sky
Like you and I.

And the orchid
Fragile as this evening's moon
Yet in the darkest recess
Enchanting
A life in bloom.

Or the empty sea
Recalling the glory and dreaming
Of that first slight bead of rain
So perfect and new and filled with a dream . . .
Of the sea.

How long mourn the empty sea?

Forever and a day
Like the sea, the oak and the orchid
And that tiniest drop of rain
Forever
And today.

I sabella was the first on the island to hear the sputtering seaplane. Lounging outside Paco's *cantina*, she was nibbling papaya when she spotted the plane as it skipped into the bay. Watching it motor to the dock she waited for Falcon to pop open his door, hop out and hook the lines like he always did. Just another delivery she thought, at least until a slender leg peeked from the plane hatch. Up perked Isabella's antennae. Leaning forward, she cooed, "What do we have here?"

She swooped down the dock before the young lady had even finished stretching from the flight.

"Mornin', Cap'n!" she hollered.

Falcon winced.

"Morning, mama bird."

Elia was caught off guard by the black pumpkin of a woman bearing down upon her.

Falcon hesitated, so Elia timidly offered her hand and introduced herself to the imposing islander.

But the big woman's voice was like velvet.

"Welcome, Miss Elia. I'm Isabella. Now what brings you to paradise?"

"She's lookin' for some writer," Falcon drawled.

"For true? Well, someone's always scribblin' something 'round here. Not much else to do," Isabella hummed. She cocked her hands on her hips and changed the subject. "How long you staying?"

"I don't know yet," Elia said.

Elia felt the blood rushing back into her calves and feet. The heat was suffocating. She was exhausted, having not slept a wink the prior night. She noticed the stains under Falcon's armpits growing. A bead of perspiration slipped down her back. Then another laced down her thigh. She smelled her own sweat. The bay looked ever so inviting.

"You'll need a place to freshen up and sleep. Come, dear, let me show you 'round," Isabella said and hooked her by the arm.

Elia noticed Isabella shoot Falcon a *how dare you* look as she pulled Elia down the dock. She glanced over her shoulder to see Falcon shrug, and then go back to stacking crates onto the dock. "Hungry?" Isabella asked.

"A bit, but mostly tired."

She was wilting in the stifling heat and didn't care where this bear of a woman took her, as long as it was out of the sun. Elia's cotton blouse and shorts felt smothery and itchy.

"Let's get you a little bit and then off to siesta," Isabella said and walked her toward a seaside *cantina*. Beside the doorway a piece of driftwood hung askew from a frayed rope. "Paco's" was slashed across the wood in crackled, red lettering. The "o" was painted in like a fishbowl, the bottom filled with a wave of blue and flecks of yellow fish. The apostrophe between the "o" and "s" was another flecked silhouette of a flying fish.

Isabella sang out.

"Paahhco."

From a narrow doorway peeked a leather-faced man wearing a tie-dyed tank-top T-shirt. His faded jean shorts were frayed just above the knee and a purple bandanna drooped around his neck. His brown feet were bare.

"More *paw paw*?" he called out before raising his eyes onto Elia.

"Hello, Miss, you hungry?" he asked.

"A bit," Elia replied.

Paco looked like a Caribbean hippie, except that his full head of black hair was neatly slicked back and cropped just past the neckline.

"This here's Miss Elia," Isabella trumpeted.

Squeezing Elia's hand she said, "And this here's Señor Francisco Dominguez."

"Please, *Paco*—I don't even know that other guy," he said.

"Good to meet you," Elia said, relieved to be in the shade.

He clapped his hands together.

"I got fresh fish, clams, *bammies*—"

"Cassava cakes, honey," Isabella explained.

"Every fruit worth slurpin'," Paco said.

Elia raised her hand to cut him off.

"Please, just some fruit."

"Coming right up, and to drink?"

"Cold water, please," she asked.

"Like the Andes," he promised.

Elia felt like she was breathing through a hot towel. She looked the place over. To her left, two sets of shutters were propped open to a stunning bay. A thicket of mangrove pressed smack against a smaller window to her right. Paco retreated into the kitchen.

"So where you from, darlin'?" Isabella asked.

The big woman dragged a chair from one of the four wooden tables that hugged the bar. Two skewed pictures of fishermen displaying their catch hung behind the bar beside a broken Red Stripe clock. One of the shirtless fishermen resembled a youthful Paco. The broken clock's hands hung in final defeat at half past five.

"Ohio, for now. I'm a grad student at Ohio State," Elia said.

It felt good to collapse in the shade, although the wicker seat pinched her butt. Her shorts stuck to her legs.

Elia looked everywhere except into the big woman's eyes.

"Ahh, the States," Isabella nodded and stroked her frazzled, black braids. "Whatcha study?"

"Literature," Elia said.

Elia's eyes began to fixate on the strange charm dangling around Isabella's neck. The braided strands of the charm looked like human hair.

"Oh, that's good," Isabella said.

Apparently picking up on Elia's stare, Isabella brushed her fingertips against the talisman.

"Just a little luck," said Isabella.

But to Elia it looked like some sort of voodoo.

Paco returned and set down a heaping plate of guava, star fruit, mango, sliced watermelon and small bananas, next to which he placed a sweating carafe of ice water. Those lacing beads of water looked heavenly.

"That's a bit much," Elia said.

Then she noticed three forks and the same number of glasses, punctuated by Paco dragging another chair across the dirt floor.

"What did I miss?" he said.

He filled each glass and offered each lady a fork.

"Just that I'm a lit student in the U.S.," Elia said and gulped down her entire glass of water. A sweet coolness gushed down her throat.

"That's sooo good," Paco said. "I've got lots of books. Here, try this guava."

He pushed the plate toward her. Elia forked into a slice. Without her even taking a bite, it melted on her tongue.

"Wow," she said.

"Grew it from a seedling; sweetest on the island," he said.

He pointed his fork at a crooked bookshelf traversing the open window and then forked into his own slice.

"Bit of everything up there. Take what you want and feel free to leave something for me too. I love it all."

Paco beamed at Elia. A golden front tooth offset his engaging smile. She was charmed by the ingratiating book-lover.

"What you reading there?" he asked.

She caught his lustful gaze at the possible new addition to his crooked bookshelf that was peeking out from her purse.

"It's *Secrets of Odysseus,* by Cameron Beck," Elia said.

Paco leaned forward.

"Read it years ago," he said. "That American poet, right?"

"That's the one," she said.

"You know I—"

Isabella cut him off.

"Falcon says she's looking for a writer."

"On this patch of sand?" asked Paco.

Even in her sleep-deprived state, something odd tweaked Elia. Paco poured another glass of water. But in a barely perceptible pause in the conversation Elia noticed that just as Falcon had done on the dock, Isabella had offered up the purpose of her trip before she could.

"Who's that?" Paco asked.

"The poet himself," Elia said.

She set down her copy of *Secrets* on the table.

Paco picked up the book and looked at its jacket. She noticed him swallow a slice of watermelon, seeds and all. The juice trickled from the corner of his mouth before he wiped it away with his bandanna.

Isabella peeled a banana and stuffed half into her mouth.

"Well, I haven't heard of him being here," Isabella mumbled through a mouthful of banana.

Paco studied the inside of the book's back jacket sleeve.

"What makes you think he'd be on Mataki?" he asked.

"One of my professors at the university knew him," Elia said.

"Nope, can't say I've seen anybody looking like this," Paco said.

He tapped the back of the book's jacket.

"But I'll ask around a little bit, let you know if anybody knows anything."

"I'd sure appreciate that," Elia said and yawned.

Isabella stood up and said, "Come on, let's get you a shower and bed, honey. This heat can suck the life out of you."

Elia wobbled up and reached for her purse.

Paco waved her off.

"It's on me, Miss Elia. My little buddy will take it from here," he said.

He whistled and a scrappy tree monkey leapt out of the mangroves. Scampering across the floor, the gangly fur-ball hopped onto Elia's chair and began eating chunks of mango with a fork.

"That's amazing," Elia said.

"That's Chuey," he said with a smile.

"Don't let him get sick," Isabella warned.

"Shoo now, take care of your new tenant," Paco said.

He fanned his long fingers at the two of them.

Chuey was still finishing his feast as the two ladies left. Wandering out the door with Isabella, Elia sensed something wasn't quite right, something more than a cute monkey eating with a fork, but she was too foggy and sweaty to start poking around. Right now, she just wanted a cool shower and long nap.

§

After the two women left, Paco walked over to the bookshelf that tilted above the window. He reached up and pulled down a dog-eared volume. He looked out the window and made sure that Isabella and Elia were far enough down the path before he dared caress the spine of the book. His fingertips passed over the worn title, *Secrets of Odysseus*. He opened to the inside cover and read the handwritten inscription, "*To Love's Fisherman, Cam.*"

It had been over a week since the poet had stepped off Falcon's seaplane. He knew Cameron safeguarded his seclusion, yet even the laid-back Paco was beginning to worry. The supplies Paco had delivered to the hilltop hut should be nearly depleted. He wanted to see his old friend, particularly given Cameron's stealthy return to the island only months after news of the film rights sale to *Secrets*, now followed by the arrival of the curious college girl.

Paco scratched his head.

Falcon's sarcastic voice drawled from the doorway, "Taking it up for another read?"

"Maybe 'bout time," Paco said.

"Let's have a beer then and you can read to me."

Falcon tilted a broken mug under the solo beer tap at the bar.

"Make it two," Paco said.

He sat back down at the table, where Chuey was still licking a fork. The mango was long gone and the monkey's stare was fixing on the watermelon. Paco grunted. Chuey looked up at him. Paco shook his head and slapped his hand hard against the table. Dropping the fork, the monkey snatched a banana and in three leaps ricocheted out the window.

"I blew it," Falcon said. "Got no idea what this one's up to."

"Trouble don't set up like rain," Paco sighed.

Falcon took off his ball cap and rubbed his head.

"Hung over?" asked Paco.

"A croc's chomping on my skull," Falcon said.

He lifted his mug.

"What's with Cam?" Falcon asked.

Paco said, "Haven't seen him yet."

"Shit, been a week now," Falcon said and took a swig.

"I know it," Paco said and took his own gulp.

"And Isabella?" Falcon asked.

"Not since you brought him," Isabella chimed as she walked through the door.

"When I took up the food he was gone, figured hiking or swimming, so I just left it on the table like always," Paco said.

"Privacy's one thing, but I want to talk to that man," she said.

"Looks like you're not the only one. Need to at least warn him she's here, just in case he starts wandering around the village," Falcon said.

The two stared at Paco, who nodded.

"I'll put together another sack and take it up this afternoon," Paco said.

He placed his palm upon Beck's *Secrets*.

"Done. I'll keep watch over Miss Elia," Isabella said.

She stacked her hand atop Paco's.

"And I'll have another beer," Falcon said.

Falcon rested his hand atop Isabella's before adding, "Think I'll stick around a bit for this one."

"Done," replied Paco.

A streak of sunlight pierced through a crack in the *cantina* roof and glinted off the golden tooth of Paco's uncertain smile.

Late that afternoon, confident that Miss Elia was tucked away in a warm nap, Paco trudged up the hillside path loaded down with a backpack of food and news of the young woman's arrival. As he walked, he drifted back to the first time he climbed the same path some twenty years ago.

His body then was even leaner, his load much lighter. Back then he carried only the curiosity of a gap-toothed fishing boy tracking a young woman rendezvousing with her lover. He remembered that the dark-skinned woman sang to herself the entire way. He couldn't quite comprehend the words to her song. They sounded like Spanish, but not quite. Her voice nonetheless enchanted him.

Isabella and Falcon weren't privy to the meaning behind the inscription in Paco's copy of *Secrets* stashed up on that shelf in the *cantina*. But Paco knew. It was a tribute to loyalty, a nod by the author to the keeper of a secret flame. Hiking up that path again so many years later, the sanctity of that flame was still aglow. At the crest of the trail, Paco came upon the dilapidated hut. He passed the spot where twenty years ago he crouched down to watch the young lovers' embrace. His old hiding place was long overgrown with wickets of fan palms overwhelmed by climbing cape honeysuckle.

Yet for Paco the weathered hut's charm hadn't changed one bit, although the palms that anchored the hammock now dwarfed him. He had restrung that hammock maybe a half-dozen times. Twenty years of life, twenty years of change, but the feel of this place still was much the same. The scent of jasmine drifted like island magic, just as it did back then.

Paco spied a hat hung on a wall peg inside the hut, but found the hut empty of life. Cameron's deflated duffle bag rested on the sandy ground. Paco's bare foot stepped on something hard. Lifting his foot he found a cork. A bee buzzed around a half-empty bottle of red wine on the table. Next to that bottle was a glass knocked on its side, and a piece of paper weighted down by the bottle.

Blank paper.

"Where are you, my friend?" Paco whispered.

He walked back out of the hut. A queasiness pitted deep in his belly.

He trotted down the path toward the cliff. Beneath a low branch of a cape honeysuckle he glimpsed what looked like a gray rag. He ran over. It was a dirty T-shirt. He crouched down, picked it up, and the jasmine dream of this place began to muddle. A nauseating thought took its place.

Still on one knee, Paco lifted his head and bellowed, "Cameron!"

Silence.

He leapt up. His backpack fell from his shoulder. He bolted down the path, right past a pair of khakis, and nearly tripped over a stray sandal as he raced toward the cliff.

CHAPTER 9

The deeper I dive
The bluer her waters
Where prisms refract
Like liquid sapphires
In an iridescent sea of mirrors
And all I can think is
Let me hold this breath
Forever.

The sultry air of a Caribbean afternoon seeped through shuttered windows. A gravity-defying gecko scurried along a pale yellow wall. Above her bed, a weary ceiling fan hummed. But as Elia's head sunk back into the sweaty pillow, she closed her eyes and thought about the verse. She swirled each word like a crisp chardonnay, mulling every nuance as the imagery settled; she imagined swimming through an underwater sea of mirrors surrounded by shimmering blue light. She wondered just how long she could hold her breath and she contemplated the man from which this verse had flowed. Each image plucked from the vine of a life, each sound a clue to his depth and character.

By comparison, she felt like a seedling tucked away in some hidden valley. Where were these wonders of which poets wrote? The verses lingered as she drifted asleep, her hand resting upon the open pages of *Secrets*.

§

Cameron felt the pulse of Aluna's heart upon his chest. The sunlight that filtered through the shafts at the top of the cave had shifted. Shade now blanketed them. But the corner with the buried nest of sea turtle eggs remained baked in sunlight. Neptune's soothing symphony surrounded them, echoing off the walls. He gazed at the vents above them, spaced about two arm-lengths apart. As the sun had passed through its arc the corner of the cave where the sea turtle had deposited her eggs had been bathed in an endless stream of direct light. He grinned as he pondered how the sea turtle had divined that spot.

He thought about the millennia that had led to this one brief moment. He thought about the endless continuum of time. Lava long ago tumbled into the ocean and simmered into crashing waves, carving out this particular, meager, hidden pocket into the rock. Some prehistoric, jade-shelled pilgrim eventually crawled into the cave, perhaps the first to ever bask in its womb-like warmth. He wondered how many ancient mariners had begun their journey from within this rock, and how many had returned home to continue the cycle. He had once read that loggerhead turtles could navigate thousands of miles to return to the exact beach of their birth. Had the mother who had just wriggled away puffed her first breath of life right here?

And then he considered the past week and the tumble of random events that had led him here. What convergence of events had brought such a woman into his arms to inspire such thoughts? And within that notion he suddenly felt fragile, adrift in an ocean of nothing more than coincidence and chance. But just as that awful feeling of frailty arose within him, Aluna hugged him tight. Her touch eclipsed those fears. And within her arms his world returned to the moment.

"How did we get here?" he whispered.

"Destiny," she replied and nestled snug.

In this snapshot, unobstructed by the past and unfettered by the future, he felt like time had actually stopped, like nothing else existed.

"Come on, we'd better go," she said.

"Yeah, the tide is rising," he said.

But from the tone of her voice he knew that was not what she meant. That precious snapshot was already fading.

He looked toward the mound of buried eggs and felt an urge to stay and protect them.

As if reading his mind, she said, "They'll be alright."

He smiled, looked one last time toward the corner of the cave and handed her the mask.

They slipped back into the sea just as they had arrived, hand-in-hand.

"On three," he said.

She nodded, he counted and they ducked back underwater, swimming through the tunnel. With the pull of the tide the passage seemed a bit easier.

They broke through the surface together. He swam alongside her the entire way, barely kicking with the fins. He climbed onto the jagged stone first and turned to offer his hand. She reached up for him, but before he could pull her up she grimaced.

"Ouch," she yelped.

He yanked her out. She hopped on one foot and then sat down onto the rock. He took the sole of her other foot into his hand. A spiky bristle was lodged in the soft underside of her foot.

"Sea urchin," he said.

She frowned and arched her foot. *Damn*, he even liked the way she frowned.

"Relax, if you can."

He massaged the skin around the black needle and circled his fingers closer and closer to the spot before glancing up at her.

"Now don't move," he said.

She nodded.

Pressing his lips against the arch of her foot, he closed his eyes and flicked his tongue over the broken spike. He pinched her foot hard, pressed his teeth against her flesh, and eyes still shut bit the needle that had punctured her skin.

She tried to jerk back, but he held her foot in place, opened his eyes and felt the bristle between his teeth like an errant caraway seed. He spit it out into the water and rubbed her foot.

"Salty," he said and smiled.

"It hurts."

"It will for a day or so, but you'll be fine. Thanks for not kicking me in the face."

"Sorry," she said.

He began to massage the puncture wound and then her entire foot. He rubbed each of her toes, pressed his thumb deep into her arch, squeezed her heel, twisted her ankle and then ran his fingers up her calf. When he finished, he picked up her other foot and did the same.

He wanted to continue all afternoon.

"*Por favor*," she begged.

"What?" he asked.

"I have to," she said and glanced toward the path up the cliff.

"Then we go," he replied and kissed her big toe.

He pulled her up to her feet.

"*Obrigado*," she said.

He raised his eyebrows.

"Thank you," she repeated in her mellifluous accent.

"For what?" he asked.

She leaned into him, caressed his neck and whispered.
"You."

And then she kissed him.

Paco was panting when he reached the cliff. There was no sign of Cameron. Squinting over the edge he peered down to the sea. It was a harrowing drop, with rocks jutting out near the water's surface. He yelled out Cameron's name.

No reply.

He raced barefoot back down the path, past Cameron's discarded clothes, past his own fallen backpack, past the hilltop shack and all the way back to the village. He had long ago learned he was faster without sandals. When he reached the *cantina* he found Falcon asleep in a chair. Two empty brown bottles of Red Stripe were on the table in front of him.

Paco grabbed him by the shoulder.

"What?" Falcon drawled.

"Come on, something's wrong. We'll take the boat."

"Why?"

"Where's Isabella?"

"Back at the cottage. What's going on?" Falcon asked.

"Good, just you and me."

"What the hell?"

"I think something's happened to Cam."

"Do we need the plane?"

"No," Paco said and paused. "Not yet."

Paco darted from the *cantina* and ran down the dock with Falcon on his heels. A jumble of images, none of them good, raced alongside him. He untied the lines to his fishing skiff and jumped aboard.

He watched Falcon duck his head into his seaplane and reach under the pilot seat. In four strides, Falcon was back at the boat with a first aid kit tucked beneath his arm. Paco cranked the motor and Falcon hopped in. They sputtered out of the bay, the boat careening along the shoreline toward the cliff where Paco had yelled Cameron's name just twenty minutes earlier.

Falcon scanned the water along either side of the boat, while Paco squinted beyond. Paco gauged the swells and recalled the tides over the past week, silently calculating how the water might push and pull a body. The sea could be merciful, but he also knew it could be relentless, and often treacherous. If what he suspected had happened, he already knew to expect nothing. He struck himself a bargain. Be thankful for anything. He mumbled a fractured prayer beneath his breath.

"Dios te salve, Maria. Llene ares de gracia . . . "

He throttled back on the engine as they got nearer to the cliff.

"El Se or es contiga . . . "

The skiff crept along the isolated coves.

"Bendita tu eres entre todas las mujeres . . . "

He pointed up.

"I think he went off there."

"Jumped?" Falcon asked.

Paco just pointed again and said, "Somewhere about there."

He slowed the engine to a hum and the swell began to rock the boat.

"Y bandito es el fruto de tu vientre . . . Jesus."

"Try here," Falcon pointed.

Paco squeezed the boat into a cove, but it was empty.

"Santa Maria, Madre de Dios, ruego por nosotros pecadores . . . "

He peered at the clear, restless water on the way out to avoid the jagged rocks beneath the surface. He pulled out again to the open sea, the water's clarity dropped into a fuller, opaque blue and the boat hugged the rough coastline past the cliff.

"Ahora y en la hora de nuestra muerta . . . "

Ahead was another inlet. He spotted a pinkish clump of flesh on its shallow beach and gulped. His throat felt dry as sandpaper.

He squinted, trying to focus.

"There!" yelled Falcon.

"*Amen.*"

Paco steered between shallow rocks into a narrow passage before beaching the craft. Falcon leapt off into the shallow water. Paco splashed behind and lugged the boat onto the sand. Falcon sprinted toward the body, first aid kit in hand, Paco only a step behind.

The body, only several feet from the water's edge, was naked. The face was in the sand, yet the torso half-twisted toward the sky, as if he had tried to roll over. But there were no other signs of movement. The man's bare skin was sunburned. Paco knew the tides. He saw the sunburn. Even before they reached the body, he figured Cameron had been there at least a day, possibly more.

They both knelt over the body.

"Cam," Paco whispered.

Cameron's left leg was battered. Deep cuts along the knee were caked with sandy clumps of blood baked by the sun, but there were no signs of gangrene, at least not yet.

Falcon placed his hand upon the man's skin.

"He didn't drown."

As Falcon said this, Paco recalled the pilot's stories of pulling half-eaten, bloated bodies from the everglades in his youth.

Crimson bruises lined the left side of his chest, stretching from under the arm to the stomach.

Paco placed his hand on the back of the body. It was warm to the touch.

"*Amen,*" he muttered.

But just as he said this he thought he felt a gentle rise in the back. He waited what seemed like the longest seconds of his life. And there it was again, like the gentlest tug on a fishing line. One shallow breath.

Paco looked at Falcon.

"He's alive."

"We've got to fix that leg and get him back," Falcon said.

"Come on, Cam," Paco whispered, "we'll take care of you."

But he said these words more to calm himself.

They rolled Cameron on his back.

"Broken ribs," Falcon said.

Falcon took off his shirt and poured alcohol from the first aid kit onto the lacerated leg. He plucked clumped sand out of the wounds. Then he wrapped his shirt around the leg and tied a knot just above the knee.

The two clasped arms below Cameron's shoulders and legs and carried him back to the fishing boat. The dead weight was heavier than Paco's prize marlin pictured in the old black-and-white photograph behind the *cantina* bar. They set him down along the bottom and used Paco's crumpled shirt as a makeshift pillow.

Paco lugged the boat's stern back into the water. Falcon pushed the bow. Then Falcon hopped in and steadied the body. Paco started the engine and backed out of the inlet until he could turn the boat around. Once in open water, he gunned the engine and the boat bounced toward the village. Paco looked down to check on Cameron. He caught Falcon's eye, but said nothing. They were doing as much as they could. He knew it still might not be enough. He felt an ominous shadow lurking alongside them on that bumpy ride.

Paco mumbled again, "*Dios te salve, Maria . . .* "

The trip back to the village took forever. He sensed the sea calming, perhaps granting one last favor, or at least he hoped.

Within view of the dock, he untangled a metal whistle looped through a socket on the skiff's frame. Isabella had forced him to place the whistle there years ago, just in case of an emergency. For years, he had listened to that whistle clink against the boat's frame, a nagging reminder that with even the slightest swirl of wind or wave anything can happen on the open sea. In the time it takes a gull's watery reflection to pass, everything can change.

He wondered whether Isabella had somehow foreseen even this. He gave the whistle a quick blast, but nothing came out. He whacked it against the boat's frame and shook it. The cork rattled and he gave it another blow. They were nearly upon the dock when the whistle shattered the calm of the bay like a screeching hawk.

By the time they had tied off the boat Isabella was running toward them, her flip-flops slapping against the dock.

Paco yelled to her, "Get the cart, a blanket and water!"

"I've got blankets and water!" Falcon shouted.

Falcon jumped across the dock into his plane and pulled out a plastic jug of water and a horse blanket.

Isabella stopped dead in her tracks. She stormed toward the *cantina* and a rusted, flatbed cart just outside the doorway. They used it to haul supplies and Paco's occasional marlin. While he waited for Isabella to bring the makeshift gurney, Paco again sensed that ever-looming shadow alongside Cameron.

Falcon handed the water jug to Paco, who stood on the boat over Cameron's body. He sprinkled some drops across Cameron's sunburned face to moisten his lips. He knew Cameron was dehydrated, but he also knew if he forced water into his mouth he might drown his unconscious friend.

Isabella jostled down the dock, pushing the squeaking cart. When she saw Cameron's naked body twisted along the boat's bottom she cried out, "*Oshun Loa!*"

Paco yelled to Falcon.

"Put the blanket on the cart. We'll lift him up and wrap it over. Isabella, go get Fatty."

Isabella froze, her eyes big as a papaya. She clutched the talisman dangling over her bosom.

"Isabella, get Fatty," he repeated.

But this time, Paco gently touched her hand to break her trance. Her sandals slapped back down the dock as she ran.

Falcon set the blanket along the cart and stepped back into the boat. They hoisted Cameron's body and thrust it onto the same spot where Paco usually tossed his catch of the day. They lifted Cameron onto the cart and placed him across it on a diagonal.

Paco pulled the blanket over Cameron to cover as much as he could, but the grotesque bruises on his ribs were still visible. Falcon propped the shirt under Cameron's head and the two of them rolled the cart down the dock. Paco had no idea if moving him would only cause more harm. But there was no choice.

At the end of the dock a few villagers had gathered.

"Make way!" Paco yelled.

They shuffled to one side.

Paco and Falcon hesitated, staring at one other.

"*Cantina*," Paco said.

Falcon gave no argument.

They rolled onto the cobbled path. The growing group of onlookers shuffled closer.

"Unless you're Fatty, I don't want to see you!" Paco yelled.

His words struck loud and clear, halting them in their tracks.

One woman, though, who looked like she had just woken up to stumble upon the commotion, peeked past several heads to see what was going on. She broke past the villagers and thrust toward the cart.

Paco sensed her innocence, but was wary whether even that light could eclipse the shadow he felt so close.

He looked at her and said, "Not now."

She stared back at him and said nothing.

The young woman's gaze finally dropped to the cart, upon which lay the broken body of the man she sought, the flesh and bones of her barely breathing thesis. There lay the phantom bard from the campus pub, the same man she hoped would unveil something of love's secret.

And upon Elia's first glimpse of the ghost poet, it was her own heartbeat that nearly stopped.

CHAPTER 10

Reason
Did not clutch me last night
Caress my brow
Suck these lips
To the seed.

Reason
Did not convulse to the floor
Rip off this skin
Split me open
'Til I bleed.

Reason
Did not thrust against me
Rock my depths
Demolish fear
In one deed.

Reason
Cannot comfort this ache
So when I weep
It's not reason
That I need.

Cameron sat cross-legged in the dirt as Aluna hurried down the path toward the village. She neared the bend that would take her from view.

"Come on," he whispered.

And just as he did, she glanced over her shoulder and looked back at him still watching her. She smiled. He raised his hand, but didn't wave. Instead, he simply held it up toward her. Aluna turned and disappeared from sight, transformed to memory, Cameron left with only the promise of her return.

The sun slumped toward the sea. Twilight cast upon the hillside's tallest palms. With his hand still raised, he gazed at the sky's tangerine glow and melted into the majesty of that Caribbean sunset. Gilded palm fronds swayed goodbye as the last remnants of her smile seemed to slip from his fingertips.

Faint bands of wispy clouds strung along the horizon. A watercolor of red and orange and pink spread across the sky. A hummingbird flittered by, and then hovered about the closing buttercups of a cape honeysuckle. The tiny bird's feathery sheen glimmered like the insides of an abalone shell. Pink and teal fused into aquamarine. He marveled at the lustrous hues. Such wonder in small things, like a smile just before it vanishes.

The muse seemed everywhere.

That same glow reflected off a puddle of salt water pooled at Aluna's feet. She sat in a wooden boat while the gap-toothed fishing boy paddled toward the *Atlaua*. Each successive trip to the yacht had occurred later and later in the afternoon. Now it was near dusk.

With each return trip, Aluna found the ivory ship less impressive. It was where she took her meals, even though her appetite had waned. It was where she slept, although her nights were now spent dreaming of Cameron. It was where she bathed, either washing away the scent of her secret or showering in anticipation of the next rendezvous. And it was where her husband obsessed over sunken Aztec artifacts, although both he and his obsession seemed to matter less and less.

She stared at the luxurious yacht and perceived a golden cage. Her gaze dropped back to the puddle at her feet.

The boy pulled the oars from the bay. The small boat bobbed in the twilight shadow of the yacht. She stared at the placid water and into her own faint reflection. In her afternoons with Cameron, she had glimpsed the extraordinary in a mutual gaze. In the evenings, she did all she could to avoid her husband's stare. The pools that revealed so much drained once again.

The young boy steadied the boat as she climbed aboard the yacht.

She heard voices.

Turning back, she whispered to him, "*Mañana.*"

He nodded and gave her a lazy salute. She watched him scull away into the dusk.

She walked along the teak-lined corridor, past the galley and toward the voices. As she stepped toward the main cabin, the magnetism that had pulled her toward Cameron all afternoon repelled her from that room with an even greater force.

The clamor inside the main cabin sounded unusually boisterous. Glasses clinked. She heard laughter. She opened the door and the room fell silent.

A gold-trimmed bottle of champagne sat upon the drawing table. An empty bottle rolled upon the floor.

"Thirsty?" Jackson asked.

His face was flushed red, and not just from sunburn. His normally square jaw slanted to the left. She could tell he, along with the rest of them, had been drinking. They huddled around the table like a band of conniving thieves.

"No, I'm fine. I'll just rinse before dinner," she said.

"We have an extra," he said.

He lifted a goblet before tipping it toward her. Rust-colored barnacles encrusted the cup. Esteban, one of the Brazilian divers, lifted up a champagne glass. The head of a green serpent tattoo above Esteban's bicep peeked from beneath his white T-shirt.

"I'll drink to that," Esteban said.

"Here, here," joined another crewmate, a pirate's glimmer in his eye.

Behind them, a nautical map of the West Indies was pinned against the wall.

"Bottoms up," hiccupped a third.

Champagne dribbled down his peppered stubble.

Splattered across the table were several coins, a metal box and two more goblets similar to the one her husband had hoisted. She could tell they were peculiar, much simpler than what he usually dug up from the ocean floor. She had seen similar images in the books littered about his cabin room and back home in his study. But these were real and, like the sweaty crew, reeked of the sea.

"Aztec," Jackson said.

He leered at the goblet in his hand.

Aluna smiled, mostly for his benefit. She couldn't recall him ever looking quite so happy, not during their courtship, not even on their wedding day, and certainly not since. His delight brought a sense of relief. It felt a welcome distraction. It allowed her to dare consider that maybe he wouldn't miss her if she left. And she began to rationalize a different life, a life where she was the treasure.

"Congratulations," she said.

The adventure of her husband's quests had been contagious, for sure, and she too had been seduced by it for a time. But she felt herself straddling some invisible threshold. This was not her dream. It never had been.

She managed another smile. Jackson filled a champagne glass and handed it to her.

"To the Aztec," he toasted.

"Indeed," she said and clinked his glass.

The crew slugged back their drinks.

Aluna stared into her glass. She imagined the hidden cave shimmering beneath the champagne.

The bubbles scratched at her throat.

"So, did you find it?" she asked.

"Not yet, but it's down there," he said.

"If it exists," she said.

He grimaced.

A pinch of queasiness panged in her stomach.

"It exists," he said.

He thrust his goblet onto the table.

"You bet your ass," Esteban said in his heavy Portuguese accent.

Snake eyes glared from Esteban's tattoo.

"Just a matter of time now," Jackson said, "just a matter of time."

"Of which we don't have much, *El Capitáo*," hiccupped the bearded pirate. He wiped champagne from his lips.

"How long?" she asked.

Her voice hinted of apology. But even as she asked, she began to wonder whether he would even care what she had done. Maybe she should just confess right now and walk the plank. She could swim back to the island. Her first trip ashore had been a novelty, promoted by Jackson as a means of breaking the tedium of life upon the yacht, his way of keeping her occupied while he pursued his *real* passion. But when she had returned again, and then again, he had said nothing. Did he even care?

"The storms are coming. Two days at best."

Her stomach clenched. She started to feel cold and clammy.

"We're diving 'round the clock 'til it hits," he said, "No choice. After that, we're gone for the season. One last swig, boys, and in the morning it's back to coffee and Cokes."

Her knees wobbled.

"To coffee and Cokes," the others toasted.

The champagne began to sear her empty stomach.

Now it was the room that wobbled.

The next thing she heard was the faded sound of her name, as if someone was calling her through a wet towel. She felt a cool moist cloth pressing against her cheek.

"Come on now," a man's voice said as she opened her eyes. But it wasn't the man she desired. It was Jackson's blurred mug. She was sprawled on the floor. The empty champagne bottle was next to her head.

"What happened?" she whispered.

"You passed out, come on."

She felt Jackson's fingertips clasp around her wrist and elbow. Esteban manned her other arm and helped pull her up.

"You okay?" Jackson asked.

"I just need a bath," she said.

"You need food. You've been eating like a sandpiper."

He put his arm around her and led her to the dining room.

"Listen," he said to her, "come eat something and then to bed. But I've got to finish this. No more day trips for you."

"No, I'm fine," she said.

She wrestled a pang of guilt.

"My stomach can't stand this boat right now, plus I want to buy some things before we go," she said.

She tried to gauge his eyes as she spoke.

"I've already arranged for the boy to come first thing in the morning."

"What things?" he asked. "We'll be out there at least two days."

She could tell from his voice how petty he considered her request. She felt her ruse slipping away.

"I'll rent a little room and watch for you."

"All right, but just take it easy."

Not even a fight. She realized how minor her request when there was treasure to be had.

"I will," she said.

From her cramped cabin Aluna heard her husband's snoring from the stateroom down the hall. His clogged nasal passages had served as a convenient excuse for her to demand separate sleeping quarters. Even with the gentle rock from the tides, she found it hard to sleep that night. Her thoughts rocketed like shooting stars. But when sleep finally came, it came hard, and she dreamt even harder.

She dreamt of packing everything she owned into a single suitcase. She neatly folded her clothes, piled her shoes and placed her jewelry into one bag. Then she turned to the furniture surrounding her, not just the things from the cabin but from her childhood bedroom, and started putting them into the same bag. And then into the bag went her bed, then her pillows. Everything fit. Its capacity seemed endless.

Next went her hand-stitched, childhood dolls into the bag. Then her two dogs, Lucia, an old golden retriever, and Doria, a young pointer, jumped in. Her mother and father appeared. They each kissed her on the cheek and then they too climbed into the bag. She gazed into the suitcase. It was filled with all that was her young life. She stared as everything started to sway back and forth, and then swish about as the suitcase filled up with water.

Fascinated, she stared at her belongings floating in the bottomless blue hole. Parents and animals swam amongst clothes and furniture, books and jewels.

Memories began to play out before her, little aquamarine vignettes from the depths. One of her schoolteachers floated by, reading a book of poems. She saw her own young face listening as the teacher read. She witnessed her first kiss. And from that kiss a sparkle of bubbles rose to the surface, percolating toward her. The bubbles clouded then cleared. She saw a sea turtle with a halo above its head swim up from beneath the bubbles.

Aluna leaned forward and tried to discern the aura that glimmered about the turtle. Leaning farther, her face dipped into the water. Warmth washed across her skin. She was peering into something she had never seen before. It felt safe here, confused, but safe. She could breathe without air. She could swim without effort.

She floated in the surreal inner space. Looking up, the portal from which she entered drifted away, becoming only a fading light from above. Then her husband's face eclipsed the light. He looked down at her, goblet in hand, and zipped the suitcase closed. And all light disappeared.

She startled awake just as her dream went black.

Wiping the sleep from her eyes, she sat up in bed, mulling the images of the dream. Leaving him would never be simple. Or could it? She climbed out of bed and began packing her things into a backpack. She looked into the pack, half-expecting to see the images from her dream. She heard a knock at her door. The handle turned and Jackson peered in.

"The boat's here."

"I'm ready," she said.

She pulled her backpack over her shoulder.

He walked her to the ladder. At the bottom she saw the welcoming face of the gap-toothed boy waited to ferry her ashore. Jackson squeezed her arm and turned to hug her.

"Get some rest now and remember to eat."

"I will," she promised.

"I'll come for you when we're done," he said.

"And I'll be watching for you."

"Remember, not a word, not to anyone."

"I know," she promised.

Then he leaned to kiss her on the lips, but before their lips met, she turned her head ever so slightly and wished him good luck.

"Thanks," he said.

He pecked her cheek.

She recalled what Cameron had said to her the day before, words he confessed were inspired by her as she lay in his arms. He had told her "there are kisses of distraction and kisses of deception. There are kisses of obligation and kisses of consideration. There is nothing like the first true kiss, and the anticipation of the next. For some, an eternity can pass between the two."

Aluna stepped onto the ladder.

"There are kisses so nefarious they have begun wars. Yet, there are kisses that quietly seal a peace," he said.

"Tell me more," she had begged.

He obliged.

"There are kisses that stop time, and those that start it again. A single kiss can forever fill a heart, yet a sea of empty kisses cannot resurrect a lost soul. There are vacant kisses and then there are kisses so filled with promise and hope that even before lips unite cosmic forces unleash."

The peck from her husband that morning, however, was the kiss of duty. And for Aluna a kiss of duty between a husband and wife was akin to the kiss of death.

By the time she stepped onto the fishing boat any memory of that peck from her husband was gone. She couldn't wait to return to the island and press her lips against Cameron. For her, there lay the kiss of paradise.

CHAPTER 11

This poison
That kills
Mirrors the passion
That saves.

Know that
Now
For it comes
In waves.

"Come on!" Isabella shouted and shook him.

The tawny man's clutch on the crocheted blanket tightened. Slumping cot springs groaned as Isabella nearly sat down atop him. He was as reed thin as she was plump.

"Wake up!"

A feeble voice drifted from under the blanket, "Eh?"

"Cam's hurt."

The right eye of the Cajun creature born François Delecroix Badeaux, and better known on the island as Fatty, squinted open. He craned up his head. Cross-stitched impressions from the blanket checkered his cheek.

"Cameron, for true?"

"Yeah, come on," she said.

"When'd that poh boy git here?" Fatty crooned.

He rubbed both eyes. When it came to talking, he was the only islander who out-sang Isabella. She had learned to decipher Fatty's hard "i's" invariably came out as "ahhs," there were no consonants dangling at the end of any of his words and, even with all his medical schooling, grammar held no quarter, French or otherwise, in *Fatty speak*.

"Never mind, come on," she said and swatted him.

Fatty propped up onto his elbows.

"Easy now, let me slide on my frog legs," he drawled.

"Frog legs my booty," Isabella said.

She grabbed him by the arm, nearly yanking him off the cot. She didn't need any sixth sense to see the skinny mullet was groggy from another spliff-induced siesta. She knew the ganja was his personal Jesus, ever since it "assisted" him out of a medical practice back in the bayou. A hurricane named life had blown Fatty a long way from the Louisiana swamps, but in the end he still landed just a shrimp toss from the sea, yet another stray finding shelter on her island.

His dirty feet squished into polka-dotted flip-flops.

"What happened, Isaboo?" he asked.

His bald noggin tilted ten minutes shy of noon.

"Paco and Falcon brought him in the boat. He looks—"

Isabella censored the thought. She didn't want to even say the word.

"Like he's sleeping," she said.

Isabella was normally as sweet on Fatty as the candy necklaces he dispensed to the children popping their brown heads into his disheveled clinic. His gentle hand, listening ear and endless Creole patience cured many an island ill. Isabella knew, however, they were going to need a lot more than that.

"Let's go then," Fatty said.

Flailing his arms, he looked scrawny as a plucked chicken trying to fly. Peering around the cubbyhole of a clinic, he grabbed a beat-up leather satchel before trotting out with Isabella at his side.

They jogged down the meandering, cobbled boardwalk, passing the cottage where Isabella had deposited Elia only a day earlier.

Isabella and Fatty burst into the *cantina* to find it empty.

She called out, "Paco!"

"Back here," a voice yelled.

She led Fatty down the hallway, past the cramped kitchen to a sparse bedroom where Paco and Falcon hovered over Cameron's motionless body. Paco's long, leathery frame was leaning over, pressing a damp towel against Cameron's face while Falcon appeared hypnotized by the rise and fall of the sheet resting over Cameron's chest.

"What happened?" Fatty asked.

Paco straightened up, towering a head above Fatty. "Found him washed up in a cove."

"Swimmin'?" asked Fatty.

"No," Paco told him and glanced over at Isabella, who was fiddling with the emerald beads of her charm and beginning a quiet chant under her breath.

Fatty sat on the bed. Leaning over, he opened Cameron's mouth and peeked down his throat. Then his bony fingers checked for a pulse, after which they combed through Cameron's scalp like he was testing a cantaloupe for ripeness.

"Went to check on him, found his clothes along the sunset path, and him gone," Paco said.

"So he—"

"Fell or jumped," Paco said.

"Jumped?" Falcon asked.

Sweat beaded down Falcon's temple.

"Place that blankey over his feet. I need clean towels and a scrubbin' pad, and some gin if you got it."

"Gin?" Paco asked.

"Poo-yee, I got to clean that leg wid sumptin'," Fatty said, adding, "and I hate gin."

"Got it," Paco said and rushed from the room.

"Isaboo, go on back to the clinic and get the bag above my fridge."

Isabella hesitated.

"Go on honey child, gonna clean and close this leg, but Cammie's dehahdratin' sumptin' fierce, need to pump him with fluids. Falcon, go with her. Grab the ahh-vee pole alongside my bed and plastic bags on bottom my fridge, way in back."

Isabella and Falcon scrambled out the room.

Fatty pried open Cameron's eyelids and checked his pupils.

"Come on, partner. Why you makin' the misery?" he hummed.

Paco returned with some towels, a scrub brush and a half-empty bottle of Aristocrat gin.

"Been coughin' up anythin'?" Fatty asked and pressed his hands over Cameron's chest.

"Not that I saw," Paco said.

"No blood?"

"No."

"*Merci*, good. Couple of crackled ribs here," Fatty said.

"Can he hear us?" Paco asked.

"Maybe bits, but he's in shock. Be sometime before he comin' round."

Fatty pulled out his stethoscope and pressed it against Cameron's chest.

"Hmm, okay there."

Then Fatty unscrewed the bottle of gin and took a long swig.

"Still hate it," he winced, before pouring it onto Cameron's gashed leg. He doused the wound again and began to scrub out the dirt and sand with the brush. Then he poured the gin over his bony hands.

"Ain't no sacrilege," he said.

He plucked out the last stubborn grains of sand with his fingernails.

Paco grimaced. Cameron didn't flinch.

In just minutes, Isabella and Falcon barged back into the room.

"*Merci beaucoup*, Isaboo," Fatty said and took the bag from Isabella. He opened the bag and retrieved a hook-shaped needle the length of his pinky finger, a long strand of black nylon suture and a set of pliers.

"Looks like it could hold a marlin," Paco said.

"Oh it could," Fatty said. "Y'all may not wanna watch."

But nobody looked away, although Isabella edged closer to Paco, who welcomed her with a hug.

"Let's see here, gonna use a continuous buried pull-out stitch," Fatty said for the benefit of his gallery. "It'll be a big one, but that's what it is," he said and he pierced into Cameron's skin with the hook. He worked it underneath and across the wound and into the underside of the opposite skin, tugging the flaps of Cameron's gashed leg together.

Isabella cringed with every stitch, each of the thirty-seven times Fatty pricked through Cameron's skin. He finally tied off a knot, cut the extra length of suture and taped nine long adhesive strips across the closed wound.

Isabella sighed.

"Okay now, let's get a bit of beverage goin'. Cammie, I'm gonna hook up an ahh-vee," Fatty whispered to his unconscious patient. He stood and hung one of the bags Falcon retrieved from his clinic onto the IV pole. He unraveled a long, clear plastic tube and hooked it into the bag. Then he pulled out a rubbery tourniquet and tied off Cameron's arm just above the elbow.

Swabbing Cameron's skin with an alcohol wipe, Fatty punctured a narrow needle into a vein in his forearm.

"This here's an angiocatheter," he said.

A maroon flashback of blood filled the tip of the catheter.

"Bulls-eye," Fatty proclaimed.

He slid the plastic hub of the device down to the skin and released the rubber strap around Cameron's arm. Attaching the end of the tube to the catheter, he released a saline drip and watched it flow down the canal, then taped the end of the contraption to Cameron's arm.

"Okay, boys, lean him up for me," Fatty said.

"But won't that hurt him?" Falcon asked.

"Gotta wrap those ribs," Fatty explained.

Falcon and Paco hoisted Cameron up while Fatty unspooled a cloth bandage around Cameron's lower chest.

"Easy now," he said.

They set him down flat again.

Cameron didn't budge, eyes shut.

"What we do now?" Isabella asked.

She was rocking back and forth.

"Now Isaboo," Fatty said, "we gonna wait."

"And pray," she added.

"Sure can," Fatty said.

"How long?" asked Paco.

"Long as it takes. He's got some bad achin', just need to keep him steady. He'll come on back when he's ready. Let's take turns sitting with him. Don't want him alone."

Isabella stopped rocking, stepped forward and leaned over Cameron placing her hand on his head. She kissed the whisk of black strands at the end of her charm, crossed it three times back and forth on his chest and then brushed it across his forehead.

Paco and Falcon eyeballed Fatty.

"Can't hurt," he said.

"I'll stay for now," Paco said.

"Me too," Falcon added. "I need a beer."

Isabella heaved a long sigh, looked at Paco and Falcon, and rested her hands on her hips.

"I best go talk with her," she said.

Elia slumped on the bed in the sparse cottage, deflated by the deceit underlying her island welcome, when she heard Isabella's voice.

"You in there, Miss Elia?"

She felt trapped.

"Yes," Elia said.

"Can I come in?" Isabella asked.

"Door's unlocked."

The rusted handle twisted open and Isabella's dark walnut frame eclipsed the doorway. She closed the door and dragged a wicker chair toward the bed. Elia sat up but looked away, still half-betrayed, half-bewildered by the turn of events. The chair moaned under Isabella's weight. Her orange sundress deflated like a parachute around her ankles when she sat, erasing any hint of the chair legs beneath her.

There was always a twist. In every story, just when she was on her way, ever so close to the *right* ending, out of the blue it would hit. The hero plunged a sword into his heart, convinced the maiden had never loved him, or that she always did, but they couldn't marry because they were brother and sister, or take your pick. Elia suspected this just might be that page. She braced herself.

She gazed toward Isabella but refused to meet her stare, glancing instead at the pale yellow wall.

"Is he?" asked Elia.

Isabella sighed.

"Dead? No."

Elia shuddered. The room seemed a little less empty, the yellow wall not so pale. For the first time Elia dared look into Isabella's russet eyes.

"Why?" Elia asked.

Isabella's fat fingers rubbed her temple. She clasped her odd charm as she talked.

"I've known him . . . seems longer than forever. He trusts me with his life. I trust him with mine. But this is *his* life, not yours, not mine, his. He comes for his reasons. I respect that. Others have come here looking for him, bother him, trying to cash in on him. I won't allow it. Not on my island."

Isabella planted her hands on her wide hips. A coil of golden bracelets slid to each wrist.

"You know what sanctuary is?" asked Isabella.

"Sure," Elia said.

Isabella told her anyway.

"It's a sacred place, protected and safe. That man, the one you're looking for, once told me *this island* is his only sanctuary."

Elia understood the need for sanctuary. She found hers deep within collected fictions. Even when the twist came, and it always did, she was always safe in that world, always able to close the book.

"I just wanted to talk with him," Elia said.

A red-billed tropic bird landed on the open windowsill. Shivering its snowy feathers, black-masked beads peered at the two women before it flew away, a long white tail streaming behind.

"Then let me ask you—"

Isabella creaked forward on the wicker chair, which nearly surrendered.

"Why?"

Elia looked down again. She scratched at the crescent moon of her thumbnail.

But Isabella pressed, "To reveal *his* muse?"

"Sure, in part," Elia said.

Isabella frowned.

"And then what? What will that do, truly?"

"I don't know," Elia said.

As Elia whispered her response, she realized how meaningless her quest sounded. She looked toward the window, as if the feathered visitor might have left a better answer, but the sill was empty.

"What do you really want from him?" Isabella asked.

Elia tucked falling strands of brown hair behind her ears.

"I want to talk to someone who believes those words," she said.

Her voice cracked.

The blanket of humid air in the cottage lulled stagnant. Elia wasn't sure Isabella understood. She wasn't sure she herself quite understood.

"Well," Isabella said, "I don't thing he'll be talking to anyone anytime soon."

Elia perceived a sliver of acceptance in her tone.

"Then I'll wait," Elia said.

Whether or not Isabella understood or agreed or accepted, Elia felt incapable of turning back. She needed to turn that next page, no matter what.

Isabella leaned back in her chair. Sweat glistened at the creases of her elbows.

"Okay then, but do one thing," the big woman said.

"What's that?" Elia asked.

Isabella raised her thick palm toward Elia.

"Respect."

"Of course," Elia said.

"You're one of the few who know."

"You've got my word."

"I got to go," Isabella said.

She got up and dragged the chair back.

"But we'll talk again."

"Thank you," Elia said, falling back down into bed as Isabella shut the door.

Elia lay there, staring at the ceiling. She sensed the narrowest bridge had formed. She hoped a bridge to this woman meant passage to that man. Long after Isabella had left, three words from the encounter with the big woman rose above the cloud of uncertainty, three words Isabella had said tantalized her: *longer than forever*.

Just maybe her being here right now was no coincidence.

Perhaps there were none.

CHAPTER 12

Float
Deep
Down
No air
To breathe
No effort
To swim
To stroke
To kick
Away
To the open
Blue
Of the sea
Within me
Again.

Then a face
Not any
But hers
Appears
A mermaid
In this sea
Of me
Again.

No help
But look
A hook
In my gill
Without will
In this sea
Of me
Again.

But
Not to float
Nor swim
Nor breathe
Nor drown
Nor feel
Nor be?
For me
From this sea
I cannot be
Nor from thee
Ever be
Away
Again.

By the time the boy tied the frayed rope from his skiff to the dock, the yacht had already slipped from sight. He led Aluna toward cottages cuddled along the shoreline. His skin was like sinewy copper. As they walked, Aluna realized she barely recalled him speaking, but the variations in his broken smile seemed to convey volumes. It was that very smile that had reappeared when she pressed a cheek across her praying hands and said, "I need sleep."

Her husband wouldn't be back for days. She decided to rent a beach cottage just to be safe. For her the portrait of their marriage was dimming into a shadowy canvas.

She figured the boy had understood her pantomime since they were approaching the last cottage, a banana-colored bungalow with crackly windowpanes peeking from beneath a drooping tin roof.

The boy opened a rickety gate to a footpath, at the end of which sat a young woman in a wicker rocking chair. Painted on a piece of hanging driftwood were two words: For Rent.

The woman looked to be in her late twenties, round and coffee-skinned. As Aluna got closer the woman's eyes looked peculiar, like they were expecting her. Those eyes remained fixed on Aluna as she stood, unlocked the door and dangled a key.

"Go on, take a look," the woman said.

Aluna turned to the boy. She felt an urge to hug him. She fished into the front pocket of her khaki shorts and pressed two pieces of silver into his palm. He smiled his broken grin, bowed and walked away.

Aluna called after him.

"Thanks again."

He turned and waved.

She peeked through the doorway. She had larger closets back home. Her cabin on the yacht was nearly as big. She turned to the woman.

"I'll take it."

"Five dollars a day," hummed the woman.

"Fine," Aluna said.

She reached for her wallet.

"Not now, later," the woman said.

She was already sitting back into her rocking chair.

"Fine," said Aluna.

Aluna stepped inside and surveyed the room. She hurried to the bed, tugged down the sheet and thrust her fist into the feather pillow. Then she moved toward the table and pulled aside the chair, but didn't sit. Instead she stepped into the cramped bathroom, tossed a washcloth into the sink and threw the towel over the edge of a tub that, at its best, might pass for a child's wash basin.

She looked at the room again.

It looked lived in, or at least passed through.

She hurried outside and locked the door behind her. The young woman was still sitting out there in her chair, stroking a charm hung around her neck and rocking back and forth, back and forth, back and forth, steady as a lazy metronome. Aluna averted her eyes from the woman's stare.

"Don't worry if you don't see me for a bit; I've got some things to do," Aluna said.

But before the last note of Aluna's pretext fell, the woman's bare feet slapped to the ground. She stopped rocking and grabbed Aluna by the arm. Aluna felt her own hair stand on end. The woman looked up and grinned.

"Follow your heart," the woman said.

Not a wrinkle creased the woman's face. Yet her eyes looked wise as a sage.

Was it that obvious?

The woman's grip relented and her fingers slid down to take Aluna's hand.

"Isabella," she said.

"I will," Aluna mumbled.

She hurried down the path and closed the gate behind her. Rushing down the cobbled path, the vibration from the woman's touch was still unsettled inside her. She nearly ran through the waking market.

At the base of the path she finally stopped. Catching her breath, she stared down at the dirt below her feet.

What was she doing?

There was nothing certain. No, it was inherently uncertain, but she couldn't shake the woman's words from her head. As she climbed the path, the words seemed everywhere, blooming in the star jasmine, etched upon the rocks, buzzing from the dragonflies: *follow your heart.* This had nothing to do with society or security or reason. No, it had absolutely nothing to do with reason at all.

Glimpses from her dream earlier that morning flashed to mind. She recalled her life swirling about in that blue hole. But some force was pulling her, heart and all, up that hill. Each step seemed more effortless. She grew lighter. She was floating. She wasn't following her heart. It felt more like she was riding upon it.

The market below was long gone, the cottage even more distant, the fishing boy and the odd woman already a memory. The yacht, with her treasure-hunting husband and crew, were another world altogether. She had slipped into a reality entirely her own. It was exhilarating, frightening and free.

She had to be with him, even if for just two more days.

She reached the hilltop hut much earlier than the previous morning. Cameron was asleep inside the hut, slumbering upon his side. Early morning light crawled through the doorway. She followed it, tiptoed in and watched him sleep. Slipping off her sandals she lay down next to him. Half asleep, he opened his eyes and smiled. As exhilarated as she was to see him, as passionately as they had made love just the day before and as crazy as this all seemed, somehow that smile calmed her.

She touched her fingers to his lips. He kissed them, and then lifted his arm. She nestled into his warmth. She pulled his arm around her own, tightening his hold. Their fingers interlocked. Not a word was said.

The scent of cape honeysuckle cloaked them. Her heartbeat again found his and in that eurhythmic embrace they fell asleep.

Cameron awoke with Aluna in his arms. Eyes still closed, his fingers began to trace her shape. He began to memorize every intricate curve. She awoke to him caressing the rivulets in her palm, following them until they branched off above her slender wrist. He charted the silky plane along her forearm, pressing into her lean muscle until he found the bend at her elbow.

And he took his time. Patience.

His fingertips strummed her arm until discovering the supple turn above her shoulder blade. He explored the base of her neck, along the spot at which he had already placed so many kisses. He stroked what he imagined to be the most precious valley of any moon.

By a slow touch he claimed all of this as his own.

And that is when the wind reappeared, quiet at first, like a woman awakening.

Aluna rolled onto her back. His hands never left her. Her hips pressed into the cot and her lower back arched. He mapped each accelerating breath along her breasts. Her hips began to rise and fall, slow and steady. His hand slid farther down, from her breast to her ribs, across her belly. He grasped her along the waist, synchronized to every lift and fall of her hips. She rose up. He pressed her down into the cot. She rose up and he pressed her back down again, until he finally cupped the warmth at her wet, luscious core. Her head turned toward him. Her eyes still closed, he heard her breath accelerate. He felt her shiver.

All the while he remained lost in her.

The palm fronds outside began an unusually early morning dance. But the clacking of the bamboo dangling in the doorway didn't distract him.

Their bodies melded, a musician and his instrument, breathing, moving, strumming and dancing into one another. Synchronicity personified. The mounting wind underscored their movements, but he was oblivious to anything outside her touch.

She asked of him, there, and faster, and yes, please there again. And he answered her every request, her every whim, with a touch, a lick and kiss along her neck, and then each breast. Her nipples rose up too, becoming harder and harder with her hastened breath.

She grabbed his arm, pulling his fingers deep into her, her thighs twisted around his wrist. No escape. In a resounding shiver, she opened herself entirely. And as she rocked out of control he felt her hot, humid wetness envelop his fingers and hand and he smelled her sea-salted scent. And what he experienced obliterated anything and everything he had ever known.

He couldn't help himself. He was throbbing now. He rolled her on her side and entered her from behind. The tip of him pressed against her still quivering walls, which begged for him, deeper and more, and deeper again. He thrust long and steady, and then deeper into her with everything he had. He grasped the side of her hips, and then her hand that clutched the side of the cot. She pulled from his grasp and grabbed his backside, pulling him into her in a primal rhythm. No more questions or answers or reasons or meaning, only perfect harmony and sweat and fusion.

And he rocketed through space and time and beyond imagination and fantasy. He rocketed into another plane of being and awareness, beyond possible and into the absolute unobtainable impossibility of this woman in his arms.

He collapsed alongside her and exhausted, he fell upon her one last time. Cradled in her arms, he succumbed back to sleep.

He felt her hair against his cheek, her dried scent upon his skin. He sat up, trying not to wake her, but she stirred. He scratched through his sandy hair before rubbing his fingers over his eyelids. The afternoon sky had partly clouded over, leaving the entire hilltop in fickle patches of sun and shade and muting the light in the hut into a haze. Without a word he reached under the cot for his notepad, tore out a page and handed it to her. She pulled herself up and cuddled next to him. On that page were words he had written the night before:

> *Yet each setting sun*
> *Left an angel behind,*
> *A mirroring pool*
> *Of light.*

> *Her reflection cast*
> *Divinity,*
> *Forsaking the dark*
> *Of night.*

Cameron watched her study his simple verse.

"It's all you," he whispered.

Aluna's eyes fell from his. She stared at the dirt floor. Her auburn hair hid her face.

"I can't," she said.

Cameron stroked her shoulder.

"Can't what? What is it?" he asked.

Wind gusted.

"There's a yacht not far from here," she said.

"So?" he asked.

"On that yacht," she said.

A single tear fell down her cheek.

"What?" he asked.

"Is a man."

Another tear followed.

Cameron had once written that every tear, like every drop of rain, forever left its mark. A single tear was part of a force much greater, a force that could carve rivers through granite and forge oceans that divide continents. He wanted to deny that truth, but it was a part of him. His own words taunted him. A single tear from this woman could drown him.

"And?" he asked.

"He's my husband," she said.

A palm frond snapped to the ground outside the hut.

Aluna curled around Cameron. She tucked her head into his lap.

His hand pulled away from the shoulder he only a moment ago had caressed.

"Then what am I?" he asked.

"You are—"

She hesitated.

"A distraction?" he asked.

His head began to spin.

"Don't say that," she said.

"Then what? Tell me then. You ask I not speak your name, so I don't. I wait here for you to come to me like a dog waiting for its master. What am I? Tell me," he asked.

"Everything," she said.

She lifted her eyes to meet his.

But it wasn't enough. Cameron looked away, stood up and clutched his head. Then he buckled over. Her confession gutted him. He glared at her, this woman he could not bear to be without, and saw betrayal.

"Everything?"

"Everything I never knew existed," she said.

"Well I fucking exist. I can't breathe without feeling your breath upon my neck. I can't open my eyes without seeing you. I sleep to dream you!"

"And I dream of you," she cried.

He backed across the hut toward the doorway, wanting to bolt out that door. He twisted around and glared at her again.

"On your yacht, in his arms, that is where you do your dreaming—how sweet for me!"

"*His* boat, but not in *his* arms, not in *his* arms, I swear it," she said.

"Do you not understand what this is, what I have become?" he asked.

"What *you* have become?" she cried out.

"Yes!"

"I risk everything, don't you see?" she said.

"You risk nothing with your *secret*."

Disdain dripped from his last word.

"Steal away to me at your convenience, while I sit here without—" he said.

"Without what?" she asked.

"Without you, damn it."

He slumped against the wall and fell to his knees. He grasped a handful of the sandy hut floor in his fist. He opened his palm and the sand sifted through his fingers.

"Without you," he said again.

Everything was an illusion. This place, this woman, himself. Everything.

Aluna crawled from the cot toward him. Reaching out, she touched his arm. When he didn't recoil, she pulled him toward her, and cried into his ear.

"Let me stay tonight," she said.

He looked up.

"Stay forever."

"I cannot stand to leave you," she whispered, "I can't."

Cameron hugged her tight.

"Then don't," he said.

CHAPTER 13

Once lustered bits of tidal bliss
caressed from crag a tender kiss
pearl divers then adrift aquatic
amid forests kelp and sways hypnotic.

Emerged two bits to each revealed
Convergent chambers anew unsealed
yet time tumbled on and bits still churn
in doubt forlorn and seas will turn.

The tempest undaunted alas spun free
And drowned drowned tides alas drowned me
Two bits in memory now lost to time
Once pearls recalled forever shine.

Elia unscrewed the silvery cap on the square glass bottle. She dabbed the tiny brush into the crimson polish. Hugging her knee to her chest, she lifted her foot onto the wicker seat of the chair. With the care of a surgeon she brushed the polish on each toenail. She pondered the concept of timeless love. Was it nothing more than myth? The quiet of dusk settled in around her. Pale yellow walls in the cottage retired into a creamy haze.

Three days had passed since she promised Isabella to respect the sanctuary of the ailing poet. The entire first day she had lain in bed, numb from the sight of him. But the second morning she swam in the bay. Her gaze became lost in pebbles along the sandy bottom. She searched for polished bits caressed by the tides. That day she took an aimless walk. There was really nothing to do, so she slipped into the island stillness. She contemplated fragile orchids and blue ribbon streams. The imagery of Beck's *Secrets* seemed everywhere, surrounding her like the sea surrounded the island.

She lifted a foot, curled her toes over the table's edge and blew across each nail. Waiting for them to dry she noticed the deepened caramel of her skin. She hadn't been this dark in a long while. She found herself picturing the contrast of her deep-tanned flesh against the pale skin of her classmate from the university. A tingle spread as she imagined their bodies pressed together. She had yet to look him in the eye, yet she had already thought of him several times since the end of the semester. Gone just over a week, she wondered how she could miss someone she barely talked to. But she did.

Twice she saw Isabella along the esplanade. The first time Isabella rushed past her toward the *cantina* and said nothing. The second time, just yesterday, Isabella promised to stop by the cottage to talk again. Each time Elia stayed the course, not pushing too hard too soon, determined to gain Isabella's trust.

She closed the cap tight and opened the second bottle, lifted the ochre brush over her big toe and painted a delicate line down the center of the red nail. With the precision of a pointillist she dabbed three golden flecks on either side of the line, and then repeated the design on each toenail. She watched each droplet dry, sixty specks in all, and grinned. It reminded her of Seurat's *A Sunday Afternoon on the Island of La Grand Jatte*. She had written an undergraduate paper on the painting in an art history course. The Post-Impressionist Frenchman, dubbed "Seurat the dot," spent two years creating his speckled masterpiece. Three days was nothing.

She blew across her toes again.

Without any immediate task at hand, other than more waiting, she had succumbed to the slow rhythm of the island. She woke to the now familiar morning song of yellow-headed warblers, absorbed ethereal sunsets and bid sweet dreams each night to the geckos that scampered across the tile floor of her room, like the one that had just darted beneath her bed.

In these small moments, she imagined herself a bit of an islander.

Her grin broke into a satisfied smile. The colors of the hibiscus outside her window now painted her toes.

A knock rapped at her door.

She instinctively checked around the room for any mess, but there wasn't much to tidy. Her unzipped black roller suitcase was pushed against a wall on the floor. A flash of a teal sundress peeked from inside her suitcase. A navy-blue bikini laced over the chair back. She pressed the cotton like a pancake between her hands. Still a bit damp along the seams, she tossed it into the suitcase anyway. She left the two bottles of nail polish on the table beside a carafe of ice water and a glass.

Hobbling toward the door, she flexed her toes to protect the fresh polish. Expecting Isabella had finally come, she twisted open the handle. Instead she found Paco on her doorstep. He was wearing the same ragged jean cut-offs and tangerine flip-flops from the day at the *cantina*. His shirt, however, was different, a faded camouflage tee with an orange peace sign emblazoned across the front. Dark circles drooped under his hazelnut eyes. His face hung low, mirroring the slump in his shoulders.

"What is it?" she asked.

"I'm sorry," he said.

"For what?"

"How we were the other day."

"Isabella sort of explained," she said.

She moved aside and he walked in. He lifted his head and stroked back his thick black hair.

"Isabella and I agree on lots, disagree on more, but her heart is right. She isn't happy I'm here, but I feel it," he said.

"What do you feel?" she asked.

"I know that book," he said, pointing to Elia's copy of *Secrets* splayed open on her nightstand, "and I know that man."

"Please, sit down," she said.

He sat and then said, "I've known him forever."

"I see," Elia said, recalling Isabella's comment and now curious whether anybody on the island knew anyone *less* than forever.

She offered him a glass of water. He accepted with his gold-toothed grin.

"I know them all," he said.

"Them?" she asked.

"The poems."

"Really?" Elia asked. "Do you have a favorite?"

Paco drank the entire glass while gazing toward the hibiscus outside her window. The creases in the peace sign on his shirt unfurled. His shoulders squared. Without further prompt he recited in a low Caribbean accent:

> *In the quiet*
> *When still life beckoned*
> *It was simple then.*
> *Do you remember?*
>
> *Daylight faded*

You there by my side
It was perfect then.
And I remember.

Reclined in a smile
Sun streams melt into you
Sculpted moment
Memory.

A dam burst open
Blue falls cascade anew
Painted canvas
Destiny.

Elia began to whisper the verse in unison.

Unveiled from a shroud
Clandestine lost
Clandestine found.
Revealed in a cloud
A fleeting glimpse
Of this time, now.

When he paused for a breath, she continued:

If wonder needs a potion
Splintered souls
Reveal the how.
If passion needs a patron
In this patina
Cast a vow.

Hail the witness candle

Time again stand quiet
Be still
Will it be remembered?
One perfect moment at dusk
It will.

The room filled with the light of that poem. Elia had read it a dozen times, but something about Paco's deliberate air made it sound like he lived each word. He served up each syllable with such dignity, held every pause so solemn. She felt drawn to this man who appeared so transported by words.

"It's time," Paco said.

"For what?" she asked.

"Come," he said.

He offered his hand. "You want to meet him?"

Elia felt her eyes begin to well up. She noticed an old scar along his forearm just below his elbow. It looked like a branding iron had seared a squatted "H" into his flesh.

"Is he all right?" she asked.

"Not even close," he said.

She exhaled.

"So why now?"

"I've lived on this island my entire life. People come from everywhere. They look at me like I've missed something out there on the other side of the blue, out in that other world, like there is so much more away from here. But I haven't missed a thing. Everything is here and here," he said and twice pointed his finger to his chest.

Elia listened as if he were a prophet.

"I'm a simple man, but there's no coincidence."

She felt as if he had just channeled her thoughts from after Isabella's departure three days ago.

"Everything is related," he continued, his gold tooth flashing when he spoke. "You and me, these poems, this room, this island, why you're here, why I'm here, it's all connected. You came looking for this man and now he lies quiet. It's time. I feel it here and here," he said and again pointed two times to the peace sign covering his heart. "With this man, I've felt this only once before, a long time ago."

"Tell me," Elia asked.

"I was just a boy fishing the bay. I met a woman like none I'd seen before, or since. Her eyes were like the sea, filled with life. She, too, came looking for this man you seek. And I took her to him."

Her body tingled.

He ran his dark fingers through his black mane.

"And?" Elia asked.

"I've seen so many walk around this sand. I look at the eyes. I watch for that look, but never again," he said and shook his head.

"Who was she?" she asked.

"*Oshun.*"

His answer sounded so nonchalant, as if she had just asked whether he wanted another glass of water or whether he had caught any fish this morning.

"Who?"

She leaned closer.

He smelled of coconut oil.

"It means *goddess* of rivers, and love, and all creation," he said.

"But her name?" asked Elia.

"I knew only her smile and those eyes," he said.

Elia asked, "What happened to her?"

"Only he knows, but now—"

"What?"

"There is something," Paco said.

Elia felt another shiver. By now the color had drained from the room. His hand remained twisted toward her. The scar again caught her eye.

"Maybe Cam will see it too," he said.

Elia snatched her copy of *Secrets* off the nightstand, shuffled on her sandals and took his hand. It should have felt odd, she thought, holding hands with a man she had so recently met, but crossing that threshold she squeezed his palm and whispered, "Thank you."

Paco managed a smile as he led her outside.

Night had consumed dusk.

Only a few random lanterns cast shadowy hints along the path. Thoughts flickered back to her like those patches of light. She remembered Beck reading at the Village Poet, chasing after him to find him gone, and reciting the newfound poem in class. She recalled the melancholy etched across Dean Baltutis's face as they sat under the weeping willows by Mirror Lake. She thought back to the bumpy flight to the island and the whale careening alongside the plane's shadow. *Listen to the whale's song.*

The peculiar, guarded island greetings rushed back and the image of Beck sprawled across that fish cart. All this, then the last three days of nothing but time, time to do nothing, time to fall into the strangest sense of calm she had ever experienced.

Two candles lit the doorway to the *cantina*. Inside, a solitary candle flickered on the bar.

"He's back in my room," Paco said.

They brushed past the table where she had eaten fruit with Paco and Isabella just days ago. He led her down the narrow hall. As they passed the kitchen, Elia picked up the scent of honeysuckle and lilac. That sweet fragrance grew stronger the closer they got to the open door at the end of the hallway.

"Shush," Paco whispered.

Elia followed his shadow into the dim room. Inside, more candles danced in pockets of light. A woman's voice hummed a low chant. Elia listened, but couldn't decipher the language.

"*Cumma na oshun loa, cumma na oshun loa.*"

The woman rocked back and forth on a low stool at the base of the bed. A maroon shawl covered the back of her head and shoulders.

Without turning, the woman raised the back of her large hand to them. Paco stretched an arm in front of Elia.

The woman continued her chant and Elia's eyes began to adjust to the muted haze of the room.

Flat on the bed was the ailing poet. A cotton sheet covered him to the chest, with only his shoulders and head visible. She could just make out his collarbone. The sheet over his chest rose and fell with each slow breath. His eyes were closed. He looked peaceful, like he was asleep. She wondered whether even now he dreamed of his love. She hoped he did.

A ceiling fan sliced the humid night air. A pitcher of water and an empty glass stood ready on the nightstand. But on the far side of the bed a slow, clear drip slithered through a plastic tube that disappeared under the sheet near Beck's left arm.

Next to the chanting woman at the foot of his bed low candles and flower petals had been spread atop a wooden chest. Shutters to the only window were open and Chuey, the scrappy monkey Elia first met at the *cantina* days earlier, crouched upon the windowsill. His hairy chin propped upon spindly mitts crossed over one knee. Apparently mystified by the somber chanting, the monkey's eyes were fixed on the shrouded woman.

The woman stopped chanting, stood and turned.

Elia retreated a half step, stunned to find Isabella staring at her.

She sounded so different. Face-to-face she looked different, too. Beneath the shawl, necklaces laced with feathers, shells and bones hung from her neck. Swaths of orange and yellow streaked her face. Her lips were painted jet black.

Pressed against her chest, Isabella held a stick with a mummified claw laced around the end. It looked the size of a monkey's paw. Elia glanced again at Chuey, relieved to confirm both of his paws were intact.

"Keep it burning," Isabella said as if she were waking from a trance.

Sprinklings of sand and shells had been spread around some of the candles, tiny rocks and small twigs tied together with twine encircled others. The sweet scent she smelled was rising from a small tray of incense.

Elia nodded, not quite sure if Isabella meant the candles or the incense. Either way, she wasn't about to mess with the juju in that room. It felt beyond question.

Isabella glared at Chuey and muttered, "In or out?"

The monkey hesitated, before jumping to the floor with a thump. Isabella pulled the shutters closed. Chuey scurried after her as she walked toward the door.

Isabella turned toward Paco and said, "Fatty will be here at dawn."

Then she leaned over Cameron, kissed his forehead and rubbed the strands of her charm across his cheeks.

"Be back in the morning too, don't you worry none," she said.

She turned to Elia.

With her painted face she looked fierce, like some sort of witch doctor. Elia's owl eyes opened even wider as Isabella extended her hand and leaned close to her, touching her forearm as she said, "He can hear you."

Elia nodded and exhaled, feeling relieved by her gentle words and calming touch.

Isabella vanished down the hall with Chuey scampering behind. Paco pulled the stool toward the head of the bed but didn't sit. He bent over Cameron and touched his right shoulder.

"Cam, it's Paco. Tonight you have a new visitor."

He motioned for Elia to sit on the stool next to the bed.

"Miss Elia, this is Cameron Beck. Cam, this is Miss Elia."

The hair on the back of her neck stood on end. She sprung up, awkwardly bowed and said, "Aloundra, it's Elia Aloundra. It's so nice to meet you."

Not a ripple passed from Cameron.

"I have to go to the kitchen and cook up some dinner. Cam, if you want anything at all, just let me know," Paco said.

No response.

"I'll be down the hall. Are you hungry?" he asked Elia. "No, I'm fine," she said and realized that he was going to leave her alone.

Elia sat back down.

In those first quiet moments, as her ears adjusted to the faint pattern of Cameron's convalescent breath, Elia thought he didn't look hurt at all. Raccoon circles ringed under his eyes but there were no wounds on his pale face or square shoulders. She had no idea what lay beneath the ivory sheet.

He looked to be in a deep sleep, like he might awaken any moment and start talking. The same thought she had earlier nagged again and she wondered whether he dreamt of the goddess, the one Paco called *Oshun*. That is what she wanted to know. There were so many more questions, but whether he dreamt of that woman eclipsed all the rest.

Graying, sun-flecked hair curled behind Beck's ears. A few days of stubble matted his cheeks and chin and an ointment had been smeared across his lips, making them glisten.

"At the end of one path," Elia whispered.

It was hard for her to believe that from this lifeless man had sprung such lovely lyrics. She had no idea where to begin, what to say, how to explain how or why she, a complete stranger, had arrived at his bedside. So many ideas spun around, but any reasoned explanation seemed out of reach.

She felt lost and nervous. She took a deep breath and fell back upon her crutch of all crutches. She reached for her safety. She reached for the word. Opening her copy of *Secrets*, Elia pulled out the single sheet of paper stashed within the back cover. She stared down at the handwriting scrawled on that slip.

And uncertain whether he could truly hear her, she said, "I'd like to read you something."

CHAPTER 14

There is a world
In which I live
Another
In which I dream.

In fleeting chance
A passing glance
Long strangers
Became the same.

Jackson's hand sifted along the bottom. Scattered sand clouded his vision. The sediment cleared. Once again: nothing. Undeterred, he kicked forward tucking his right arm back under his chest, an unexplored seabed ahead.

A buoyancy control vest clung around his torso. The expandable bladder and integrated weights allowed him to maneuver as if weightless. Long yellow and black split fins propelled him past sea grass that swayed among pockets of volcanic rock littered with the sparse, barnacled remnants from the wreck.

His primary regulator looped over his right shoulder. His alternate remained tucked into a clasp on his vest. He heard the controlled rhythm of his breath flowing through the mouthpiece. His breath sounded like the labored breathing of an invalid on a respirator. It was a sound he still associated with his grandfather's final days trapped within a sanatorium. Looking into the old man's longing eyes that last time, Jackson decided he would rather perish undersea than in some stark infirmary. Submerged for nearly two hours, he needed to ascend soon or his romanticized finale could come true.

Several meters away what looked like an oversized lobster trap rested upon the sea floor. From its top, a yellow rope slithered like a serpent into the blueness above him before it altogether faded from view. At this depth everything still felt calm, with no hint of the oncoming storm.

He checked his air gauge. It was only two clicks from red. He had maybe ten more minutes. He blinked a dive light toward Esteban, who turned and flashed ten fingers. He signaled *thumbs-up*. Esteban gave him the okay sign.

What concerned him more, however, was another clock ticking away. The storm would soon hit and they would need to abandon the site altogether. There weren't many hours left to explore the wreck. With each successive dive he straddled the edge between patience and urgency, particularly because the pouch clipped to his vest was still empty. The lobster cage was for anything and everything else they might find, such as the rustic goblets hoisted yesterday from the sea floor. But the yellow netted sack clipped to his vest was reserved for one treasure. That pouch was meant for a dream, the Aztec bracelet.

Through his underwater headphones a ping pierced the drone of his breath. He peered. The mask sucked against his face. He extended the aluminum clasped to his forearm toward a rock. The state-of-the-art metal detector didn't look all that different from the simple contraptions used by beachcombers rummaging for buried coins and lost wedding bands. The rubber-sheathed coil at its end resembled a peace sign. He hovered the device above a small sand drift at the rock's base.

Once in a hundred times the sand might conceal something other than an old tuna can, stray fishing lead or corroded rivet. Floating above the drift the metal detector sung in a flurry of pings.

His pulse quickened.

With the care of an archeologist, he began to brush away silt. Not even a palm length down, his fingers grazed a curved rim. He traced along the rough edge half the length of his forearm, giving it a tug. In the flurry of sand he followed the object as if reading by Braille. He discerned a narrow shaft bisecting the arc. Then his fingers slipped through two hollowed triangles on either side of the crusty shaft.

As the sand cloud settled, a flat bronze quarter-circle was revealed, much of its surface coated in a green coppered patina, part of a broken arm fused in place along its scale. He gripped an antiquated quadrant. It was a Spanish navigation tool from the 1600s, a predecessor to the sextant.

He couldn't help but smile.

He dug deeper into the shallow grave to search for the broken arm. He felt another odd edge, although it seemed too long. He traced along, felt it broaden and gave it a tug. Sand flaked away until a shiny black surface reflected in his light.

But it wasn't the quadrant's missing piece. Instead he gripped a chiseled blade. Even underwater he immediately sensed the object's purposed balance.

Peering through his mask, the glassy sheen looked like obsidian. He knew what that meant. This wasn't Spanish. His fingertips caressed a rough handle sculpted into the form of a crouched body. Forearms and thighs hugged its base. A menacing head with bulbous eyes stared down the shaft.

Even more remarkable than its existence, though, was that the dagger appeared nearly pristine. Barnacled critters clung to nearly everything else he found undersea, including the fragmented quadrant. But only a couple of tiny mollusks were tucked into the creases of the carved handle. The blade was almost spotless, damn near perfect.

Images flooded to mind. His breath quickened. He'd seen pictures of similar daggers in books and museums. This was Aztec. He was certain of it. And he knew its intended purpose. The rituals were legendary.

Two masked sentinels escorted a maiden to the *Teocalli*, the "house of gods." Frenzied throngs danced like a copper-skinned sea of hungry piranha. At the peak of the pyramid-like temple was a stone slab. A high priest waited, standing by the crimson-stained altar and wielding a dagger. The maiden, rarely more than sixteen years old, climbed a hundred steps only to be splayed across that slab. The high priest raised the dagger. The clamor of thousands neared climax. Down came the dagger, thrust through human flesh and bone, disgorging a human heart. The high priest hoisted aloft the still-pulsating organ to appease the gods.

Jackson fought the urge to hold his breath. If he gave in, that would only lead to him taking in too much compressed air upon his next breath, and that would be deadly. He clung to the diver's mantra: slow and steady. Still, when he remembered to check his air gauge it wasn't the single click from red that set his heart racing. Instead, it was the ancient obsidian dagger now gripped in his palm—likely more than five lifetimes since its last use.

He imagined the souls lost to this blade. He pictured a young maiden about to be sacrificed and envisioned a bracelet upon her wrist as she lay down. A harsh sun burned overhead. This dagger eclipsed even that sun. He pictured the maiden's eyes falling to the bracelet. She, clinging to a promise of eternal life, and believing in an ancient secret he now dreamt would be his own.

In the next instant her body convulsed, her last breath exhaled, and her innocent life ended while a throng cheered.

In his hand he gripped the antithesis of immortality.

Yet it felt no less powerful.

His heart pounded. He opened the sack at his waist. He slid the dagger in and cinched it closed. If the bracelet ever existed it had known this dagger. He marked the spot with a weighted flag. He flashed his light toward Esteban, who signaled back. Time was up. They needed to surface. He swam toward the cage, secured its lid and the two divers began their ascent.

The scuba divers broke the surface. Only miles away two lovers plunged into the sea.

But those same waters now churned the two lovers. Where only days earlier they swam in a tranquil sea they were now jostled by heavy currents and chop, one moment thrusting them toward each other, the next ripping them apart. They scuttled any hope of revisiting the cave. Cameron grabbed onto Aluna and guided her back to shore, where they climbed from the turbulent sea.

She clung to the rock like a marooned castaway. She sat down to catch her breath.

"It's so different," she said.

"Yeah," Cameron said.

But he wasn't looking at the water or thinking about the weather.

"So rough."

"It'll get worse," he told her. He squinted toward the clouding horizon.

"The storm comes soon?" she asked.

Cameron nodded.

Palm trees were beginning to extend into windswept arcs. Island birds darted about, shoring up nests. A day away at most, he figured. The sea lurched against the rocky shore.

Signs everywhere, but he had jumped in anyway.

Her matted bronze hair began to dry in the sun. Loose strands split away in the wind. She brushed a wisp from her face.

"How long will it last?" she asked.

"A couple of days, maybe a week, but then another and another," he said. His voice trailed off. He watched the distant clouds.

"Until?"

"Spring," he said.

"April?" she asked.

"May," he said.

May was seven months away. He knew what seven months of wind and rain would feel like, but now he imagined seven months of solitude. Seven months without her. Seven months of lies and deception until she might return to him, if even then. Seven months of waiting and wasting time.

"Can we go back?" she asked.

Cameron looked straight at her. He sensed her uneasiness. "Sure, come on," he said.

Helping her up, he felt her skin already dry and warm. They climbed up the cliff and trekked back to the hut without holding hands. Aluna said nothing. Cameron had so many questions, but all of them seemed unanswerable, or maybe the answers better off unknown. So he too kept quiet. Where their silence had once been filled with seduction, now it just felt awkward.

Inside the hut, Cameron carved open a black-skinned avocado, losing himself in the task. He squeezed one half until its heavy seed dropped into his palm. He backhanded the seed out the window into the bushes. The ripe fruit squished from its skin onto a small plate. He sliced some golden carambola, spreading the star fruit along the plate, and added a pocket of goat cheese and several rips of bread.

He felt her watching his every move, but she said nothing. He poured two squat glasses full of wine and handed her one.

She finally broke the silence. "How long will you stay?"

He looked up at the thatched roof.

"This will hold for a couple of weeks."

He shook his head and swigged the wine.

"Then what?" she asked.

"Back to the States," he said.

He looked at her, perhaps for the first time appreciating the true distance between their lives. Her caramel skin, pointed cheekbones and hollowed eyes were culled from southern latitudes beyond his travels. Her polished Portuguese accent and mannerisms hinted of privilege. He caught himself searching her left hand for the pale trace of a wedding band.

"I don't want to leave this place," she said.

But he could tell by the defeated tone of her voice she was leaving, and soon. He stared into her green eyes, hoping to find at least a hint of a struggle. He saw only sad resolve.

"This will exist forever," he said.

He watched her eat a slice of yellow star fruit. Everything she did now seemed even more significant, each movement another grain of sand filtering through an hourglass. The way her lips parted and met each time she chewed. The way her fingers moved over the plate as she pondered which piece of fruit to choose. The way her elbow rose from the table as she lifted the fruit to her mouth. The way she bit into the fruit, her lips revealing the sweet satisfaction of the juice dissolving upon her tongue.

Yes, this will exist forever, he promised himself.

Even in slow motion lunch passed too fast. He wanted to paint each moment so each would last, so this space they occupied, just as he'd promised, would somehow remain, so they would forever be together. His mind clicked a hundred snapshots. He'd find the words later. Right now, he could not spare a detail, each grain of sand too precious.

The sun began to sink. He settled next to her upon the cot. Like a still-life painting, next to the empty bottle of wine atop the table rested remnants of fruit and a lone piece of bread.

Hugging her in his arms he gazed out the window.

A burst of crimson coated the underbelly of the gathering clouds. He looked back at her. The tangerine glow illuminated her features. Her green eyes dazzled like emeralds, her skin was a silken stream, her smile effervescent ivory. The fiery finale permeated everything, but to him the only purpose of the day's extravagant farewell was to enlighten her and only for his eyes. In that last light of day she became his masterpiece.

This will exist forever, he vowed. He would dedicate his life to making sure of it.

Cameron finally asked, "How long will you stay?"

But before she answered, she said, "Make love to me now."

"Like my life depends on it," he said.

"Like both our lives do," she said.

And the two of them again became one, snuffing out the last light of day in the salted sweat of their primal dance. But somehow, this time to him felt different, almost fatalistic. This time, at least initially, sadness resonated in that union. It felt to him almost as if neither of them wanted to let go, but perhaps each had to face the possibility of doing just that. And this thought angered him, manifesting in him a fierceness previously unfelt between the two of them. This time he wanted to obliterate them both forever right here and now, resolve everything once and for all, howl straight into the darkness approaching the island. Rip each other apart. Fate be damned.

§

Cameron woke once that night.

It was pitch black. He didn't know whether they'd slept for minutes, hours or days. Clouds blanketed the night sky. Not a hint of a star blinked overhead, but he felt her breathing upon his neck. She nuzzled alongside him. Her head lay upon his chest.

He fought to remain awake, tortured by the thought of no future, yearning to capture every last nuance, but soon the calm rhythm of her breathing lulled him back asleep.

He sank into a dream filled with underwater caves and a mermaid swimming among turtle hatchlings. A light shone from the mermaid's wrist. He swam toward her and the baby turtles. As she raised her right arm toward his face, Cameron felt warmth from her glowing wrist.

He awoke to Aluna's kiss upon his cheek. She squeezed him tight.

"It must have been nice," she said, "you were smiling."

"You cannot imagine," he said.

The two lay beside each other in near pitch black until the scouting light of dawn discovered them.

The cloak of night lifted like an impressionistic painting easing into focus. First he divined her eyes and lips. Next her body, pressed against his, became visible. Gentle hues filled in soft as watercolors at first, creamy pigments flowing into the palette of early day. Eventually even the emerald curve of the empty wine bottle across the room sharpened into focus.

He wanted to stay there all day, content to watch a spectrum of light and color paint the day until fading again to dark, as long as she remained in his arms.

"Tomorrow," she said.

"What?"

"That is when I must go," she said.

He rolled over.

"I'll be by your side 'til morning. Know that," she said.

Those words were her only promise.

He shut his eyes.

And his world returned to black.

CHAPTER 15

Let me perish
one gasp past
this peak, in love,
nothing to yearn.

Beyond the gorge,
rivers black
despair, roiling
for its return.

Straddling the squat, three-legged stool, Elia arched her back. She cleared her throat as quietly as she could. One long breath, and then she read aloud:

A flicker lost beyond myth

She glanced up at Cameron. She looked close for any hint of recognition, the flick of an eyelash, a gulp in the throat—but nothing. She lofted at him the same words he had recited at the Village Poet. She crawled into those words as if her own, hoping to stumble upon any hidden key within, something or anything maybe buried in the rhythm or even the spaces in between. Her voice strengthened a bit with the second line.

danced in those eyes

She squinted in the dim candlelight for any sign. She paused to listen for even the slightest stutter in his breath. Nothing. How could this comatose man unlock anything? She had the odd latitude to study him without reproach. And the more she stared at him, the more he appeared anything but prophetic. His breath was steady, but weak, like a tiring metronome that might stop without notice. Patches of reddish-gray stubble covered his chin. Uneven cheekbones poked from his angular face. His long nose tweaked to one side. His whole visage seemed slightly askew, like he had been smacked with a shovel and his face never reset. He looked weak and fragile. He looked utterly human.

like a nascent sea
of rippled reflection.

She waited. The slightest remnant of "reflection" faded into nothingness. She had fantasized about him waking, his eyes ready, willing and able to reveal everything. But he didn't. The sheet over his chest lifted and fell, but barely.

Elia scooted the stool closer to the bed. One of the stool legs lifted off the uneven floor. She bent forward on the wobbly stool so that she could hover nearer to him. The candles on the nightstand dipped in a hypnotic dance.

Something inside her stirred. She picked up his limp hand. Maybe he would awaken to her touch. His palm felt warm. Jagged scars streaked across his freckled knuckles. His limp fingers were soft, without callus. She pictured them scripting the verse she had just read. But he gave no response. She kissed the back of his hand and placed it back upon the sheet.

Her palms began to sweat. She cleared her throat. New words struggled from within. This time the words were hers.

"Your poems mean so much to me," she whispered.

She felt the warmth of the candles on her face.

"I saw you at the Village Poet that night. You came in and read this poem. Something drew me there that same night."

Some fissure within widened. Tears began to follow every word. She began to rock upon the hobbled stool.

"I don't know why I came that night, why you came, why you read or why you left this paper behind, but here it is in my hands and here I am on this island in the middle of nowhere."

Paco's words came to mind.

"I don't believe in coincidence. I saw a whale while reading your words. *Listen to the whale's song.* That's what you wrote. That's what I read. That's what I saw. That's why I'm here. Damn it, I'm listening."

She stopped rocking and leaned even closer.

"Tell me everything."

A pan crashed down the hall. Cameron didn't flinch.

"Where is this love?" she asked.

She raked her fingers across her forehead and pushed back her hair. Her words trickled to a whimper.

"Is it just some phantom?" she asked.

"You're no ghost."

Elia swiveled around and wiped her face. Paco stood at the doorway. He balanced a bowl on a tray. Puffs of steam from the bowl clouded the candlelight upon his face.

"I'm sorry," she said.

She rubbed her eyes as she hurried to get up.

"I don't know where that came from."

"Come on and eat. Let's give him some quiet. Between Isabella's chanting and your crying he's probably reeling inside."

An oniony aroma rose from the bowl.

"Just look at him," Paco said.

The tip of his gold tooth reflected in the candlelight. Something wet was splattered across the peace sign on his shirt. Elia felt her face flush. She had just broken down and begged an unconscious stranger to explain love. *Great.*

"Soup?" Paco asked.

She peeked into the bowl. It smelled—*ugh*, she gagged. It *was* fish soup. Years ago in New Orleans she had eaten a bowl of gumbo. Only after gnawing on the rubbery piece of what she thought was white okra did she learn it wasn't white okra at all. Not even close. She had swallowed a fish eyeball. It took days to shake the thought of that eyeball slithering down her gullet, and nearly blasting back up, equally as disgusting. Ever since, she gagged at even the scent of fishy broths.

"I'm really not hungry. Please, can I stay? I'll keep quiet."

Paco took a hard look at her. He nodded.

"Okay, but let him rest."

"I will, I promise."

He inched toward Cameron. "Cam, I'm just down the hall."

Paco muttered beneath his breath as he left the room, but loud enough so that Elia could hear, "That will be enough small talk for now."

Elia understood. The confessional was closed.

She felt embarrassed by Paco's comment. She sat back down, a long silent night ahead.

Pulling her feet up she crossed her legs into the lotus position. She balanced upon the worn stool so that her spine extended again. Every once in a while she uncoiled herself and stretched, but a lifetime in libraries had trained her to endure long periods of stillness. Seconds slipped into minutes that became hours, and she drifted into a peaceful vigil.

She absorbed into the calmness of the room. Her mind began to wander. She began to emulate the slight sway in the candles. She noted every change in the faint breeze as it combed across her skin. She slowed her breath to synchronize with Cameron's.

And as she played this game, in that near dead calm and quiet, she began to notice small, odd things. In the shadowy candlelight the outline of the cotton sheet that draped him and the bed resembled a sarcophagus. The dimly lit, languid room felt like a crypt. She recalled reading about pharaohs buried with their family and servants all in the same crypt.

She imagined the candles to be infinite stars of a galaxy. Each flickered independent of the other. Each burned at different rates. So did planets, and people and even thoughts and feelings. Billions of stars made up the universe. How rare that two might collide. How rare that two people ever meet. How rare that two ever share the same thoughts or feelings. How rare? She had no idea.

An inverted gecko curled its head between the window shutters. It climbed through, scampered down the wall and across the floor toward her. It seemed to be considering whether to scale the stool leg. She froze perfectly still. She wondered what it might feel like against her skin. But the gecko darted beneath the bed. She lost it in the shadows.

The scent of incense had faded. She found a box of matches next to the pitcher of water on the nightstand. On one side of the box, a hand-etched picture depicted a court jester holding a chalice. On the other side of the matchbox a Spanish-looking knight posed with a sword. Each side bore an alternating yellow and red wax-beaded frame and the signature "San Pancho Nay." But even with all that elaborate detail, the matches inside were thin as toothpicks. The first match broke when she struck it against the box. The broken tip landed upon the sheet near Cameron's covered legs.

The second match flamed and she lit the incense. She held the tiny flame over the sheet and pinched off the broken match. Her fingertips brushed against the thin cotton. It felt like bare skin underneath the sheet. She felt the urge to peek. What was she thinking?

She sat back down and resumed her cross-legged pose. Eventually even the occasional shuffle of night noises in the bushes outside the shuttered window faded. She stopped noticing even the small things. It seemed the entire world, even her mind, had surrendered. She felt her eyelids dropping.

She startled to a stranger clutching a leather satchel.

"Hello darling, been here all night?" the odd man crooned.

His feet were filthy. It looked like he might have shambled right out of the bushes.

"Yes I have," she said and rubbed her eyes.

Those *were* polka dots on the flip-flops squishing under his dirty feet.

The scrawny sack of bones slid past her. A scent of marijuana cut through the incense. He took up Cameron's hand and pressed his fingers along his wrist. The man's beady eyes and beak reminded her of a turkey. His ribbed tank top must have been an extra-small, yet it still hung loose. The strange bird leaned forward to press his hand against Cameron's neck. A faded, Rastafarian-colored belt cinched his baggy shorts to his skinny frame.

"Not so bad," the man croaked.

Something about him reminded her of fish gumbo. She must have looked a bit dumbfounded.

"Fatty, *Medicinae Doctorae*," he said with a sly grin.

"Elia," she said and stood up.

Feeling tingled back into her thighs.

"May I borrow that?" he asked.

His big toe was already hooked onto the stool's leg.

"Sure," Elia said.

She had at least two inches and ten pounds on him.

He sat down, opened the satchel and wrapped a blood pressure cuff around Cameron's bicep. Clasping the earpieces of a stethoscope around his neck, he placed the silvery disc that dangled from its rubbery tube over the inside of Cameron's elbow. His bony fingers pumped the little black balloon. He propped the earpieces into his drooping ears. Just before he twisted open the pressure release, he glanced back at her as if to confirm she was watching. She was.

He turned back toward his patient and listened. The cuff released a slow hiss.

"One lucky crawdad," he said.

He got up, walked around the bed and fiddled a bit with the IV. He lifted back the sheet where Elia had pinched off the broken match in the middle of the night. A gauze bandage wrapped Cameron's left leg. She was glad she hadn't peeked earlier, but didn't look away as Fatty unraveled the gauze to inspect the stitches. She gasped. Taut black stitches held together a long, red crest of flesh.

"Laced gators," he said.

Isabella bustled in with a sack in her hand. She smiled at Elia and bellowed, "Time for some fresh air."

Isabella opened the shutters. Morning filtered into the room. Chuey hopped onto the windowsill, banana in hand.

"And?" Isabella asked.

"Stable, Isaboo," Fatty said.

Isabella pulled new candles from her sack, set them in place of the old ones and sprinkled a jarred, yellow powder alongside them. Humming and stroking her charm, she rearranged the pebbles, shells and twigs around the candles.

Intrigued by the juju, Elia nonetheless backed away. She leaned against the doorframe not quite sure who was in charge, the scrawny doctor or the overbearing island matriarch. Her face felt puffy. Isabella finished and then stared at her. By that look alone, Elia felt Isabella telling her to get some rest. But she didn't want to leave, even though she felt lightheaded and dead tired.

Elia heard a familiar voice behind her. "You did a nice job last night keeping quiet."

She hadn't.

"You'll need your rest if you want to do the same tonight," Paco said.

Elia noticed Isabella frown.

"I'll be here," Elia said and yawned.

"Then go get some sleep and a swim. We'll see you tonight," Paco said and prodded her out the door.

"Okay," Elia said.

As tired as she was, Elia gleaned that Paco was somehow the one in charge.

Fatty called out after her in a sweet drawl, "And yes, darlin', it's true."

"What's that?" Elia asked, her eyes barely open.

"I'm available," Fatty said and chuckled.

Isabella moaned.

"Thanks," Elia said, polite as she could muster. She snuck one last look at Cameron before leaving. He hadn't flinched.

That was how it went for the next three days. Elia would eat a light breakfast of mango to get something in her belly after her visit, crawl into bed and sleep to mid-afternoon. She hiked or swam, sometimes both, and then gobbled down dinner before returning to the backroom of that *cantina*.

Except one thing did change.

With every return visit Paco's welcoming hugs seemed a little bit stronger. She didn't mind. In fact she liked it. After those hugs, Paco always announced her arrival by telling Cameron "Miss Elia's back now." Then he would leave her alone and disappear down the hall. After he left she would retake her perch atop the bedside stool. Paco never returned during those three nights. But she always sensed him close by.

The second night, lured by the faint sound of snoring, she found Paco dozing in a hammock slung along the far side of the *cantina*. A worn paperback copy of Steinbeck's *Cannery Row* fanned open upon his chest.

She did not read any more poetry to Cameron, nor did she make any more weeping confessions. Instead, each night she fell into her own simple ritual. She whispered hello to Cameron and then sat in complete silence. A couple of times a night she lit those long incense sticks with the spindly matches. She didn't necessarily believe in Isabella's voodoo, but she wasn't about to cross it. Western religion had failed her long ago. She had migrated spiritually toward Eastern philosophies. Still, Isabella's magic, like the big woman herself, unsettled her.

Each night Elia played the same game too, slowing her breath to match the poet's, syncing up each inhale and exhale. Without any communication and without him likely even aware of her presence, she imagined a relationship budding. This was the precious time only she and Cameron shared even if nobody else knew it, not even Cameron.

Then even those thoughts fell away as she let go. Not even books to fill time. Instead, she started to drop into some sort of meditative calm. A peacefulness rose. She trusted that she was exactly where she was meant to be. There was nothing else she could do. She controlled nothing. And as she realized her utter lack of control she finally let go of any expectations. It was an odd feeling, but somehow she felt liberated, in a sense as naked as that barely breathing man beneath the sheet.

And with every successive night this feeling grew a bit more. She began to crave this quiet time together, but for a much different reason than she had ever anticipated. Something was happening in all this nothingness. She wasn't sure what it was but she didn't care. It felt right to just sit there all night, silent, and do absolutely nothing but stop thinking. Even the allure of Paco's crooked shelf of books down the hall didn't trump this new feeling.

On the fourth night, overwhelmed with a sense of gratitude she kissed Cameron's hand after she entered the room. Without even speaking, he had already taught her something. Those long silences had slowed her down. She hadn't read in days, but even that was okay. Now she wanted to give him something in return. But what had she to offer this man? She knew every word he had written so long ago. And she knew every breath he had taken these last four nights. But she knew so little else.

So she decided to give him maybe the simplest, most precious gift one can ever give to another. She wanted him to know something, maybe as much for her as for him. She longed to be with him now. He had not spoken a word. He had not lifted a finger. Yet she needed this time. And she hoped that maybe in some way he did too.

So on that fourth night, after kissing his hand, Elia leaned over him and gave him her word.

"I will be by your side until morning. Know that," she said.

She sat back on the stool and shut her eyes.

"Stay with me forever," a voice whispered.

Her eyes startled open.

She looked back at the door. Paco wasn't there.

"What?"

She squinted in the candlelight for any sign that his lips had moved. She locked onto those eyelids and waited for them to open. They didn't.

§

Cameron huddled next to Aluna on the cot. His eyes were closed. Their last day together had been anything but tranquil. One solitary thought coursed through him. It felt stronger than even the gusting winds. He needed to topple her resistance.

"Your life will be empty," he said when he opened his eyes.

A candle flickered inside a squat glass jar on the table.

"Don't say that," she said and sat up. She tucked her head into her hands.

"You know it will."

"Don't make me angry at you," she said.

"At me?"

He sprung from the cot and paced toward the table. Damp sand clung to his feet.

He hovered over that defiant candle.

"Why, because I speak the truth? Turn your back on this, even for an instant, and then what? How will you breathe each day?"

He grabbed his spiral notebook. He flipped to the page he wrote just earlier that night while she had slept. The words that ricocheted through his mind had obliterated any chance of sleep. But that wasn't enough. He tilted the notebook toward the candlelight and taunted her with raw verse:

> *Where will you go my love*
> *When demons dance on your pillow*
> *Whispering doubts as you lay awake*
> *The impostor by your side*
> *As alley cats wander home*
> *The delivery boy tossing dead words*
> *A muffled thud heard only by you*
> *And the barking hounds.*

His fingertips crumpled the corners of the page.

> *Where will you go my love*
> *When insanity pierces reason*
> *Slicing like a knife*
> *When paranoia sneaks into bed*
> *Curling up for another night*
> *Dallying until morning*
> *And even then*
> *Lingering.*

He glanced at her. She was hunched over and cradling her head. Her elbows on her knees, but her eyes fastened to him. His voice dropped.

> *Please tell me*
> *Where is it?*
> *Where shall you go my love?*
> *Tell me*
> *So I can find this place too.*
> *This place I so desperately crave*
> *This place*
> *That is your voice*
> *Your touch*
> *Your smile*
> *This place that was you.*

Tears streamed down her cheeks.

"How dare you?" she cried.

"Speak the truth?" he asked.

"Make me suffer even more. Torture me with your words when all I have is love for you."

"Love?" he asked.

He shook his head.

"Yes, love. Damn you," she said.

"Then what else matters?"

He knelt down before her. His knees grounded into the sandy floor of the hut.

"So much you do not know. If I disappear now, he'll never leave this place. If I tell him, there's no telling what he might do. You don't know him."

He took her hand.

"And you don't know me," he said.

"I'm yours. Know that. But I've got to go."

"Why?" he asked.

She stared at the floor.

"I can't just run away from my life," she said.

He sensed doubt.

"And your heart?"

She lifted her eyes.

"It's yours."

There should have been splendor in that declaration. But he felt only despair.

It would have been so much easier had he never seen her in the island market that first day, had their eyes not met. It would have been so much easier had they not wandered off to hike and swim together, had they not kissed, had they not discovered together the mystery of the cave, made love in the sand and fallen into this clutch.

Life was so much simpler without this.

She began to tremble. He crawled up and hugged her. He couldn't help himself. She buried her head into his bare chest.

"My god," she said.

"What?"

He felt her trembling subside. He pulled back. She was gazing out the window.

"Can you see it?" she asked.

"What?"

He squinted out the window. Patches of an eerie fog seeped along the hilltop. But all Cameron saw were elongated shadows dancing in the moonlight.

"Those two, that shimmering light," she said.

"What are you talking about?" he asked.

"Please tell me you can see it," she said, still fixed on the window.

Whatever she saw, it calmed her.

Cameron stroked her hair.

"We're going to be okay," she said.

"We are?"

"No, I see it," she said and turned back to him.

"Really?"

He wanted to believe her. Her fingertips clenched into his. She stared again out the window. He tightened his hold on her.

"I can see it," she said.

CHAPTER 16

The day we stopped time
Now cold and gray
A fog veiled
Shoreline
Lost harbor, one day.

The day we stopped time
High above blue
Frail promise
Upon
Rock, jagged as you.

The day we stopped time
Windswept to yearn
Lone petal
Aloft
A vow, its return.

Cameron stared from atop the cliff as the yacht slashed across the slate canvas that engulfed the island. The boat shrunk to nothing more than a pallid speck on the horizon before dissolving into an ocean mirage. He closed his eyes and searched the muted orange blackness of the back of his eyelids for any last figment of that image, but that too vanished.

He curled his toes into the moist sand. In the past week, he had trekked over this path seven times with her at his side. He looked down. Any remnant of their passage had been erased. Above him, the stringing clouds that deflected the orange glow upon her just the day before were long gone, replaced by heavy pillows of muddy gray. The palm fronds still rustled, but now seemed resigned to a state of mourning.

Nothing seemed the same.

A scouting droplet flicked against his cheek. The spark prickled his skin, as if to remind him of her promise to return. He plodded down the path. With each step the reality of her departure sunk in deeper. Walking back into an empty hut just emphasized that vacuum. But he didn't want to leave.

He squatted down near the wall opposite the doorway. He unfurled a dingy patch of canvas rolled up in the dirt. Three of its tattered corners bore discolored copper grommets, two with old shoelaces tied around them, the third with a rusty wire looped through it. He stood up and held the gray bit of sail over the window opening. Close enough.

He laced one of the shoestrings around a top corner of the bamboo window frame and cinched it tight. The shoestring was long and flat. He grinned. By the pattern of blackened eyelet markings, it looked to be pulled from a pair of Chuck Taylors, his favorite high-top sneaker as a kid. He pulled it tight. He knew the knot would be nearly impossible to undo, particularly once it was rain-drenched. But he didn't expect to be around for the task. He tied off the opposite corner with the other shoestring.

The sail flapped like an angry flag. He grabbed the flailing end and twisted the brittle wire around the bamboo, pricking the pad of his thumb as he secured the wire. As he pressed a knuckle into his thumb, a pinhead of dark blood poked through his skin. He licked it off and sucked the end of his thumb, contemplating the final corner, the belligerent sail still snapping in the wind. There were no more grommets, shoestrings or wires.

He untied the drawstring in the waistband of his shorts and yanked at one end. It cut into his waist. His shorts twisted to the side before the drawstring pulled free, leaving only a loose snap to support his sagging shorts on his absent hips. Stretching the final corner in each hand he rubbed the sheet against a splintering bamboo reed. A hole punctured through the worn sheath and he laced up the last corner.

The wind buffeted against the makeshift shutter. Gusts sucked the sail in and punched it back out of the window, but it held.

Storm clouds burst and raindrops pelted against the canvas. In a blink, sheets of rain swept across the island hilltop from every direction. The three bamboo shoots hanging in the doorway flung about in a sodden frenzy, their tan skins glistening wet. Rain blasted through the doorway like a scattergun, muddying the sandy dirt. He dragged the cot away from the soaked window patch to the farthest corner of the shack, now transformed into a dank cavern before even the first clap of thunder.

He clung to that hovel like a life raft.

Water punctured through the roof. He lugged the table underneath the leak, climbed on top and grabbed a palm frond to shift it over the hole. The rain smacked against his face. The frond sliced his palm. Blood dripped down his wrist. He hopped off the table, smeared his hand against his shirt and assessed the cut. Not too deep. Fishing around his duffle bag he pulled out an old bandanna and wrapped it around his hand.

He repeated the tabletop repair every time a new leak spouted, careful not to slice another hand or finger. But on the sixth or seventh effort, the futility of the situation began to sink in. Each time he shifted a frond another two new holes appeared.

The storm showed no signs of letting up. As a kid back in Ohio he had learned to count the "Mississippis" between lightning and thunder to determine how far the strike. The "M" barely passed his lips before a rumbling bolt illuminated how pointless his efforts were. He could no longer ignore it. He decided to abandon the shack.

He hoped the yacht had left soon enough to outrun the deluge. He wanted her safe, even if she was gone.

He thought about changing into swim trunks, but he was already drenched. So he stuffed his trunks, a dry pair of shorts and a few T-shirts into his canvas duffle bag and squished down on the cot. The rain now pierced the roof like bullets. He cradled the leather journal in his hands, hovering over the poems and scribbles to keep them dry.

He stroked the journal's spine, raised it to his face and kissed the worn Italian leather. It smelled like an old baseball glove. He turned to the entry written after their first meeting at the marketplace. Crouched down in the hut, with the rain closing in on him from all sides, he read every detail of their time together. Lightning flashes punctuated the muddy light. In oft-times floundering words he found her smile. He gazed again into her eyes. He traced the small dimples of her lower back, reveled in her laugh, and he felt her gentle breath again upon his neck.

When he had finished he circled the last entry.

I can see it.

He took one last look around the hut. He listened hard for even the slightest lapse in the torrential rain, but there was none. He took out the dry pair of shorts and put the journal inside them, wrapping his last three dry T-shirts around them. He took off his t-shirt to wrap the bundle one more time, but instead wrung it out like a mop. He ended up tossing it into the mud. Then he slid the clothes-bound journal into his duffle bag, cinched it closed and stepped into the rain. He slipped and slogged down the path back to the village, rain-soaked, in drooping shorts, barefoot and shirtless.

It was late afternoon when he got to the village. The flooded streets were empty.

Cameron ducked under the overhang of a tiny cottage near the bay. The rain pelted off the corrugated metal roof. It sounded like a cacophony of brass drums. A dark, dry face peeked around the corner at him. She giggled and pointed to the cottage.

"You want?" she asked.

"Yes. How much?" he asked.

Water dripped down his face.

"Two dollars a day," she said in a sweet Caribbean accent.

She looked in her late twenties, with cherubic cheeks, strong arms and a big, knowing grin. Something about her reminded him of cinnamon cocoa.

He reached into his duffle bag, unbundled the journal and retrieved his wallet from his dry shorts. He placed three crumpled twenty-dollar bills into her hand.

Her eyebrows arched high over her brown eyes.

"*Papa yo!* That's *en'less hototo pesh.*"

He looked at the rain.

"Not sure how long I'll be here."

"No problem, boss, stay long as you want. You need *any ting*, you ask for me."

"Will do," he said.

He followed her to the door.

She twisted open the handle.

"Isabella," she said.

"Okay, Bella," he replied.

He shook her big hand.

"Cameron," he said.

Isolated in that cottage Cameron wrote. He purged as much as he could onto the page. Rain pelted the metal roof. But even that drone was incapable of distracting him. The brightly painted yellow walls did little to lift his spirits. He hunched over the wooden breakfast table for hours on end, padding the wicker seat of the chair with a towel when his legs and buttocks went numb. Most nights he brought his journal with him into the narrow bed, lying diagonal on his stomach. He wrote to exhaustion just to fall asleep, waking the next morning only to start again. Form, rhythm and rhyme came and went like the intermittent rain, but he was never short on substance.

Some nights he lay awake replaying their time together, mulling over every detail. He tried to slow down his mind to play out their every interaction in real time. He wanted to capture the slightest nuance of her. He debated the precise fragrance of her hair. He remembered how soft her skin was against his and dwelled even on those spots that weren't so soft. His journal was always close on the nightstand, always within reach.

He left his room around lunch for one daily meal, a bowl of white fish mixed with rice, black beans and peppered hot sauce served from a stand near the market. His weight dropped along with his appetite. He started to notice a protruding rib cage. He drank only water and an occasional Red Stripe beer, the two at times indistinguishable. On his empty stomach three beers got him buzzed. The fourth put him asleep well before he could get drunk. Late one afternoon he bought a bottle of rum from a boy lazing in a ramshackle *cantina* at the far end of the bay.

"Five," the gap-toothed boy said.

He held up a dusty bottle of mud-colored liquor.

Cameron handed over a crumpled bill.

"Do I know you?" he asked.

"No," the boy said.

Yet something about the boy seemed familiar.

"Francisco," the boy said with his broken smile.

"Cheers, Francisco," Cameron said and tipped the bottle at him.

Cameron lugged the bottle back to his room and drank more than half before sunset. He wrote late into that night. The vision of his muse was pierced by cavalier thoughts of Hemingway scribbling about bullfights and marlins. The next morning, he awoke to a hazy thought of Aluna and reached for his journal. He gripped the near-empty bottle instead on the nightstand. He sat up. A vice tightened around his temple. His mouth was parched. His stomach churned. He limped to the table. No water, only the cap to the rum bottle and his journal.

Upright his stomach only worsened. He broke into a chilled sweat. *Fuck*. He felt it coming. He stumbled into the bathroom, knelt over the toilet and gripped its sides, splattering the rusted bowl with throat-scorching, murky brown bile. He crawled back into bed and tried to read what he had written in his drunken flurry. The puke in the toilet was more appealing. He rolled over and clutched his pillow to ease the pounding inside his head. His waking thought of Aluna left unwritten.

That afternoon he poured the last few gulps of rum into the toilet.

In the infrequent gaps between storms he tried to retrace their path up the cliff, but that path had reduced to muddy slop. When he did venture out, though, he kept his solitary promise. He never spoke her name, nor did he write it in his journal, staying true to his word. He convinced himself by doing so she would keep her vow and return.

But as days passed doubts arose, spreading seeds of insecurity. In the short breaks between storms he swam in the bay. He wondered whether it was all a dream, whether he was clinging only to a *duppie,* what the locals called a ghost spirit. She had another life. She had a husband. He swam between decrepit fishing boats. She had a yacht. He had never even been on a yacht. Why would she return? Even if she still wanted to so many things could happen. Demons whispered to him. *You are obsessed. You know nothing of her. You* are *nothing to her*. Nights grew longer and harder and fears crept into his journal.

> *I wish I could show you*
> *All that I miss*
> *But suspect I'm the only one.*
>
> *I wish I could kiss you*
> *Forever, and more*
> *But the lips I once kissed are gone.*
>
> *I wish I could tell you*
> *All that I feel.*
> *But the moment has slipped to the past.*
>
> *I wish I could hold you*
> *Just one more time*
> *But I fear even that might not last.*

Days later Cameron sat in his room and reread this poem. It had surged from him nights earlier as if his life depended upon it. But now, reading it again in the stark light of afternoon, it seemed nothing more than common drivel. He feared his words were diminishing, their import haplessly adrift.

A knock tapped at the door. He got up and twisted the doorknob. His young landlady, Isabella, stood there. She held a small package in her dark hands. It was wrapped in plain brown paper, taped on all sides and tied with twine. She looked up at him and smiled.

"Came for you, boss," she said.

She offered it to him.

"Please, no more boss—Cameron."

"Came for you, Mister Cam," she said with an even bigger smile.

He considered the odd package. Few knew his whereabouts. He had never before received a delivery on the island.

"From?" he asked.

"The plane. Your name, right?" she said.

She pointed to the name scrawled on the package.

It was indeed his name etched across the brown paper. The handwriting was unfamiliar.

"That's me," he said.

"Here you go," she said.

She handed him the package.

"Thanks, Bella."

She nodded at him.

And then in her heavy island accent she said, "Gonna be okay."

He thanked her again. She turned to leave. He shut the door, sat down on the bed and stared at the package.

Below his name was the name of the island, but nothing more. There was no street address. He ran his fingers over the orange and red stamps posted across the upper half of the package. Each stamp depicted a different leafy plant. But they all looked like tobacco. Along the bottom left corner of each stamp it read "Brasil," and along the top right corner, "1,80." The postmark was too faded to read.

He untied the twine and found a cigar box inside. *Great.* He didn't smoke. Maybe he would start. He ran his hands across the light wood and slid open the lid. Only the faint scent of cigar remained. Inside, an olive piece of paper was neatly folded in half, nestled atop a yellowed bed of straw.

He unfolded the paper.

"I meant what I said my love, I am yours."

There was no signature. He didn't need one. He could hear her voice.

He fought back tears. He rubbed each cursive letter. Something shiny tucked within the shredded packing caught his eye. He fished out a silver wristwatch.

Lifting the watch from the box, he balanced it in his palm. An elaborate swirling design was etched along the watch's edge. Raven-black roman numerals emblazoned across a pearl-white face. The second hand ticked. He smiled and then laughed. The watch was set to island time.

He shifted the watch about, feeling its weight in his hand, sliding it back and forth upon his wrist. Then he flipped it over in his palm. Loopy scratches arced across its back. He tilted it in the light to make out the inscription.

"'til the end of time."

Nothing seemed insurmountable. No distance too great. Time again was irrelevant, merely a diversion until the next embrace. He felt her again with him.

Gonna be okay.

Isabella was right. Somehow, she knew. In a tick, he believed again. She loved him. She would return and they would be together *"'til the end of time."* He held the proof in his hands.

And the tiny second hand on the silver watch ticked away.

CHAPTER 17

Yet that trough
Of a thousand years
Dead reckoning
Alone.

Knew the crest
Opiate eyes, Venus
Beckoning
Him home.

"What?" she asked again.

Cameron heard a woman's voice. Consciousness cavorted like a tempest bent on ruining his dream. Each shallow inhalation stung his constricted lungs. It felt like an elephant's foot pressed upon his chest. Between aching breaths his leg throbbed. He felt heavy and weak, helpless under a thin veil that he began to sense covered him.

He clung to the dream, but the honeyed voice would not let go. The vision of his lover evaporated. His eyelids crept back and his pupils adjusted to a thick, gray cloud of space. Everything was blurred. He gazed at fuzzy lines that gradually focused into bamboo running along a ceiling. He rolled his eyes to the left, an unfamiliar, shuttered window. Elongated halos danced across a wall.

Dry grit coated his tongue. A crack split its tip. His mouth was parched. He gleaned he was on his back, the thin veil he felt actually a cotton sheet covering all but his head and neck. Rolling his eyes to the right he saw the silhouette of a young woman sitting at his bedside. A muted, golden aura washed across her. The soft lines of her face revealed in the candlelight. In that waking moment she looked ethereal.

Elia swallowed when their eyes met. She felt the wings of a hundred butterflies brushing against her insides. She strove to stay calm. He looked dazed. She didn't want to startle him.

She placed her hand atop the sheet over his right hand.

"You're in Paco's room," she said.

His dry lips parted.

"Water," he said.

"Of course," she said.

She felt his eyes follow her as she stood and took a half step toward the nightstand. A glass pitcher with a splintered crack near the mouth was three-quarters filled with water. The ice had long melted but the nicked handle was still cool to her touch. It reminded her of the pockmarked pitchers from which the undergrads at the Village Poet chugged beer while lofty grad students huddled around cheap wine bottles.

She lifted the pitcher above a candle on the table and picked up a squat drinking glass. As she tilted the pitcher, the water cascaded over a tiny starburst near the end of the crack. The starburst glistened in the candlelight. She recalled that the boy from her class at the university drank beer. Somewhere she had stored away this random detail until now. She envisioned his face. She wished he could see her now. She picked up a short, fat, black straw from the table and stuck it into the glass of water.

"I'm Elia," she said.

She placed the glass near his chin and bent the straw toward his mouth.

"I'll be here 'til morning," she said.

The corner of his lip curled a bit. He barely turned his head. Without lifting off the pillow he took a sip. His lips released the straw. She watched him swallow that first drink of water and waited, leaning over him, and felt his eyes studying her. Something within that simple, intimate moment calmed the wings of her butterflies. He took another sip and rolled his head back.

She put the glass on the table and sat back on the stool, but shuffled it even closer to his bedside. Paco's snoring cut the night air.

"How long?" he asked.

He stared at the ceiling as he spoke. His voice was brittle, any waking change in his crooked visage barely perceptible.

"Seven nights now," she said.

He sighed. She wasn't sure if it was just his asking the question or her answer, but the exchange seemed to exhaust him. He sucked a shallow breath as if uncertain he could trust his lungs.

"I wanted to die," he said.

Her butterflies turned into locusts.

Another hollow breath.

"I expected to," he said.

Tears began to well up. She both longed and feared for him to look at her. It sounded like he was speaking more to himself than to her. But she was the only other person in the room. She was the only one to hear him say, "I was ready."

Yet as he said this, it was from *his* eye that she saw a tear form and cascade down the side of his pale temple.

"Please, don't," she said. She wiped away her own tear.

She slid the sheet aside and slipped her hand under his limp palm. Bent over the bed, she rested her cheek against his knuckles. She stared up at his languid profile. He gazed toward the ceiling. Her tears fell upon the back of his hand.

She raised her head.

"I want to know of love," she said.

If nothing else, she'd put to the poet that one question. She waited, not knowing what else to say. Her words hung in dead air. They threatened to vanish into the shifting shadows. It seemed so long she wondered whether he even heard her, and whether he was even still conscious.

She perceived the faint flex of his fingertips under her cheek and raised her head. His hand shook as it lifted off the bed. His palm rotated upward and he held it there. The inches between her face and his hand disappeared and he cradled her cheek in his palm. His flesh was like a salve against her skin. His head turned toward her. His dreary, cobalt-blue eyes fixed upon her longing stare. He looked fragile and uncertain.

His mouth opened. She felt those butterflies again take wing.

But not one feeble word slipped past his lips. Only one breath passed before his eyes closed. In just moments he fell asleep. She watched him drift away, all the while feeling like a spring had just trickled to the surface in the stillness of that room. For the first time in four nights, she crawled off the stool, knelt on the plank floor and rested her head against the soft edge of the bed, right next to his hand. Her eyes shut and she finally succumbed, following him into a world of dreams.

Elia heard muffled footsteps. Light pestered against her eyelids. She awoke as dawn sifted through the shutters. She was still cuddled against the edge of the bed. Her head nestled alongside Cameron's hand. His long fingers rested in her hair.

Her back and neck were stiff, having slept sitting on the floor with only her head, shoulders and arms resting upon the bed. Since childhood she had developed the ability to sleep in awkward positions and strange places. A hand pressed upon her shoulder. It felt like a nun waking her younger self that was splayed along a cushioned kneeler of a church pew after falling asleep with a Bible.

"So you do sleep," Paco said.

"I'm sorry," Elia said. She lifted her head and her hair pulled from beneath Cameron's hand. Arching her spine, she rolled her neck in an extended loop. Paco was wearing the same old shorts, but now his damp white tank top had a rainbow of letters scrunched together, the letters forming the shape of the word they spelled, *Parrotfish*. His shirt stuck to his skin and his hair was a wet, black mat. She shrugged back her shoulders as he opened the shutters.

"He woke up," she whispered.

Paco spun around.

"When?"

"Couple hours ago," she said.

Paco asked, "Did he say anything?"

"No, just opened his eyes," she said.

In that incalculable instant she felt an allegiance to Cameron. If he wanted to tell Paco anything, that was up to him.

He grinned and stared at Cameron. "That's a start."

Paco shook his head like a dog after a swim, scattering ringlets of drizzle.

"Lobster," he said with his gold-toothed grin.

"Makin' bisque?" crowed a Cajun voice.

Elia swiveled to see the polka-dot-sandaled island doc slapping through the doorway, a familiar waft of resin lingering right behind.

"Sure," Paco said.

"Good, 'cuz I'm already hungry. Now how's our sleepin' crawdad?" Fatty asked.

He scratched his bald noggin.

"Sore," Cameron murmured.

Fatty cackled with delight. He puffed his chest like a rooster. "What'd I tell ya? He'd come 'round when good 'n ready."

Elia felt butterflies again as Cameron's eyes opened.

"Papa yo!" Paco said.

"And thirsty," Cameron said.

He sounded dry as cinders. Elia refilled the glass on the nightstand and offered him another sip through the straw. This time, he lifted his head a couple of inches from the pillow, a faint hint of recognition in his eyes.

Fatty kicked the stool over to the bed, saddled down and snatched up Cameron's hand. He pressed his fingers along his wrist. Then he propped his stethoscope against Cameron's chest.

"You're gonna be damn sore for awhile, especially them ribs and that leg. I stitched you up a bit down there," he said and eyeballed Cameron's leg. His words rambled up and down like a drunken roller coaster. "Gonna need to change them bandages. Ticker's ticking fine. You'll be on your back for a bit but you've got to start eating, just no bisque."

Fatty shot a glance at Paco.

"Snapper?"

"Yep," Paco said.

"Ooh wee, let's scrape together some *étouffée*."

Fatty's last word was downright jubilant. The word reminded Elia of her trip to New Orleans.

"Spice on the side," Paco said.

"Well, most of it, but go on 'n leave in a couple pinches, gets the blood flowing," Fatty said with a sweet whine hard to deny.

"What can I do?" Elia asked.

Before either could answer, Isabella towered through the door. "What did I say about those candles?"

Only two were still burning. Elia realized the others had all snuffed out during the night while she slept. The incense had burnt out as well.

"I'm sorry," Elia said.

Isabella frowned and Elia felt a reprimand coming.

"Isaboo."

Fatty's inflection could have softened a long-horned toad.

"What?" Isabella shot back at him.

Fatty gulped.

"Bella," Cameron whispered.

"*Grand Bois!*" Isabella said.

She pushed past Elia and Fatty.

"For true, there you are," she said and hovered over him. She placed her fingertips against his cheek. Her other hand stroked the braided strands of her charm.

"Why don't you help me with that *étouffée,*" Paco whispered as he offered Elia his hand.

"We'll take it from here. Go on, git," Fatty said and winked at her.

"I'll be back," Elia said to Cameron. She thought she saw the corners of his mouth turn up again.

"Just 'cuz he's awake don't mean them candles shouldn't be burning," Isabella said. She reached for the matchbox on the nightstand.

"No, let me," Elia said, but Paco tightened his grip on her hand.

"Come on, let's go bang some pans," he said.

As they left, she heard Fatty tease Isabella, "Looks like the ol' gator's got another admirer."

Elia followed Paco down the narrow hall to the kitchen, grateful to escape Hurricane Isabella, at least for now. She noticed how graceful the barefoot *cantina* owner's gait was. He treaded with a sleek felinity. A few extra lives would certainly come in handy around Isabella.

A long, discolored butcher-block table covered with divots dominated the kitchen. Every scrap ever sliced or diced on that table had left its mark. A square metal tub sat just beyond, its faucet in a lazy drip. No stove. Only two electric heating coils sat atop a banged-up pushcart, its wheels long gone. Black cords dangled down the crippled cart's legs, which in turn were plugged into an orange extension cord that slithered out the door.

A disarray of pots and pans hung from a bamboo slat. Assorted knives, no two with the same handle, were jabbed into a quarter-moon of cork. It was rustic, to say the least. Elia had seen more elaborate kitchens around a campsite.

Paco leaned over a black pot on the butcher table.

"Not today, my friend," he said.

A brown claw snapped out of the water at his nose. He reached in and grabbed the crustacean, pulling it out of the pot by the back of its spine. Every claw snapped and its legs scurried in midair. Its tan chest was as long as his forearm, almost the same color and nearly as thick.

He set the lobster into the sink and poured the pot of water over it. Then he turned on the faucet and let the water creep up to the edge, dumping a cup of sea salt into the basin.

"That'll do for now, Ernesto."

"Ernesto?" Elia asked.

"Crusty ol' papa, don't you think?"

"I guess so," she said.

Paco put his hands on his hips.

"For him, the bell tolls tomorrow."

Elia stifled a laugh, but she wanted to be back in that room with Cameron, minus Isabella. Paco slid out a battered metal cooler and flipped the lid open with his big toe. Inside the cooler was a long, reddish fish packed in ice.

"Lunch," he said.

He handed her a yellow pepper, a bunch of green onions and three stalks of celery.

"Chop, chop, chop," he said. Elia grabbed a knife out of the cork and started slicing the vegetables. Paco gutted the fish right next to her on the same table. The serrated knife he used was thinner than the fish's spine.

"You like Hemingway?" she asked.

Paco stopped, blade in hand, and rubbed his brow with the back of his wrist.

"Not him so much, the magic."

"Magic?"

"Some see it everywhere, even on this table," he said with a grin.

She watched him chop off the head just behind the gills, relieved when he chucked the fish head, bulging eyes and all, into a bucket on the floor. The tail and guts followed with a wet thud. Flies buzzed about the bucket of fish scrap. Before she was done chopping the pepper he had filleted the snapper.

"Let me help," he said and picked up the celery. She took awkward, deliberate strokes, one to every four of his. He flicked the cut ends into the lobster's tub with the end of the knife. An occasional claw snapped at the morsels.

"And Cameron?" she asked.

"Fatty once said he could tell me everything he knows about *étouffée*, but it's still up to me to pick up that spoon and taste it," Paco said without looking at her.

Something about his allegiance to the poet appealed to her. By telling her nothing he had told her something, just about himself.

Done with the celery, he sliced the onion in two and pushed half toward her, finished his half as her eyes stung all the way through hers, and chopped some garlic cloves.

Paco wiped clean his knife, while Elia checked for fingertips.

He rubbed the fish with salt and red and black pepper before dropping about a quarter of it into the black pot and dousing it with olive oil. Then he dumped some of the chopped vegetables over the fish, along with bay leaf plucked fresh off the stem that he ripped into smaller pieces and some dried, bluish sprinklings of thyme. He squeezed some lemon and poured water over it all.

"Go on and open that," he said, pointing to a can of tomato sauce.

At least she could work a can opener.

He poured some tomato sauce over the whole mess, placed another layer of fish, vegetables and sauce, repeated it and flipped on the heating coil, tossed in some parsley and squeezed some more lemon on top. He winked at her and flicked in a couple of pinches of a reddish powder from a small glass jar. He offered her a taste.

She obliged. A singe torched her nostrils. Her eyes flamed.

"Don't you worry about Isabella," he said.

"Is there something going on there?" she asked.

She had noticed how Cameron's mere whisper had calmed Isabella.

Paco shuffled the pot, giving the whole thing a good shake, and set it back down on the coil.

"Never stir, breaks up the fish," he said.

He grinned.

"Hope not," he said.

About an hour later Elia carried a steaming bowl of rice-smothered *étouffée* and followed Paco back into the room. She held the bowl like an altar boy carrying a chalice of holy bread.

She was stunned, and a bit proud, to have played a small part in making something that smelled so good. Paco was right. She'd witnessed every chop and pinch of preparation, but the spoonful she just savored in the kitchen was a delight beyond description. It was like magic.

That sweet spice was still on her tongue when she saw Isabella sitting alone on the bed next to Cameron. A metal bucket of soapy water was at her feet. Like a mother with a toddler, Isabella sponged his pale face. Elia watched as she ran the sponge along Cameron's narrow forehead, dabbed his sandy hairline, then swept across his closed eyes, the bridge of his crooked nose, and washed his cheeks and lips. She soaked his stubbly chin and neck and patted him dry with a cotton towel.

The taste of *étouffée* on her tongue disappeared. She wanted to be the one holding that sponge and towel.

"Tomorrow, I'll give you a shave," Isabella said.

"Thanks," Cameron said.

Even his weakened gratitude toward Isabella pinched Elia.

"Fatty's in the *cantina* with lunch," Paco said, "and there's a bowl waiting for you."

"I'll be down the hall," Isabella said to Cameron before she lumbered up.

Isabella finally left. It felt like a storm cloud had passed without bursting. Paco looked toward Elia. She relinquished the bowl, but stood close behind him as he sat down on the bed and spoon-fed Cameron. She studied his every deliberate swallow. His eyes were open, but he didn't speak. His slight movements appeared more compliant than grateful.

Elia picked up the glass of water with the straw. She was more than ready to do her small part. She gave him three long sips of water, the longest at the very end. Throughout the remaining spoonfuls and sips Cameron stayed quiet. Paco didn't ask for any explanations, either. It was a tacit, triangular pact of silence.

The bowl was soon gone. Paco motioned for Elia to take it to the kitchen. Cameron's eyes were fading, but she was confident he saw that it was her hands holding the glass and straw that quenched his thirst.

She walked out the door with the bowl, but lingered outside a moment. She heard Paco say in a surprisingly stern voice, "She's been here every night, in case you're wondering. Now listen here. Not again. The sea ain't got no back door."

CHAPTER 18

Verse.

Mired between
empty dawn
and pallid moon,

Once bellowed
from whispers
in gloried bloom,

Incarnate,
collapsed, one
breath, its ruin.

Elia walked from the *cantina* into the smothering heat of afternoon. The village looked like an overexposed postcard. Only a few blotches of shaded refuge broke up a skillet of harsh brightness. She felt sluggish. Any morning breeze had long surrendered. The humid air was woolen. It felt like breathing inside a sauna.

The market to her left was vacant. Vendors had retreated for siesta. She squinted ahead. Alabaster stones marked the cobbled promenade that hugged the bay. She discerned but two choices, either back to her cottage or down one broken step to a fishing boat overturned beneath a low-hanging palm tree. The tree's spine swooped low, as if thirsting for a sip of seawater.

Sweat dribbled down her thigh. She didn't have her bikini. But she could at least wade into the water. Heck, it was hot enough to jump right in wearing her halter and shorts. Another suffocating forty yards to her cottage seemed unbearable. For the first time in days she wasn't sleepy.

She headed for the shade of that palm. It was only after she had committed to her course that she noticed a sight more oppressive than the heat. Isabella was crouched behind the boat.

It was too late. Isabella's big eyes had already caught hers. Isabella stood up straight, dropped her sandals and planted her hands on her ample hips. The two women were roughly the same height. But Isabella dominated Elia in sheer mass, even with the capsized dinghy between them.

Isabella didn't blink. She looked to be searching for any hint of weakness, the twitch of an eyelash, a nervous swallow or the scratch of an ear. Elia did all three. For one long, awkward moment, it felt even hotter in that shade. Isabella slid one thick arm at a time out of her orange sundress. She slipped it off to reveal the largest one-piece swimsuit Elia had ever seen. Elia figured two of her could fit inside the big woman.

She heard a snicker. She glanced up to see Chuey. The owl-eyed monkey sat with his long tail coiled around the palm trunk.

Isabella folded her sundress on top of her sandals. She then placed her charm, the one with the whisk of braided black strands, on top of the orange pillow.

"Come on," Isabella said.

Her tone was neither inviting nor condemning. She walked toward the water. Chuey let out a low howl. It sounded like a moan of disappointment.

Stripped down to that expansive piece of black nylon, there was an unabashed, regal magnificence about Isabella.

She appeared more than comfortable in her skin, every last coffee-colored inch of it. She looked like some great, exotic species approaching a watering hole, perhaps dangerous only if provoked. In that glimpse, it was the rest of humanity, including Elia, who seemed small and weak. Watching her amble toward the bay, Elia perceived something about Isabella she had previously missed: a certain splendor. And it made Isabella all the more formidable.

Elia slid off her sandals and followed Isabella into the bay. It felt like submersing into liquid silk, first around her ankles, then her calves and thighs. The water was almost flat, except for the languid ripples emanating from Isabella, who deftly rolled onto her back like a beautiful, black manatee. Elia felt the squish of sand beneath each deepening step and an odd sense of reluctance and relief.

"Come on," Isabella said.

Elia dipped down to her shoulders. She cupped the warm water, and stroked it aside to glide nearer. She was careful to stop where her toes could still touch the sandy bottom. Isabella could drown her like a mosquito. Only Chuey would witness. Their two heads bobbed ten strokes past the end of the dock, beyond one lonely, tethered rowboat. Flecks of sun-scorched, teal-blue paint covered the boat's hull. The color mirrored the shallow island waters that Elia had first viewed from the backseat of the seaplane. Elia noticed the plane was gone.

Only the rustic skiff hugged the dock. Scrawled in white brushstrokes across the stern was the name *Pilar.* Perched on the bow was a muddy gray-brown pelican. A captain's hat of white plumage marked its head and neck, setting off a long, rusty beak.

Isabella waded closer. Only an arm's-length separated them. Elia's chin dipped into the water.

"Listen," Isabella said.

Elia sunk to her nose. The pelican bristled its mighty wings and resettled.

"Best not ask too many questions," Isabella said.

The words themselves sounded merely suggestive, but Isabella's scowl made them seem much more of an edict. Isabella hadn't drifted an inch, but just by her words she felt even closer.

"I'm sorry about the candles. If he doesn't want to talk, fine, but maybe it would help," Elia said.

Isabella frowned.

"Help who?"

A mullet flashed into the air and torpedoed back into the bay without a ripple. Elia felt like ducking her head under too. Telling Isabella what Cameron had said would only fortify her opposition. She again kept quiet about Cameron's waking confession.

"Sitting with him these past nights, in the quiet, watching him and wondering how I came here, to this place. It's hard to explain," Elia said.

But as she spoke Elia realized how inadequate her words sounded. Like a cautious ballerina her toes buoyed up and down, not willing to lose touch with the sandy bottom. Her hands sculled back and forth beneath the surface.

"I'm not trying to replace anybody," she said.

All those candles, incense and voodoo chants only reinforced what Elia perceived to be Isabella's obvious feelings for the poet.

Isabella threw back her head. She let out a chortle that echoed throughout the bay. The pelican leapt into flight. It flapped right over them, nearly grazing them with its wings.

"Well, that's good," Isabella said.

Elia felt like a fool.

"Come on, Missy, you might be getting sunstroke," Isabella said.

Isabella sculled back toward shore. She left behind a wide wake. Elia dunked her head underwater before following.

Isabella emerged from the water. Her skin glistened like a midnight pearl. Only a step behind, Elia noticed Isabella's spongy black hair already looked remarkably dry. Isabella glanced over her shoulder at Elia.

"Paco says some fish better with the hook still in."

Just then Elia stumbled on a submerged rock and fell forward. Isabella caught her by the arm, breaking her fall. Elia regained her balance but Isabella didn't let go of her. A tingling shot up Elia's arm. It felt like that twinge when smacking her funny bone, but her elbow hadn't struck a thing. She felt like someone had just dumped a bucket of ice water on her. Isabella relaxed her grip. The shiver subsided as fast as it came.

Elia stared at Isabella, but the big woman had closed her eyes. A few seconds later, Isabella opened her dark walnut eyes. They looked altogether different, not so much in color or shape but in clarity. Isabella's intense scowl was gone.

"*Oshun loa*, things *are* hidden," Isabella said.

She bent down to snatch her charm.

"What?" Elia asked.

"Tread lightly," Isabella said.

She caressed the black strands of her charm. "But be prepared."

"For what?" Elia asked.

The big woman's change of demeanor set Elia off balance.

Elia rubbed life into her numb arm. Isabella leaned against the overturned boat. All of a sudden it looked like it was Isabella that needed the support. Isabella shook her finger toward Elia.

"Just keep those candles burning."

"I will," Elia said.

§

Elia replayed Isabella's warning as she strolled down the promenade toward the *cantina*. The night winds had returned to scatter the ashen remnants of a sunburnt day. A billowing blanket of relief caressed the island. Fatty huddled at a table under the market tent. A gray stretch of sail lifted and fell under warm drafts of air. The tired sail and gentle wind danced like two old friends, perhaps reminiscing about life at sea.

Across the table from Fatty a young boy deliberated over a rectangular, wooden board. A row of six shallow wells stretched across the longer sides of the board. Two larger depressions were carved out at the shorter ends between each row. Yellow and gray nickernuts, marble-like seeds from prickly island shrubs, were pooled about in the various basins. *Nickernut* had become Elia's favorite island word, particularly when squealed from the smiling Caribbean children who found all sorts of uses for them, from game pieces to mock currency to necklace beads to slingshot artillery.

Fatty crooned when he saw her.

"*Mon cher*, come sit."

His Cajun drawl filled every last syllable with playful seduction.

Fatty's adversary, a barefoot reed of a boy with a short mane of thick, curly hair, allowed only a quick glance. His long fingers were interlaced in front of him. He was focused like a hawk on the game. It looked like a cross between chess and marbles.

"No thank you, I'm heading over to see him," she said.

"C'mon. Let me teach you how to play Warri," Fatty said.

He made it sound like his heart might otherwise break.

The boy reached over one of the wells. He picked up one of the yellow nickernuts like it was a precious diamond, and placed it down across the board. The boy exhaled and feigned a confident stare.

"Maybe next time—looks like you've got your hands full."

Fatty giggled. He bounced as if trying to contain a burst of uncontrollable hiccups.

"Next time it is," he said.

She walked away, but heard him whisper to the boy just loud enough so she could hear, "Gonna teach her next."

When she arrived at the *cantina*, Paco was in the kitchen. He was staring at the lobster in the tub of water with a look of clemency. A faint scent of *étouffée* and stale beer hung in the air.

"He's been quiet all day, mostly napping with bits of food in between."

"Cameron or crusty ol' Papa?" Elia asked.

Paco smiled.

"If you need me—"

"You'll be down the hall," Elia finished.

"Don't let him ramble too long now," Paco said.

"Oh I won't," she said.

At least one of Cameron's sentinels seemed to be letting down his guard. She wondered whether Cameron had said anything to Paco about her or what she had said to Cameron, assuming that he had even heard her. But she remembered Paco's quiet allegiance to the poet. She didn't ask. She left Paco in the kitchen to decide whether the bell would toll for the main ingredient of tomorrow's bisque.

Elia tiptoed to the room. She didn't want to disturb Cameron if he was asleep. She noticed a brighter-than-usual yellow glow tinged the room. His eyes were closed. But they opened when she neared the bedside stool. Cameron turned his head, looked at her and raised one eyebrow. She had the warm feeling that he had been waiting for her. She hoped he had.

The candles seemed to have multiplied, along with the incense. Isabella had certainly been busy. Elia viewed the new reinforcements as a challenge to her resolve, and her promise to keep them all burning. In the increased candlelight she could see the weariness in Cameron's eyes was gone. She noted a shade of pigment in his cheeks. He no longer looked as pale as the sheet covering him.

Cameron whispered, "Please sit."

"Thank you," she said.

"Want anything?" he asked.

His head turned toward the water pitcher on the nightstand.

"No, I'm fine. Do you?" she asked.

She reached for the pitcher.

Up to that point all that really bound them was a pitcher of water, her evening vigils and a few shared words from the middle of last night. Yet she felt more connected to him than ever. She wanted him to know what *Secrets of Odysseus* meant to her, why she was here, what was happening to her. She wanted to tell him everything so he would understand that connection. And then, maybe just then, he would tell her things.

He shook his head no.

"There's a market," he said.

His speech was slow. Shallow breaths parsed every word. *Shut up and listen*, she thought. *Let him talk about whatever he wants.* Isabella's edict echoed. No questions.

"Been there long as I know, sea beans, nuts, bananas, melons piled in baskets. Cayenne, chili and basil spread across split burlap sacks, fresh fish every morning, warm flatbreads."

His words gained strength. It was almost as if the images replenished him. But he stared at the ceiling like he was telling her a story playing out above him.

"Birds perched on splintered ropes. A handful of shoppers under the shade of a gray canvas sail tied to rusted hooks screwed into rickety poles, and pomegranates. Why pomegranates? I have no idea, a morning dream."

A faint smile curled his lips. She realized he was talking about the island market where she had just left Fatty and the young boy squaring off over a board of nickernuts. Paco's warning took hold: "Don't let him ramble too long." She wondered if this rambling was already too long. But she wasn't about to stop him.

"A wrinkled woman with a craggy smile will slice one open for you. Inside are these pesky black seeds in red mush. She'll even give you a spoon to scoop out some pulp," he said.

His eyes closed and he licked his lips. He looked to be recalling the taste of that pulp. She had never eaten pomegranate seeds. She couldn't even recall tasting the juice. Pomegranates were for nutritionists and cleanses and squatty bottles at health food stores.

But the word she knew well. It came from the French, for "seeded apple." Most importantly both Chaucer and Shakespeare had extolled its virtues. No less than Juliet had admonished Romeo that it was indeed the nightingale that nightly "sings on yon pomegranate tree."

Still Elia had never tasted one.

She recalled a mention buried in Homer's *Odyssey* too, which she had never fully read. Beck's work came to mind, *Secrets of Odysseus*. She suddenly needed to taste of this mysterious pomegranate.

Not asking questions was getting easier.

"A little island finch—I think it's a finch, I don't know birds well, but they're tiny with a yellow-green underbelly. Well, they'll dive toward a pomegranate in your hand. Sometimes they might even land on you, like a tamed bird. And sometimes they'll swerve and flutter off to harass somebody else. You never know whether to flinch or not."

She couldn't think of a single literary finch, other than Atticus. She wondered if the references were everywhere, just like the tiny bird, and too often unnoticed.

"There are dried seeds too, bags of them, sunflower, pumpkin and sesame. You can open the bags and sift through them, smell them, taste them. I've seen finches peck seeds out of a hand."

He looked euphoric. But the whole conversation was odd. Here he was awakening from shock or coma or wherever to only delve into such minutia.

"Hop, hop, hop right down the arm."

His eyes opened. He stopped talking. Elia poured the pitcher of water into the glass at his bedside. She had a flood of questions readying to burst, but now they included pomegranates and arm-hopping finches pecking seeds from the palms of unsuspecting market visitors. Her dam held. She offered him the water. He took a long sip through the straw.

He closed his eyes again.

"Everything is a just reflection," he said.

"Reflection."

"Yes," he said.

He stared at her.

"Tomorrow morning, go to the market, you know the one, at the end of the promenade. It's open every morning."

"I know it," she said.

"Find the woman selling pomegranates. The old woman, every morning, selling pomegranates and melons all this time. Look in her eyes. Touch her hand."

"I will," Elia said.

"Go to the market. The smells, squeezes, tastes, the weighing, and buying and selling, it all seems so mundane, but it's not. Watch the finches diving in and out. Sift sunflower seeds in your fingers."

His voice faded.

"I will," she said.

"And one last thing," he said.

"Anything."

"Bring me a pomegranate."

"Of course," she said.

"I haven't had one since," he whispered.

Then he drifted off asleep.

Elia hadn't asked a single question, not even "since *when?*"

CHAPTER 19

If a kiss cannot heal
an embrace not reveal
the muse is she real
where then to go?

If this heart unopened
halts withered, unbroken
time, a mere token
never to know?

Emerald waves unfurled in an endless rhythm. A few naked children leapt in the waves and bodysurfed toward shore. Aluna liked watching the little ones. Their playful shrieks pierced the constant swish of surf and the steady stream of bossa nova sauntering from a beachside café. A rush of water gurgled across her legs and then the tide washed back to the sea. A handful of speckled pebbles marooned atop her caramel skin. Pipalito beach was only a short drive from her home in Natal. But it was a world away from the overcrowded sands of Rio de Janeiro.

The beach was a rolling canvas of speckled stone fragments. The tumbling stones scored each wave like a symphony of rain sticks, blanketing her legs beneath a new wash of pebbles. Each rejuvenating chill of pebbles would then bake dry under the high sun.

Aluna scooped the tiny stones in her hand. Shades of brown, orange, black and white glistened in her palm. Dapples of blue, green, yellow and red flecked as well. Each speck seemed so randomly unique, so insignificant, yet together they had been churned into the softest, most perfect beach.

She opened her hand. Damp flakes sifted through her fingers, their remnants clung to creases in her palm. She rubbed off the reluctant stones. She scrubbed several against the light stripe of skin around her ring finger. She brushed away the last granules and collected another handful.

She thought about the random flecks of time that made up a life. She wondered how many handfuls of time remained to be cherished. A woman shrieked. She looked up to the sea to catch a nervous mother pluck a giggling boy by the arm seconds before he would have been toppled by a wave.

Aluna nestled back into the grainy bed. She massaged her slender form into the pebbles. It felt like sprawling into a sack of beads, minus the sack. She scooped handfuls of stone over her thighs and pelvis. The wet chill made her tingle. She spread some across her bare stomach, just above her teal bikini bottom, and rubbed the pebbles across her skin. Each cool stone quilt became tropic warmth as the pebbles dried upon her skin.

She imagined Cameron's hands upon her skin. Each pebble became a facet of his touch. He was a thousand miles away. But she had come to Pipalito for a reason. The sea reminded her of him.

She brushed away the dried pebbles from her brown stomach. A moist well filled her belly button. Her eyelids closed. She circled her fingers across her brown skin. The well dried. She felt even warmer, and then hot. The sound of playing children, lilting bossa nova and crashing surf faded. She imagined a cord at her core, tugging at her. That pull felt as real as the pebble-filled tide bathing her legs. Her fingers traced down her slender belly toward her bikini. And she felt a faint throb inside. And then that throb grew stronger.

Fear evaporated. Reason soon followed. The note and watch she had sent Cameron wasn't enough. She needed more and she knew it. Her next words to him would be delivered with a kiss. Every speck of life was precious. She had to do something. Today.

She stood up, sweaty and draped in stones. Tiny pebbles caked to her back and legs. She peered over the heads of the playing children, past the breaking waves, and looked toward the horizon. A green shell arched from the water. She squinted, but just as fast the arch dipped out of sight. She strained to hear that familiar puff. She needed to hear it.

She waded into the water and her mosaic gown washed away. The throbbing tug at her core grew even deeper. She waded past the mother clutching her young son. The child's legs were wrapped around the woman's waist. She stroked past the breaking waves, duck-diving under each crest, looking for the sea turtle. The farther she swam from shore the stronger that pull seemed.

Elia tumbled a pomegranate in her hand. It was blockier than she had pictured. It looked like a baseball flattened on four sides by a heavy bat. Compared to an apple or orange, the pomegranate appeared downright archaic. Its imperfect contours defied uniformity. At one end a bristly-puckered stem sprouted. The stem resembled the top of an old Christmas tree ornament absent a crowned hook, likely the spot from where it had been plucked from "yon pomegranate tree."

Holding the odd fruit pleased her.

So did its color. Shades of purplish-red onion, with a patina of rusted red streaks and muddy pinkish brown, painted its skin. It reminded her of finding a dusty book tucked in a hidden rack at a used bookstore.

Elia felt a tug at the hem of her white cotton sundress. Fatty's young adversary from the day before was staring at her. The boy clutched a wooden board to his bare chest. A fishnet full of nickernuts was cast over his shoulder.

"Warri?" the boy asked.

Elia realized the wooden table beneath the bushel of pomegranates was the same table from yesterday's Warri tutorial given by master Fatty to the young boy. She scanned the market, but didn't see Fatty anywhere.

A hunched-over woman appeared like a wisp of smoke. A bright orange and green bandanna wrapped her head. The old woman looked like a Caribbean gypsy. The old gypsy shushed at the boy, but the youngster held his ground.

"No," Elia said.

"Champion," the boy said.

He tapped his thumb against his chest. The gypsy woman fanned her wrinkled fingers at the boy. Only after Elia declined a second challenge did Fatty's protégé relent. The boy eyed Elia before walking away, his confidence evident in his youthful swagger.

Elia smiled as she watched him wander off. She turned to the old woman. Elia got the feeling she had been watching her all along. She looked into the woman's eyes. The old woman's face became animated, apparently delighted by the attention. Her eyes danced and her lips puckered before breaking into a spindly smile. A few yellow teeth dangled from her rusty gums.

Elia glanced at the bushel. She was about to put back the pomegranate and pick up another. But the woman waved her hand. The old woman leaned in close over the bushel.

"This one," the woman said.

She had a thick West Indies accent. She curled Elia's fingers back around the first pomegranate Elia had picked up, the one she had spent so much time inspecting.

"Really, are you sure?" Elia asked.

The woman squeezed their hands around the fruit. Her leather-looking skin was actually as soft as suede, and her grip quite strong. The old woman spoke in lilting, broken English.

"From a seed it dreamt of you," she said.

Elia felt herself blush. The woman didn't blink. Elia fumbled into her purse and fished out a few coins. The old woman shook her head.

"A gift," the old woman said.

"No, I must—" Elia said.

She offered the old woman the coins.

The woman's stare alone froze Elia. There would be no argument. The old woman bent over in a slight, slow bow.

Elia noticed a table with all sorts of seeds spread upon split burlap sacks. It looked just as Cameron had described. She walked over and began to sift sunflower seeds in her hands. She glanced back toward the pomegranate lady. The old woman's gaze was still locked upon her.

Know that space for me.

Elia heard Cameron's voice inside her head.

Just then a yellow-and-green-bellied bird swooped over the old woman's head. The bird appeared out of nowhere, almost as if it had fluttered from an illusionist's sleeve. The bird swerved right toward Elia. And as it did everything slowed. She could see every flap of the bird's wings. She watched the bird pull back its short wings. It shifted its clawed feet forward. Its black beady eyes locked on her and the tiny bird landed on the shoulder strap of her sundress, so close it could have pecked her right on the cheek.

The tiniest tuft of feather smoothed its thumb-sized head. The bird hopped down her forearm. There it perched on her upturned hand that held the seeds. The tiny claws felt like the slightest pinpricks along her skin, yet the bird's weight was almost imperceptible. At her palm, its head craned toward Elia and then back at the seeds. She could have closed her fingers around the bird.

Elia froze, even though she wanted to say aloud "it's happening." The bird peeked up at Elia, then back down at the seeds. It checked both her and the seeds again before it ducked its feathered neck and pecked at a kernel. It glanced at Elia, bead in beak. Elia looked over at the pomegranate woman. The old woman's hands were clasped in front of her chest.

Elia floated back toward the *cantina*. She clutched the pomegranate. When she got to the *cantina* she found Paco inside, slurping a half-moon slice of watermelon.

"Everything all right?" he asked.

He spit out a seed.

"Yes," she mumbled.

"You sure? You look a bit strange."

"I am," Elia said.

She glided past him to the backroom.

Cameron was still on his back, but awake. He smiled when he saw the pomegranate in her hand. She hooked the stool with her foot and pulled it to the side of the bed. She collapsed onto the stool and plopped the pomegranate into his waiting hand. He turned it over and over.

"Tell me," he said.

He was clean-shaven. The color in his uneven cheekbones had deepened.

"It was just like you said," she said.

She told him what happened in the market, one flapping finch wing at a time. She waited for Cameron to show some sign of awe or surprise, all of which she was feeling as she told her story. But he didn't look at all astonished. Not one bit. He just looked pleased.

"Let's open her up," he said.

Elia felt an odd reaction. Part of her wanted to keep this particular pomegranate as a souvenir, some evidence of the surreal events that had just happened.

Cameron motioned toward the nightstand. On top of that table was a knife, a fork, a spoon and a wooden bowl. Elia handed him the knife.

"Oh no, you'll have to chop it open," he said. He made a cutting motion with his hands. Elia noticed a new command in his voice. His arms were more deliberate when he gestured.

She hesitated at the thought of ruining what she now felt to be the pomegranate's odd perfection. But she could feel him waiting. She leaned over the end table and thrust the knife into the fruit. The rind was stiff. She had to saw back and forth to cut through the center.

"Don't worry, like all matter it cannot be destroyed," he said.

It was as if he sensed her consternation over slicing into the pomegranate.

"I've heard that," Elia said, not really sure she had in fact heard anything of the sort.

The knife finally split the fruit. She had expected pulp or juice to stream out, but all she found inside was a dry catacomb filled with purple and pink seeds, a labyrinth of little jewels each about half the size of a kernel of corn.

Elia put both pieces into the bowl.

"Please, scoop some out for me," he said.

He craned his neck toward the bowl on the table.

"The seeds?" she asked.

"Yes, the seeds," he said.

He let out a little laugh.

He dropped his head back upon the pillow.

Elia dug into the ruby seeds. That was pretty much all there was inside. She scooped some seeds out with a fork and offered them to him. She watched as he chewed them. He sighed.

She scooped more seeds from the other half and slipped them into her mouth. The taste was bland until she bit into them and then a bitter, almost tart sourness puckered the inside of her mouth. She offered him another spoonful. He took the whole spoon from her and dropped the seeds into his hand.

"So all matter lasts forever?" she asked.

He grinned and handed her the spoon.

"Well, all that matters does," he said.

Elia picked out several seeds and rolled them between her fingers. Their glazed edges were nearly translucent. Yet the centers were blood red.

"You never know," he said.

"What?" she asked.

He tilted his head at her.

"When you might taste a pomegranate again."

She laughed.

"Maybe it's only life that is fleeting," he said.

He stared at the seeds in his palm and whispered, "Red dirt and water."

Elia noticed his gaze shifted to the ceiling.

"There's a path just past the market. It leads up a long hill. I've walked it a hundred times. I know every switchback, every stone, each drooping tree branch, the red dirt, the bugs and butterflies along the way."

He turned his head and reached toward her.

"Open your hand."

She opened her palm. A few sticky seeds clung to her fingers.

"It's the path—" he said.

He let the seeds from his hand tumble into hers. He stirred them together with his index finger. The pad of his fingertip tickled her palm.

"To Ithaca."

But the sensation of his finger stroking her flesh somehow soothed her. He lifted his finger from her palm. He closed her hand around the seeds, those from his hand and hers, and squeezed her fist closed. His hand around hers reminded her of the grip of the old woman from the market, just stronger.

"At the top is a hut. Outside that hut are three white rocks in red dirt. In the soft place beneath those rocks plant these seeds."

"I will," she said.

She longed to stay with him. Even his slight touch felt so good.

"Come back when you're ready."

"Of course," she said, not quite understanding. Ready for what, she wondered? She had been with him every day like clockwork. She felt more than ready for anything.

"Then I'll tell you," he said.

And he closed his eyes.

"About forever."

CHAPTER 20

More
Trusted
This quiet
This fear.

Since
Music
Might vanquish
Me here.

Aluna's arms sculled just beneath the surface. Warm seawater slipped like silk between her cupped fingers. Every ten or so strokes she stopped. She let her legs drift down. She dunked her head underwater and opened her eyes. Suspended beneath the water she pirouetted like a languid ballerina. She swished the sea with her hands to pivot in each direction. Her hair swirled as she spun. A burst of bubbles percolated from her lips to the surface.

The salt water stung her eyes. She couldn't see more than two bodylengths. Beyond that the water faded into an emerald fog. A school of sabalo hurried past her. Their shimmering scales were the color of her teal bikini. Without goggles covering her eyes the shapes and colors underwater looked like an impressionistic painting.

She lifted her head to suck in another breath of air. Treading at the surface, she scanned the water line for a head, flipper or shell. She listened for that familiar puff, convinced she had indeed heard a sea turtle. The swell bobbed her up and down. The current nudged her toward the beach and then pulled her away again.

She took another look, but saw nothing. She scissor-kicked her legs and began to swim back toward the beach. Her arms fanned above the water like elbowed windmills. She gasped for air to her right side with every second stroke. After her third twisting breath she dipped her face into the water. A dark mass rocketed beneath her. Her fingertips almost skimmed its shell. She nearly choked. The turtle disappeared behind her.

But for her it was the sign. She swam on elated. Cameron was calling her. She was more convinced of it than ever. The entire universe was conspiring with them. A couple of meters from shore her toes pressed into a cushion of pebbles. She wobbled a bit. Tiny stones displaced beneath her feet. As she emerged she gazed at her glistening brown skin. Her sheen seemed reminiscent of the iridescent sabalo. And her skin tingled. In that brief moment she imagined herself Venus.

The water receded to the knot of her bikini, and then to her slender calves, and then to a silver anklet she wore. But as she walked from the sea, it was the water that seemed stable. The beach began to roll like an earthen wave. She could not find her balance. A beach umbrella tilted on its axis. Then the sky began to spin. Everything swirled, slowly at first but then faster and faster, until she collapsed onto the pebbled beach.

A damp towel pressed against Aluna's forehead. She opened her eyes. A green and yellow striped canvas billowed, blocking the afternoon sun. Aluna felt the familiar plastic slats of a beach chair from the seaside café pressing into her backside.

"Easy now," cautioned an unfamiliar voice.

The man had bushy black eyebrows and a bald, sun-blotched head. He spoke in fragmented Portuguese. His chest was covered in a slick scramble of black hair. His protruding belly formed an oily shelf below his drooping nipples.

"Who are you?" she asked in English.

Astrud Gilberto's voice hummed from the café's speakers.

"Your guardian angel. Here, drink some water," the stranger said.

He slipped into an easy English of unmistakable North American origin.

One of the servers from the café, a round-faced teenager that she had always tipped well, handed her a long, slender glass filled with ice water. The sweaty glass felt cool against her palm. She pressed it against her cheek and then tilted it to take a sip.

"Too much sun," she said.

"See a doctor, just to be sure," the stranger said.

"No, I'm fine."

"I'll drive you," he said.

He stood up. A series of red creases striped the top of his expansive gut. His protruding belly threatened to burst his black Speedo. He looked like a red-skinned Buddha.

She stared at the odd man, speechless for a moment. She wondered if he had carried her from the sand to the café chair. She prayed he hadn't, but dared not ask.

"Just to be safe," he said.

His eyes glinted with a carnivorous twinkle.

Aluna sat up.

"Tomorrow," she said.

"It's no problem," he said.

The round-faced server raised an eyebrow and smiled.

"I'll have my husband take me," she said.

She caught the stranger glance toward her empty ring finger. He bowed to her.

"But of course," he said.

He took a step back and gave her a lazy salute.

"*Atey a vista*," he said as he left.

Elia rambled along the crimson path. Crumbs of powdery sand sifted between her toes and the front of her worn sandals. About halfway up she kicked off the sandals and carried them in one hand. The pomegranate seeds were still pressed in the other. The soft, cool dirt tickled the soles of her feet as she walked. A canopy of wispy blue jacaranda, giant birds of paradise, banana trees and looming palms shaded the trek.

A shrill cry screeched from behind. She spied an orange, yellow and blue macaw flash from beneath the overhead branches. It careened over her left shoulder like a winged roller coaster before it darted out of sight around a turn up ahead. Tracking the aerial daredevil, she stepped into a clearing at the top of the path and caught her breath.

There leaned the hut Cameron had described. The macaw perched atop the hut like a splashy exclamation point. She stepped from the brush. The king of parrots flew away. She crept around the perimeter of the abandoned shack. Two rowboats, side by side, would have filled the inside of the hut. But she could see through the doorway that the hut was nearly vacant. She saw only an old cot, one small table and a chair. Yet a palpable energy resonated. The sun-bleached hair on her forearms prickled up. She had the oddest feeling that she was treading upon sacred ground.

And as this notion crystallized some switch deep inside her was tripped. She slipped back into the quiet girl of her youth, the girl Sister Rita Magdalena had once so doted upon. In a blink of her mind, she witnessed herself again pacing upon the mosaic floor of an empty church. Hollow clicks and clacks of patent-leather shoes echoed against the cathedral ceilings. Vacant pews aligned a long, processional corridor. Stained-glass saints towered as sentinels. She edged forward and crossed the transverse at the church's center.

She felt Saint Jerome's watchful eye. She stepped around a marble stone on the floor. The stone was inscribed with words she couldn't read. She had heard a cardinal was buried beneath that stone. Sister Rita Magdalena had explained to her that it wasn't a dead red bird buried beneath the marker, but instead an important, saintly man of the church who once wore a red hat. To her young ears, that sounded even more gruesome. She made sure not to step on the stone.

She craned her neck upward. Her awestruck eyes stared at interlaced vaults that arched so high they might as well be heaven. But the omnipotent grandeur of the church paled to the yearning within her heart, a heart no larger than a font of holy water.

The nuns had told Elia this was the place to ask her questions. They assured her that this sanctuary held *all* the answers. And that was all the reason she had needed. She climbed the steps to the altar. The scent of incense enveloped her.

Behind the altar hung a gold-framed painting of a gaunt, bearded man. A shining yellow halo floated above his drooping head. The nuns had taught Elia his name was Jesus. They told her He had the answers. They taught her He *was* the answer. Armed with this belief, she crept closer. Spikes nailed his hands and feet to a wooden cross. Purplish blood seeped from his wounds. A spear sagged from a gash in his ribs. He wore only a dirty loincloth and a crown of thorns.

He looked hurt, feeble and weak. Yet at the same time his face appeared peaceful, almost resigned to his pain. She didn't want to make Him speak too loud. One ethereal whisper would suffice. She tiptoed around the lace-covered table. A shiny golden chalice sat atop it. She stopped at the foot of a heavy oak throne with bear-claw feet and a regal, velvet cushion. Perched next to the throne was a golden scepter. Atop that scepter was a sparkling orb. To young Elia it looked to be some sort of wizard's wand.

Her heartbeat quickened. Surely this was the kind of place where answers to important questions were found. The nuns must be right.

She knelt down upon the scarlet carpet. She clasped her hands in front of her, just as the nuns had taught her, and just as she had watched others do when they became purposeful and silent with their own important questions to ask. Her eyes lifted above the throne. She peered into the man's sorrowful eyes, eyes that seemed to mirror what she felt.

Surely He would know.

Her angelic whisper broke that holy stillness.

"Why?"

Elia waited, but she heard nothing. Maybe He would speak to her in her head. The nuns had told her that. But nothing came. Maybe He would speak to her in her heart. But she felt nothing in her heart, other than emptiness. Maybe He would speak to her in her soul, but she wasn't even sure where that was or what that would feel like if He did.

So, just to be sure He had heard her, she asked again.

This time her voice grew a little bolder.

"Why?"

Her question sliced through the silence with the purity of a Tibetan prayer chime.

Yet again, no answer came. Nothing came to her mind, her heart or soul.

So she waited, and she waited, and she waited some more. Her knees began to ache. Her prayerful hands began to get clammy, but she held that dutiful pose like the tiniest soldier refusing to break rank.

A tear fell down her cheek and salted past her lips. It clung against all hope until it finally dropped from her chin. Then another, but still no answer came. An eternity seemed to pass. Yet the man in the painting remained silent. The man they called Jesus offered nothing to a six-year-old girl who wanted a mother.

The nuns were wrong. That was what Elia learned that day. She never again asked them, or the man in the painting, for anything.

Floodgates burst. Tears came like never before. Elia fell to her knees onto the dirt floor of the hut and convulsed in heaving sobs. She cried for the love of a mother she never knew, the void decades deep. She wept for every wanting stare she never dared return. She wailed for the lonely nights cloistered in towers of words, hiding between pages, grasping for life and love in the turn of a phrase, instead of a heartfelt gaze, or the touch of another vulnerable soul.

She cried like a newborn torn from the womb.

And within that exhausting purge the high-flying buttresses supporting her fragile life crumbled. A startling emptiness deepened. She retreated to that vulnerable girl kneeling on the floor of that church.

She grasped for the frame of the cot and she pulled herself up from the ground. She drew her knees to her chest. Her breath steadied and eventually slowed. Her defeated eyes surrendered and closed. And, tucked into a fetal position, she finally passed out on the cot.

When Elia awoke it felt like a hundred-year storm had passed. Afternoon had dimmed to dusk. A full moon catapulted above the horizon. She sensed a pulse faint as a butterfly's heartbeat. A barely perceptible tingle resonated within her palm. The pomegranate seeds, after all of this, were still clutched within her hand. Her fist was tucked against her face. She unclasped her fingers and studied the seeds. One of the seeds had split open and crushed within her palm. A small splotch of deep red marked her palm. She licked the ruby stain. It tasted less bitter than before.

Dusk faded. A majestic moon rose high. She stared up at that moon. The same nightlight that summoned lost mariners to safety, quelled dancing tides and cast a silvery sheen over sleepless sorcerers cast upon her. She had read the moon was capable of lifting lovers and lunatics. The moon was paramour to both pagans and poets alike. She had an idea, perhaps nothing more than a spark of lunacy. Just maybe that moon had sprinkled a bit of dust upon her.

Of course, she thought. The thought sprang from no rational place. But she felt revived by the whimsy of it all.

She crept outside the hut and surveyed the scrub brush about the clearing. There must be something she could use. She crouched down beneath a palm trunk and inspected a broken piece of coconut. Her fingers ran along its clawed edge. *Perfect.*

She turned back toward the hut with the broken coconut shell in hand. A triad of ivory stones shone like pearls in the moonlight, guiding her. Just as Cameron had described, those white rocks were nestled in the dirt not far past the doorway to the hut. As she inched closer, she peeked over her shoulder. Only the moon was watching.

She knelt down and grazed her hand across the dirt. She picked up one of the oblong stones. Its surface was slippery smooth. If felt like it had been tumbled to a polish. Even in the moonlight she noted a remarkable translucence. The veins within the rock seemed to suck in light. She picked up the second and the third rock. Each bore these same facets. These were not random bits.

She set aside the stones and began to dig with the coconut shell. She scooped out loose soil into a powdery pile. Six or so inches down seemed deep enough. She opened her hand. The pomegranate seeds, minus one, were still clutched in her palm.

She patted down the hole. Her finger glanced against something hard. She brushed the soil aside and felt a cool, sterling clasp. She tugged at the clasp and pulled out a silver wristwatch from the soil.

What the hell?

She rubbed the watch face with her thumb. The tiny second hand still ticked. She pressed it against her ear and listened. Cameron had never mentioned any watch. What type of man buries such treasure, guides her so close yet leaves the actual discovery to fate?

She scrubbed more dirt away and studied the watch. It was heavy, with a pale round face and black roman numerals. Five interwoven rows of links slunk together, like metallic snakeskin, forming a silver band. Across the bottom of the face, nestled between the roman numerals VII, VI and V, were two tiny words she could not discern. Near the top of the face, centered under the numeral XII, was a larger word she could read. Omega.

Simple, balanced, flawless, she thought—*and buried in dirt*.

Elia slid the watch onto her wrist and closed the clasp. It dangled there as she pressed the seeds into the dirt. She peered into the hole before covering the seeds. This would be the last time the seedlings saw moonlight. She spit three times into the hole. The seeds' first watering would be her saliva. She pushed a pile of dirt into the hole, patted it down again flat and replaced the three stones to mark the spot.

Any thought of returning to the *cantina* tonight succumbed to a sense of obligation. She needed to water those seeds. Cameron's words came back to her. *Come to me when you're ready.*

This wasn't a race.

Elia gazed up at the moon. She stared at the milky brilliance, just like she used to do after Sister Rita Magdalena would turn out the light and close the door to the orphanage's cramped sleeping quarters, leaving young Elia lonely but not alone to stare out the window until she fell asleep. The night wind whispered to a hush. The tropic air felt as warm as an old quilt. Elia walked back into the hut. She curled up on the worn cot. She looked out the window and stared at the moon. She slid that watch up and down her wrist, alone but not quite so lonely, until she fell asleep.

CHAPTER 21

Spell upon me
Gypsy heart
Pirouette
Eurhythmic rain.

Bind about me
Gypsy vine
Quintessent
Beyond refrain.

Nestled in cotton linens on a hand-carved, mahogany four-poster bed, Aluna stared at the wrought-iron pulls of the sixteenth-century Spanish armoire across the room. Each handle had been worn smooth by generations of chambermaids. She kicked aside the sheet and slid from bed. Her feet planted upon a maroon carpet of Turkish origin. On either side of the headboard's swirling posts, cream chiffon curtains fell from a plaster-and-beam ceiling. Those curtains framed tall French doors and pooled upon oak plank floors.

She walked toward the armoire. With each step her toes pressed into the abstract weave of ram's horn and human figures with arms akimbo. The wardrobe dated to the time of Catherine of Aragon, daughter of Isabella and King Ferdinand of Spain, before Catherine married Henry the Eighth. Aluna imagined vibrant lives both grand and small survived by the forged permanency of the inanimate, mundane handle that she tugged.

She swung open the left door. Inside was a row of six drawers beneath a marble shelf. Upon the cracked marble top leaned an antique doll in a formal hoop dress. Modeled after a Portuguese princess, the infanta's gown bore an intricate design of glossy black satin, burgundy fabric, gilt and lace. The doll's gold, filigreed headdress attached to a black veil with pearl-tipped headpins. The doll had been an engagement gift from Jackson, her husband. It was no less than a thinly veiled promise of a life that would be hers.

She caressed the top drawer's handle. Inside were her velvet-lined jewelry boxes. In front of those boxes were bottles of her favorite fragrances, her two "Jeans." With every pull of that drawer, Jean Patou's Joy and Jean Dessés's Kalispera clinked against one another like jousting swordsmen. The lower drawers were stuffed with silk undergarments and an array of blouses.

Her favorite dresses splashed across the clouded oval mirror snugly framed inside the armoire's partially ajar right door. It was as if each generation had left behind its own particular film to further dull the luster of that looking glass. More than once Aluna had found herself staring into the mirror thinking she had just seen another set of eyes reflecting back at her.

Morning sun spilled into the room through French doors, illuminating three antiquated tapestries on the far wall of her bedroom. The tapestries hung just to the right of the armoire.

In the first tapestry, a crusading knight charged into battle atop a furious steed. The intensity of the beast's eyes was matched only by the apparent resolve of its rider. Castle spires rose in the distance. In the second tapestry, a maiden with cascading brunette curls stared into a hand-held mirror. The looking glass reflected a dove taking flight from a window ledge behind her. The third tapestry depicted a pastoral scene of a rustic valley with ripened vineyards beneath hills dotted by shepherds tending their flocks. Aluna had long imagined the triptych symbolized what would become of her life.

Now each tapestry reminded her of Cameron. And everything else in the room reminded her only of his absence.

Aluna sifted through the clutter of her privileged life. She was surrounded by fulfilled promises, now all meaningless. She mentally sorted her possessions. What she wanted, or thought she had once needed, fell away to a most elemental desire.

Jackson's voice bellowed from downstairs. He barked into a telephone about the newly found shipwreck. Since their return from the remote Caribbean waters his quest had consumed him even more. She was used to it by now. She knew his pattern. Jackson was a twenty-first-century conquistador. He would stop at nothing to collect what he now considered *his* rightful treasure.

"I'll double your pay!" he yelled.

She reached for the doll. She hadn't picked it up in years. It smelled musty. The gilt trim of the doll's skirt scratched her cheek. Other than its porcelain complexion, the doll's features were not unlike hers. Almond eyes, exaggerated to the point of caricature, dominated the doll's high cheekbones. A refined, inconspicuous nose centered the face. She set down the doll. Its frozen beauty would outlast her, like it had so many others before her. She tightened her grip on the cool wrought-iron drawer pull. She opened the top drawer. Her two Jeans clinked against each other.

Tucked in the front left corner of the drawer was a red velvet box. Inside that box was her wedding band. There was a time when she had only begrudgingly removed that wedding band from her finger, too worried that a sacred spell might be broken. She stared at the ring she had now avoided wearing for weeks. She felt like she was being watched and glanced to her right. But only her clouded reflection stared from the wardrobe's mirrored door.

And then the floor began to sway. The top drawer pulled from its track. The corner of the drawer banged into her thigh. The drawer's insides spilled onto the oak floor.

"What's going on?" Jackson shouted.

The drawer crashed to the floor. The full weight of Aluna's body followed with a thud.

She regained consciousness with Jackson kneeling over her on the floor. He cradled her head in his hand.

"Are you alright?" he asked.

"I think so," she said.

But she didn't know what to think. Fear dripped into a foggy pool of consciousness. What was going on? She saw the concern upon Jackson's weathered face. But she sensed he was just irritated at having to cut short his phone call.

The drawer handle was still in her right hand. Just beyond Jackson's head she saw the fallen doll. The doll's eyes stared down at her from the marble dresser ledge within the armoire. She smelled lilac and mimosa, remnants of the splattered Kalispera. Joy, the victor, lay intact next to her head. Her leg ached.

All of her jewels had catapulted from their tufted beds. Scattered across the oak floorboards and the Turkish rug were a pearl necklace, diamond-studded earrings, a jet-black, oval onyx ring, and a nineteenth-century ladybug broach with ruby spots and emerald eyes. Next to Jackson's bent knee was her wedding band.

Within the hour, an old gentleman with big ears and the drooping face of a basset hound loomed over her bedside. Doctor Silva pressed the long fingers of his familiar, oversized hand against her wrist. He wrapped a blood pressure cuff around her arm, squeezed the little black ball and then released the air until he appeared satisfied. She watched his thick eyebrows. He pressed a stethoscope against her silk pajama top. He probed a lump near the back of her head. A cold compress balanced across her forehead. Jackson stood behind the doctor, watching.

"I'm fine," Aluna said.

But she wasn't so sure.

She saw Jackson's eye catch her overnight bag beside the armoire.

"Planning a trip?" he asked.

His hands were on his hips.

"Shopping in São Paulo for a couple of days."

Jackson just stared at her.

"Just woke up and decided to go?"

Jackson stroked his thinning black hair.

The only sound coming from old Doctor Silva was his sucking on a piece of hard candy.

"I told you but you didn't hear me. You've been so busy. You won't even miss me."

Another lie, followed by the truth, finished off with a bit of both.

Jackson stepped in front of the doctor.

"I know I've been distracted. To think it's right there after so many years, just waiting for me, it's just so—"

"Addicting?" she said.

"Overwhelming."

She pictured him on some beach, grinning like a pirate atop trunks overflowing with Spanish coins and gold chalices. She saw him gloating over his prized bracelet. But she envisioned herself on a different beach in the arms of another. How could she begrudge his passion? His passion and unwavering confidence had once won her hand, until it eventually smothered her. He still had the swagger of a man destined for greatness.

He crossed his arms.

"Follow the doctor's orders," he said.

"Of course," she said.

He seemed unsure whether to say or do something more. Aluna, for the first time in a long time, glimpsed a hint of helplessness. It was the same look she saw in the rare instances he spoke to his father, the retired ambassador Jonathan Gray. His name alone, *Jackson*, seemed to have sentenced him to a life in his father's long shadow. Jackson turned away. She exhaled with some relief when she heard his feet race down the stairs. The heavy doors to his study closed with a groaning thud.

"Has it happened before?" Doctor Silva asked.

She smelled peppermint on the old doctor's breath.

"No," Aluna said in a voice as delicate as the doll's embroidered sleeve.

"I mean other than yesterday at the beach," he whispered under his candied breath. He didn't bother to raise either of his bushy gray eyebrows. Aluna was instantly reminded just how fast gossip spread.

"I need to run some tests," the old doctor said.

She looked down, embarrassed to be so easily exposed.

"Okay," she said.

"Before you go—shopping," he said.

"But I—"

"But nothing. My nurse will take a blood and urine sample. Until then, rest and patience," he said.

He wagged his finger.

"We don't want you falling ill on your travels, now do we?"

He walked to the door, turned and nodded.

"*Nao se preocupe*—you're my patient, not him."

§

Elia's eyelids were sealed tight when the earliest birds chirped into her dream. A yellow-bellied finch swooped into the hut. The bird fluttered to a cluster of chattering hatchlings in a nest no bigger than her fist. The nest was tucked into a narrow eave between the roof and wall. The hovering finch landed in the nest and dropped a wriggling worm to the outstretched beaks, the clatter momentarily silenced. The finch craned its neck and spotted Elia.

The finch flew out the door. It returned with a longer worm. It glided toward Elia with its wriggling catch. The bird dropped the worm just above her head. She caught it and felt its cool jellied body writhe in her hand. But when she opened her palm there was nothing. She felt the worm slithering up her forearm. She awoke to find the silver watch sliding down her wrist. No worm. She looked at the corner eave. No chirping hatchlings. No nest.

She slid the watch from her wrist. She brought it close to her face. The casing felt cool against her fingers. She turned the watch over in her hand and rubbed its smooth face like a wishing stone. Her thumb brushed across a scratchy surface on its backside.

To her drowsy eyes it looked to be nothing more than an erratic scribble of elongated loops. She squinted. Cursive lettering began to take shape. Tilting the watch toward the light, she whispered, "*til the end of time.*" She repeated the inscription. Cameron's words echoed. *I'll tell you about forever.*

Still cuddled on her side, she spotted an empty wine bottle on the dirt floor beneath the table. She had one last task. She heard waves in the distance. She crawled across the dirt floor. Maroon silt clung to the inside of the bottle. She picked it up. The label read zinfandel. She sniffed. It smelled more like musty sea silt, with only a hint of stale wine.

Elia got up and stepped into the morning light. The silver watch was on her wrist. The empty wine bottle was in her hand. She followed the sound of the sea to a steep path. She squatted in the bushes to pee, using the wine bottle to help her balance. A furry orange caterpillar clung to an accordion-like frond of a Mexican fan palm. The brilliant creature inched up and down the grooved ridges.

She couldn't recall the last time she had peed outside. The thought of crouching down in the weeds to pee while propped up by an empty wine bottle made her giggle. She looked up. The faint moon was fading into a blue sky.

She stood and noticed the path forked. One track led to a ledge overlooking the ocean. The other terraced down the cliff to the sea, anchored by rocks and exposed tree roots. She stepped to the cliff's edge and peered at the water. From her vantage the sea looked like a rolling blanket of shimmering blue diamonds.

A pelican drifted below her. Ivory wings skimmed along the water's surface. It landed with barely a splash. Then another pelican, a bit smaller, followed. The second pelican glided down and slid into the water alongside its partner. The two floated side by side. The large pelican's yellow beak scratched into a tuft of feathers along the other's back. The smaller pelican craned its head up toward the sky.

And out of the blue somehow it was her classmate's pale face that flashed to mind. Elia smiled.

Hiking down the steep path proved tricky. Several times she had to switch the wine bottle from hand to hand to better grip a rock, a branch or an exposed root. Her sandals skidded along the dirt and rocks. Halfway down she took them off and hung them on a stubby branch of a cape honeysuckle. After half a dozen tight switchbacks, she reached the bottom. She climbed over an outcropping of jagged rock. The pockmarked surface pinched her bare feet. She found one smooth spot that dipped into the water at a gentle angle. That mossy rock brought some relief to her prickled feet.

She inched along the slick stone to the water's edge. She bent down to dip the wine bottle into the water but slipped. The bottle flung toward the stone. She jerked her hand back. Her elbow banged into the mossy rock. She slid on her butt into the water. The salt water stung her elbow. She lifted her arm out of the water and twisted it around. Blood traced from three long scratches. She dropped her elbow back into the sea and rubbed it clean. The salt water stung.

She pushed clear of urchins embedding into the rock and treaded water a few feet from shore. She dipped her face beneath the surface. The bottom quickly dropped away. Air bubbles gurgled from the bottle's mouth when she held it beneath the surface. Seawater filled the bottle. More bubbles percolated up. Her head bobbed just above the surface.

A haunting sound echoed from the water. It was like nothing she had ever before heard. The sound rippled right through her. She dipped her head below the water again and listened.

She heard it again. This time it was even louder: a piercing, lilting, harmonic cry, and then a long guttural moan. She swirled around and looked out to sea. The two pelicans took flight. But she already knew what she had heard. It sounded like the soaring climax of a hundred cellos. She was certain it had come from the goliath she had spotted from the seaplane weeks ago. It just had to.

Elia listened.

And the whale's song was glorious.

CHAPTER 22

And on this day
I give my hand
Hold close this moment
Without demand
Coarse from life
Yet soft in strife
Since when I grasped
She gave me two.

Elia paused outside the *cantina*.

The whale's hypnotic cries had stayed with her, triggering a peculiar sensation. She had floated beneath the water's glassy surface and listened. Yet as she did, she felt like she had gained the vantage point of a drifting seagull. She looked down at the moss-draped rock upon which she had slipped. She could see her own honey figure scull below the water. In her periphery, the massive cliff offset an infinite blue sky.

That surreal perspective continued as she walked up the trail. She hovered above her own body while she poured the wine bottle of seawater onto the dirt to water the buried seeds. She watched from outside herself while she traipsed down the path to the village.

Now, she stroked the watch. The glint of late morning sun reflected off its silver. She felt its weight upon her wrist. This was real. She turned her elbow. Her fingertips traced the three short, parallel scrapes on her flesh. She didn't want them to heal. She wanted the mark of this island upon her.

Her shorts and halter were nearly dry. She wiped sweat from beneath the damp ponytail that tickled the back of her neck.

"Allow me," she heard a familiar voice say.

But that offer had come from inside the *cantina*.

Elia peeked through the doorway. She spied Paco sitting with Isabella at a wooden table. It was the same table she had shared with them upon her arrival to the island. On the table was a white plate filled with a pink guava, two green mangos and a papaya. Next to the plate was a mound of discarded banana peels. She heard an infantile wheezing coming from Paco's hammock. Chuey was tucked under a bar towel. The little monkey's head was pillowed upon a dog-eared paperback book.

A pitcher of ice water and two glasses sat on that table between Paco and Isabella. Elia was thirsty. But she waited.

Paco was clad in crumpled shorts the color of a weathered sail. His tie-dyed tank top was one size too big. As usual he was barefoot. He sat with his back angled to the doorway and his elbows resting on the slatted tabletop. He reached for a mango. Sinewy bands of taut muscle flexed along his triceps. His loose tank top revealed the dark-skinned shoulder blades of a fisherman. Elia pictured him capable of reeling in any fish he hooked.

Paco peeled the mango with an ivory-handled buck knife. Isabella was watching his hands, which moved with the deftness of an illusionist. Neither spoke. Four chairs circled the table, but Isabella was nestled beside him. She appeared lost in his dexterity. Watching Paco reminded Elia of the time she had helped him prepare the *étouffée*. He sculpted the fruit like it was a piece of art. Elia felt herself smiling.

He rotated the skinless mango between his thumb and forefinger. *This is when it turns into a dove,* she thought. Instead he simply sliced off a piece.

Isabella's arms sprouted from a canary-yellow sundress. Her slinking armor of gold bracelets coiled along her wrists. A necklace of teal-blue nickernuts shifted when she leaned closer to him and opened her mouth. Paco pulled back the wedge and teased her. Then he relinquished the mango into her waiting mouth. Elia had never seen Isabella so tame. She first accepted the mango like it was nectar. But then she bit it in half and let a small chunk fall from her fleshy lips. It seemed to fall in slow motion. Paco caught the chunk before it dropped to the table.

Isabella trapped his forearm against the table. Paco nevertheless flicked the piece into his mouth with only his fingers. Isabella let go a hearty laugh, loosened her grip and began stroking the inside of his forearm. Their mutual delight was apparent. Their intimacy reminded Elia of the two frolicking pelicans.

Isabella traced her fingertips along the inside of Paco's forearm. Elia recalled Paco's scar she had noticed days earlier. That branding along Paco's forearm she had thought to be a squatted "H." Now it looked much more like an elongated "I."

Isabella.

Elia had had no idea. Now she had no doubt. The whole world seemed to be shifting, or maybe for once in her life it was just coming into focus.

She kicked her sandals in the sand, coughed, and knocked on the doorframe. She feigned a surprised "good morning" when she walked into the *cantina.*

Paco flashed his gold-toothed grin.

"Miss Elia, there you are," said Isabella.

They didn't budge, which only made Elia feel more intrusive. Isabella's eyes looked at her as all-knowing as ever.

Maybe she knew Elia had been spying on them all along. She continued to caress Paco's scar.

"That's an 'I' isn't it?" Elia asked.

She pointed toward Paco's arm.

"Huh, sort of looks like it," Paco said.

"Hmm," Isabella said. "Jus'so, maybe a little bit."

"Nah," Paco said.

He looked up at Elia.

"See now, this is me," he said.

He took Isabella's thick index finger in his hand to stroke it along the bottom ridge.

"This is Isabella," he said.

And he ran her finger along the top mark.

"And this long line connecting the two—" he said.

"That's the *moyo*," Isabella whispered in her singsong accent.

"*Moyo?*" Elia asked.

"Sure, let's just say it's an unbreakable cord," Paco said with a smile.

Chuey chattered something as if in a dream. The monkey peeked out from under the bar towel to eyeball the three of them and then resettled.

"Nah, maybe it's an 'I,'" chuckled Isabella.

"Could be an 'H,' Paco said. "Henrietta?"

Elia laughed.

"How is he?" she asked.

"Suspect he's waiting on you," Isabella said.

"Or Halley, like that comet?" Paco said.

"Want some mango?" he asked.

"No thanks," Elia said.

She still felt more than a little awkward, but she liked hearing Isabella say Cameron might be waiting for her. She also felt more than a bit embarrassed for having been jealous of

Isabella. Isabella's defiant belly laugh at the beach the other day now made better sense.

"He's better," Paco said.

Elia noticed him glance at the watch. But he said nothing of it, nor did Isabella. To Elia it felt as if they were ignoring a jeweled tiara atop her head.

"May I?" Elia asked.

She pointed toward the hallway. The watch slid down her wrist. Their eyes seemed to follow, but still not a single remark from either of them.

"Of course," Paco said. "He should be awake by now."

She walked down the hallway. Just around the corner she slowed to eavesdrop.

"It's happening," Isabella hummed.

"What kind of *cunumunu* carves an 'I' on his arm?" Paco asked.

"Only a *ragadang chupidee*," Isabella said. "And wit' a bony knife, too."

"More mango?" he asked.

"You're back."

Elia discerned an unmistakable welcome in Cameron's tone.

Things looked different. A thick pillow propped up his head. He was cleanly shaven. His hair looked freshly washed. An old T-shirt, blue as a postcard of the Caribbean, covered his shoulders and chest. The shirt rippled into a fold of white sheet near his waistline. Sunlight streamed through the open window. The T-shirt provoked the blue in his eyes. She had never before seen eyes so keen. His gaze disarmed her.

The offerings at the foot of his bed had thinned to three coconut-shelled candles. The candlewicks flickered in puddles of orange wax. Clumps of twigs and leaves and several feathers were scattered around the candles. The bright orange, blue and yellow feathers hadn't been there before. Yet those feathers looked remarkably similar to those of the macaw she'd seen perched atop the hilltop hut. Sage incense laced the warm air.

Isabella had been busy. But her feelings toward Isabella had shifted and now Elia felt grateful for the big woman.

"You look so much better," she said.

His eyes locked on her. She slid the watch from her wrist. She had no idea if he was right- or left-handed. He raised his left hand from his chest. She leaned over. She noticed that both of their hands were trembling. She slipped the watch past the freckled veins along the top of his hand. She felt a palpable magnetism between the two of them and that watch. The pull alleviated only after she clasped the watch to his wrist. His hand seemed to steady.

She noticed a weathered copy of *Secrets of Odysseus* tucked beneath the sheet. She recognized the first-edition scarlet cover. He took a deep breath. To her that breath alone sounded wonderful. She fought off a sudden urge to kiss his cheek. She straightened up. He stroked the watch, inspecting it like he had never before seen it.

Two glasses were atop the bedside table. One was full of water. The other was upside down. *Isabella again*, Elia thought.

"May I?" she asked, still flustered by her impulse to kiss him.

He nodded. She poured a glass of water and gulped the whole thing down. She scooted the stool closer to the bed. She wanted to tell him everything. She wanted to tell him about the hut, her collapse, the moon, the seedlings, the watch, her dream and the whale's song. But that odd feeling returned. She felt outside herself again, like she was witnessing this whole scene from above. She held her tongue.

And it was his words that then came, slow but deliberate.

"She swept me away like a wave carries away a speck of sand. There was never any choice. That is the only way I can explain it."

A streak of sunlight worked its way up from the floor to his mattress. The ray stretched toward the silver watch that now rested against his blue shirt. The watch's silvery sparkle glimmered onto Elia.

"And this watch?" she asked.

"*A poet's death is his life*," he said.

"Gibran," Elia whispered.

She knew the story of the dying poet. The great Arabic poet and writer Khalil Gibran had written that an angel had appeared at his bedside with a wreath of lilies. She embraced him and then closed his eyes so he could see no more—except with the eye of his spirit.

"Gibran," he said.

Cameron heaved another deep breath. He reached down and pulled the book from beneath the sheet.

"I looked for her everywhere. I saw her in everything. And the watch, you ask," he said.

He thumbed toward the back pages of *Secrets*. The cracked scarlet cover had nearly dislodged from its binding. It looked battered but had somehow survived every single second of over two decades.

He drew in another breath and read:

> *To hold dear words,*
> *But not me.*
> *Cherish my verse,*
> *But not thee.*
> *This then you ask?*

Then how harbor my gift?
Will you cultivate it with care?
Safe in your soul?
Or lock it in a silver box,
Lined with crushed velvet,
Tucked away in a closet,
To peek at,
When you,
And you alone dare?

He seemed to become lost in those words. But he didn't rush through them like familiar alleys of an old neighborhood. He still dwelled upon the rhythm and imagery. It sounded almost as if he was exploring them for the first time.

Will you carry them in your pocket?
Crumpled and torn.
Secrete along a cobblestone alley?
And only then,
Furtively press to your heart?
Careful,
Lest the world see, and mourn.

Or will you declare,
Look at this meager gift,
From my forlorn,
Such trite words,
So sad,
Don't you think?
Torn down,
Revealed fakirs
In the house of love.

As he read, Elia's own underlying sense of abandonment rose up, but her loss was so different than any such romantic notions. To her, that poem struck a very different chord. It evoked the memory of a long-lost childhood locket, a locket she had worn around her neck, a locket without any picture inside.

Tell me, how will you nurture them?
Because I know too well,
You will not nurture,
Or stoke their fire,
Instead only neglect,
Like all you acquire.

If I am wrong, then show me,
Paper your walls with my verse,
So that you live,
Breathe,
And dream,
With this love as the curse.

And then
Off to the square,
To the clock tower at midnight,
To scream aloud,
Then again,
At noon and every hour,
Declare love's import,
Because that is what I have done,
But you dare not.
Do you care not?

As he stopped reading, Elia felt immersed in her loss. She was still haunted by a faceless image. She could only imagine the face that should have filled that empty locket.

"And then, this watch," Cameron said.

She stared down at the watch she had worn for one mystical night and morning.

"My fears were trumped by five words more potent than anything I had ever written," he said.

Elia stared into his blue eyes.

"'Til the end of time," he whispered.

"'Til the end of time," she repeated.

"It's real, this forever," he said.

It sounded like he was confiding his most precious, long-guarded secret.

"Where is she?" Elia asked.

A tingle rippled through her.

"Everywhere," he said.

The dust that flickered in the late morning sunlight seemed to suspend. The chirping birds outside the window hushed.

And Cameron whispered, "She's dead."

CHAPTER 23

And on this day
Behold the smile
Returned the captive
Oh mystic isle
Eyes past to present
Reflect iridescent
Time tarnished
Familiar, but new.

Aluna gazed at Machado de Assis's *Dom Casmurro*. The book was propped atop her embroidered blouse, her back cushioned by goose-feather pillows crammed against the mahogany headboard. She cradled the old book's embossed leather cover. Her thumbs were pressed against its parchment-like pages. But not even de Assis's remarkable Portuguese prose could keep her attention. She had no idea how long she had been lost on the same page. Her thumb peeled from the translucent paper. The oil from her skin had discolored the honeyed page. A smudge fingerprinted beneath the sentence, "Not everything is clear in life or in books."

The classic tale of unresolved jealousy collapsed upon her stomach. It was no use. All she could think about was the nurse's visit that afternoon. The demure nurse had looked barely beyond high school age. Her sleek black hair was pulled into a bun. Not a blemish marked her face. A hint of down shaded the turn of the young nurse's jaw, perhaps her only imperfection. Her face looked like a charcoal artist had over-shadowed just that one feature. Except for a small medical bag and patent-leather shoes the girl could have been mistaken for a maid. At most maybe five years separated them, but the moment the young nurse reached into her satchel she was all business.

The girl tied the elastic tourniquet around Aluna's bicep. The thick black rubber cinched her skin.

"Clench your fist," the nurse said in a monotone.

Her bedside manner was a far cry from that of Doctor Silva.

Aluna felt the cool gauze wipe across her forearm. She caught a whiff of rubbing alcohol. She stared at the tingling patch of shiny skin. She studied the needle, about the length of her small finger, for even the slightest tremor of uncertainty. The silver needle navigated above a bluish vein just below the crease of her elbow. Then she felt a prick followed by a slow, burning sting. She shuddered when the first drop of blood seeped into the clear vial at the back of the syringe. She watched a steady maroon trickle when she opened her fist.

The nurse pressed a cotton ball over the puncture. She taped it into place and handed Aluna a plastic cup.

"*Por favor*," the nurse asked.

Aluna kicked free of the sheet. She glanced toward her ghost-like reflection in the armoire's mirrored door. She walked barefoot, carrying the cup in front of her. She closed the door, set the cup on the antique vanity and looked at her face in the mirror. Her eyes looked no different. Her cheeks maybe a bit flushed, but the air had been humid. Her thick, dark hair looked as full as always. She felt no cravings, other than for a certain man on a certain island. She untied her pajama bottoms and let them slip to the cold tile floor.

She had always considered her shape just round enough in all the right places, which included her waistline. Several kilos beyond any Paris runway, she still maintained a natural Brazilian confidence. She had grown accustomed to at least a second glance wherever she went. Satisfied her tanned stomach was no different she sat on the toilet, grabbed the cup off the vanity and dipped it beneath her.

How odd, she thought, when she handed the urine sample to the nurse and watched her leave: any secrets hidden within were now tucked in a satchel carried by a girl with whom she had shared less than a dozen words.

For the rest of the afternoon she found little distraction from mulling over her physical state. She didn't feel nauseated. She counted the weeks since her last period. A spectrum of maladies darted through her mind, any of which threatened her escape. She fended off thoughts of pregnancy, cancerous tumors and malfunctioning glands by mentally packing and repacking her overnight bag, paring down her outfits, culling her toiletries to the barest necessities. The less she took, the more easily she could disappear.

A wrought-iron knocker thumped against the front door. She heard her husband downstairs greet Doctor Silva. Their voices were low. She bolted from bed, grasped the glass doorknob and twisted. The bedroom door groaned. The men's conversation came to an abrupt halt. She froze, conscious of her own breath, and listened to a pair of deliberate footsteps climb the stairs. She pranced back into bed and stashed de Assis's novel in her nightstand drawer on top of her grandmother's old rosary. The silver crucifix and black prayer beads peeked from beneath the book. She shut the drawer.

A knock rapped on her door.

"Come in," she called from bed.

"*Muito bem*, you're resting," the old doctor said.

He walked into the room. He had a long face with drooping eyes yet the elegant demeanor of a stage actor. He moved with a gauged efficiency.

"How do you feel?" he asked.

"Better," she said.

She wondered what he had told her husband.

"May I?" he asked.

He pointed toward her writing table.

She nodded. He pulled a frail chair from beneath the single-drawer table off to the side of her bed and sat down. The table had been in her family for generations. Its cracked cherry top and serpentine legs glistened from heavy layers of lacquer. The lip above the drawer was yellowed from years of use. Following family tradition, she had etched her name on the inside bottom of the drawer. No less than half a dozen names were scrawled there. Her own name was scribbled directly beneath her deceased mother, Rita Adelina, and her grandmother, Francesca Olivia.

"I suspected it when I saw you, but wanted to be sure."

His voice had lowered.

"Of what?" she asked.

She grasped at naivety.

The debonair, basset-hound-looking doctor took her hand in his wrinkled fingers.

"*Parabens*, you're pregnant."

His words fell with unequivocal certainty, like he was telling her the time of day, or that it was raining outside. There was no "might be" or "perhaps." Her next exhale felt like she had been holding her breath ever since the nurse had left. Her cheeks felt warm, her feet clammy and her hands tingled, both the hand in his grasp and the other resting on her stomach, the stomach that hours earlier looked and felt no different than ever. She stared at the ceiling.

A flurry of images raced to mind: the nurse, the cup, the first drop of blood, the satchel, the shimmering sabalo and sea turtle. Was that her reflection in the armoire mirror? Was that her face in the bathroom vanity? She felt herself tumbling over a waterfall. Yet in the next moment she felt an incredible lightness.

"How long?" she asked.

Her gaze locked on the beamed ceiling as if he were divining the answer from above.

"Maybe seven, eight weeks."

His gaze shifted back to her. "You tell me."

But she had already escaped into a vision of Cameron wrapping her in a blanket and carrying her from the mountaintop hut to the sea.

"Did you tell—" she asked.

"Nobody," he said.

His smile filled with grandfatherly affection. She had known him her entire life, from first tooth to tonsils to teenager to this.

"You're my patient, not him. All he knows is that you're going to be fine."

Aluna grimaced.

"Which, by the way, is true," he added and squeezed her hand.

But she wasn't so sure.

"The rules are simple, lots of rest. Come see me in a week," he said.

He got up and closed his bag.

"But—"

"No appointment, just call me when you're coming. Until then take your time and think things through," he said.

"All right," she mumbled.

"One week. Promise," he said.

He returned the chair to the writing table.

"Of course," she said.

A feeling of imprisonment slowly overtook her.

She listened to make sure his footsteps tracked down the stairs and out the front door without interruption. She got up from bed, pulled out that same feeble chair and sat down at the small writing desk. She opened the drawer and removed a sheet of stationery.

Secluded on the storm-battered island, Cameron served time without Aluna like a prison sentence. He chalked off the days in endless strokes of his pen. Torrential rain had forced him to surrender the mountaintop hut for drier shelter. Tucked in the bayside cottage he fell into the life of a hermit. Days passed with barely a solid meal. He ate very light, mostly mangos, bananas and an occasional sliver of the cassava cakes his young landlady had brought him one morning.

"Calaloo bammies," Isabella said when he opened the door to find her standing there, barefoot in the rain.

She held out a plate of steaming flatbreads. Her skin was slick as oil, and only a shade lighter, but somehow the plate was almost dry. Stringy green flecks dappled the pale cakes. He smelled coconut and a hint of spinach. Rain dripped from her elbows as she offered the plate to him. Her tangerine dress sucked against her cello-like curves. A spongy black ponytail slithered around her neck. Its end clung to her chest. She was panting and looked positively vibrant.

He didn't need a mirror to know he was withering. It was evident from the concern in her eyes.

"*Jeez-an-ages*, go on," she said.

She stomped her foot into a puddle. He glanced down at his bare chest. His ribs jutted from beneath his skin. Hers was a mission of mercy. His stomach grumbled. He took the plate. She dashed off into the rain.

"Thank you," he shouted.

For weeks he had bathed only in the sea, during infrequent gaps between the rains, and slept only upon exhaustion. His hair took on the texture of matted straw, crackled and stiff. A pallid haze of sea salt and stale sweat coated his skin. His body odor sunk to that of a seafarer, a scent more akin to clams and oysters. Barnacled stubble tangled into a bearded thicket. Yet he clung to the inscription upon the back of the watch like a life preserver.

"*'Til the end of time.*"

Those five words sustained his vigil.

He scribbled down every last remnant of their passion, contorting it into verse. Disgorged, dissected, contemplated, magnified and sometimes, he worried, manipulated. The demarcation between reality and memory blurred. Were her eyes truly like jade or was it his memory that colored them so? Was he preserving her or creating some ethereal creature spawned from memory? He withdrew into himself. He debated aloud his obsession. He muttered, ranted, laughed and wept. He contorted along with his words.

At night he filled the cottage with candles. He wrote under flickering dots of defiant light. He traipsed perilously one word from silence, from the empty page, from her. He distrusted sleep, afraid that she might not visit his dreams. But she always appeared to cavort with him so he could obsess even more.

Stroke by stroke he continued. Each brushstroke seemed critical. But he began to doubt the final portrait. He reread the poems. Words he had scribbled as if his life had depended upon them later seemed dead, like dried-up hibiscus petals crumpled along a dusty hillside path. Would anyone perceive how deep the scarlet, how perfect the bead of dew that glistened upon it like a translucent pearl in the morning sun? Would she?

Rain pelted against the corrugated metal roof. It sounded like frenzied brass drums. He grew accustomed to the cacophony. It rained so often it became the lull that disturbed his sleep. He slumped over the table, his face down in half-written verse. He rubbed drool from his whiskered chin. He twisted upright from sleep's rigor. A rusty file grated against his spine. His neck popped. He rubbed his eyes, scratched his flaking scalp and stared at the watch.

Ten past two and daylight, it was afternoon.

In the unusual quiet he heard an even more unusual whirring, like a dragonfly buzzing in his ear. The sound grew into a rattling whine.

He stepped to the window. The cracked tile floor chilled the bottoms of his dirty feet. Rain still cried down the glass pane. He leaned against the splintered sill and stretched his back. Isabella stood on the dock next to a shirtless young boy who held a bamboo pole. Both Isabella and the boy were barefoot. The boy wore cut-off jeans cinched around his narrow waist with a knotted rope. Isabella wore that same tangerine sundress he had seen days ago. Two red jugs with black spouts sat atop a flat pushcart.

The boy appeared almost as tall as Isabella, but given his wiry frame looked a few years younger. His chest bore the concavity of an early teen. A black mop of hair slicked back behind pronounced ears. Except for his crowning tuft he was slim as his fishing pole.

The two gazed at the sky, but whatever they were looking at was blocked from view by a flush of dripping mangrove trees and two stubby palms just outside the cottage window. The boy tried to nudge Isabella off the dock and into the water. She flicked the boy's ear. He recoiled. Cameron smiled. The boy waved into the air. When Isabella looked up again he mocked pushing her once more, then broke into a broad, gap-toothed smile. Cameron recognized the boy. He was the same kid that had been sitting under the palm on the beach. He had not spoken to the boy then, or since, except when the kid had sold him that five-dollar bottle of muddy rum. Francisco—that was the boy's name. Cameron noticed the boy seemed to always be near the water.

The drone of propellers reached its climax before cutting back. A gray pontoon plane skipped into the bay. It sputtered over to the dock and blocked his view of Isabella and Francisco. In just minutes the engine coughed again. The propellers began to spin and the plane chugged away. One red canister lay on its side on the dock. Another floated in the water. Francisco deftly hooked it with his fishing pole and pulled it up. He put both canisters atop the three plastic crates now stacked upon the pushcart. The plane disappeared behind another clump of mangroves. Cameron watched Isabella, Francisco and the crates wheel down the dock and out of view.

Cameron sat back down at the table and stared at the half-filled page. He couldn't shake the images of Isabella, Francisco, the plane, the pushcart and those crates. The waterfront vignette had piqued his curiosity. A world existed outside his roomful of memories. He needed to clear his mind. Maybe he needed to refill it. Either way he needed a swim. He fished his trunks off the towel peg in the bathroom and slipped them on. They sagged around his waist. If not for the drawstring they would have dropped to his ankles.

He opened the front door. There stood Isabella again, about to knock. She nearly rapped him in the nose. She seemed even more startled by his appearance.

"Thank you, again, for the cululu—" he said.

He reached down and picked up the empty plate he had left by the door.

"Calaloo bammies," she said.

"They were delicious," he said.

He handed her the plate.

She rolled her eyes and shook an envelope at him.

"*Mama yo*, Mister Cam, you got to eat something more. Can't just be bammies and bananas. You look like a needlefish. Paco gonna catch you some red snapper."

Who's Paco?

She thrust the envelope into his hand.

"Came for you while you was watchin' us on the dock," she said.

She shook her head and stomped off.

"Crazy *po-po*," she muttered loud enough for him to hear.

He hadn't noticed her even look toward the cottage from the dock. But that detail was lost to the envelope in his hand. He knew the handwriting. He had seen those tobacco-leaf stamps before. The postmark was faded, but this time he could make it out. The words "SHOPPING C. IGUATEMI DR SP BRASIL" encircled some numbers "13 9 76."

"Thank you," he said.

But Isabella was already gone.

He sat down upon the step to the cottage and worked his fingernail beneath the glued flap. Pressing open the envelope he took a long inhalation. Layered hints of jasmine and peach and sandalwood; she was safe in his arms again on that cot in the mountaintop hut. He longed for any trace of gardenia. He yearned for even a single strand of her hair.

The note's brevity pained him at first, but its salutation reassured him. Her slanted, cursive lettering was fluid, without break or blotch, like a stream confident of its course.

My love,

My first and last thought is to run to you. I cannot describe what rises within me, but I believe it, now more than ever. Time exists only in

relation to you. I will return, soon, I promise. If I wrote all I feel this
would go on forever.

I trust it will.
I love you.
Yours,
A

"Time exists only in relation to you," he whispered.

He walked into the bathroom and picked up his razor. He wanted to feel the sea against his face again.

CHAPTER 24

And on this day
Of memory
Amidst sandstorms a
Caravan fought
With fragile blooms
Enamored moons
Doubt settled
Upon wishes true.

A display case was tucked against the corner of Doctor Silva's office. Its glass-enclosed shelves tiered like a wedding cake, all buttressed by a crown of dark walnut ribs. The cabinet reminded Aluna of the windowed cases at the *pastelaria* her grandmother took her to after Sunday morning Mass. She recalled the incredible feeling of lightness when Avo hoisted her off the floor. Her shiny black oxfords were always loose around her feet as she dangled beneath her grandmother's grip. Fingertips smudged the curved glass while she deliberated between the cinnamon *pasteis de nata* and custard *malasadas*.

But instead of sweet pastries, a collection of antiquated instruments and devices filled Doctor Silva's display. A tortoiseshell-handled lancet with a center-grooved blade rested upon the top shelf. The old doctor explained it was used in the 1800s to administer smallpox vaccinations. Below that was a brass bloodletting scarificator with a dozen protruding spikes. Next to the scarificator was a wooden speculum that looked a bit like a baker's rolling pin, except half the length and tapered to a roundish tip. None of them looked like instruments of healing, particularly not the elongated silver forceps at which she was staring.

"We don't use that set anymore," he said.

"Of course not," she said.

It had always befuddled her why this man, the gentlest of caregivers, displayed such macabre devices. She grew up dwelling upon the dichotomy between those devices and the sweet old doctor. The odd collection reminded her that Doctor Silva was privy to a grisly world. His ability to dispense care in such a world with such exquisite grace made him all the mightier. She had spent the last week pondering the inevitable heaviness of her own world. Those trips to the *pastelaria* with Avo had never seemed more distant.

"So?" he said.

The physical exam was complete; now for the real probing.

"I cannot deny this heartbeat," she said.

Doctor Silva's bushy gray eyebrows arched. The corners of his drooping mouth curled upward.

"*Muito bem*," he said.

He pushed up from his armchair. The worn leather sounded relieved of the old man's weight. He stood still there for a long moment. He had reached the age where upon rising one waits that extra beat to assure blood flow to the legs. But even his slight hesitation exhibited elegance. Circling the desk, he settled into the chair next to her. He put his arm around her. His long fingers pressed into her shoulder.

"Because this life needs you," he said.

"Is it possible?" she asked.

"What?" he asked.

"To meet someone so briefly, yet be so entirely consumed?" she asked.

His hand slipped from her shoulder. He reached into the chest pocket of his linen jacket. He took out a mud-colored wallet only a thumbnail longer than a Brazilian *real*. Tan stitching dimpled the leather seams. A few loose strands unraveled at its dog-eared corners. Three initials branded upon the leather were nearly worn smooth.

He opened the wallet with his usual grace. He slid from the wallet a sepia-toned photograph. He took a long glance at the photograph before he handed it to her. It was an old portrait of a young woman. The edges faded into a cloudy oval that encircled her body. An ivory-laced, Victorian-collared blouse offset the woman's dark skin and hair. A silver butterfly broach gleamed above her heart. Full lips pouted from beneath a slightly crooked nose. But it was the woman's eyes that dominated her face. Fierce, spirited, mysterious, seductive, wholly lacking of doubt. Those eyes reminded Aluna of Cameron. She had seen before pictures of the doctor's deceased wife. The woman in the vintage photograph was someone else.

"Most definitely," he whispered.

He reached for the photograph. Even those few moments without it seemed to bother him.

Aluna stared at him. She wanted to ask a hundred questions. But he had already told her what she most needed to hear.

"Most definitely," she said.

She handed him the photograph.

It felt like her feet might again leave the *pastelaria's* floor.

She stood up. She waited for him to get out of his chair and straighten up. Then she hugged him. Her cheek pressed into his linen lapel. His shoulders felt surprisingly strong. For the first time she could remember, he gave her a bear hug.

"How soon, before—"

"You start to show?" he asked.

"*Sim,*" she said.

Her hand dropped to her stomach.

"Maybe another four, six weeks tops."

She patted her stomach.

"If you need anything, I'm here," he said.

"*Muito obrigado,*" she said and walked out of his office.

She heard a voice whispering in her ear. She knew what she had to do.

Aluna listened to Jackson's muffled voice coming from behind two huge mahogany doors. Wrought-iron handles thrice the size of her fist and elongated black hinges dominated the splintered wood. Dating to the fifteenth century, the ominous Spanish doors guarded her husband's study.

Convinced the doors came from an Inquisition-era castle, Jackson had become so enamored with those doors that he had the entranceway to his study demolished and reconstructed to retrofit them. The project took six months. Ever since, he kept the doors shut. Visitors to his study, including Aluna, had no choice but to abide their massive weight. He always insisted they be closed behind any visitor to his study as well.

Great men make great plans behind great doors.

She had heard him say this on several occasions, no doubt taunting his father's lifelong shadow. Yet the old door bottoms were uneven and split. A mouse's haunch could easily pass beneath their gaps and the tile floor. Thus, every great word of every great plan spoken within the study echoed out along that tile floor beneath the doors. With all that historic weight the doors were little more than an extravagant facade.

"Not yet, but we're very close. It's mine," he said.

She pictured him a conquistador. She had never heard him say "it *will* be mine." Never. His fate was preordained. To him it was always just a matter of collecting what was predestined. But to her, and now more than ever, his hunger for greatness warped reason.

She stood outside and listened. A silk shawl draped any hint of her growing secret, although she doubted it really mattered. She could have pranced about naked. He seemed more enamored with the newly found treasure, particularly the obsidian dagger. The subtle changes in her feminine form were lost on him. The dagger had become his appendage, a constant reminder of what still lay in wait for him at the bottom of the sea. She pictured him dagger in hand behind those massive doors.

"We can't waste any time. It'll be rough, but not impossible."

Aluna recognized that unmistakable tone of his voice. Another great decision had been made.

"We leave next week then," he said.

Life sometime lines up so perfectly, she thought. She heard him hang up the telephone receiver. She scurried up the stairs to her room.

Later that evening at dinner she pushed a pewter spoon through a plateful of striped bass *galinhada*. He raised a glass of red wine and announced from across the table what she already knew.

"I'm going back," he said.

She looked at him with feigned astonishment. She set down a spoonful of the fish paella, raised her glass and took the slightest sip.

"You call that a toast?" he asked.

His cleft chin dropped. His hollow eye sockets were never more apparent.

"It tastes like mud to me," she said.

He gulped down his glass.

"It's the finest Malbec from Mendoza. You're surprised?" he asked.

"Just that it's taken this long," she said.

Jackson wiped the corner of his grin with the back of his hand. His chest puffed out like a robin's. She noticed that just the thought of the trip seemed to add color to his otherwise pale face, or maybe it was the effects of the depleting liquor cabinet behind the great study's doors.

"How soon?" she asked.

"Next week," he said.

"I don't know if I can be ready by then. I've got things to—"

"Not this time. It's going to be even rougher seas. We could be months. That spit of an island will be deserted. You'd either be seasick or bored sick."

Life does line up so perfectly, she thought again. She knew he really just didn't want to be bothered with her, but even if his words were genuine she had already spent the afternoon weighing her options. On the one hand, she fancied the irony of her husband unknowingly delivering her to her island lover. She pictured the gap-toothed fishing boy taking her ashore to surprise Cameron. That embrace alone nearly swayed her. She craved his touch.

But she also knew she'd eventually end up waiting for her husband to find them, or track them down if they fled. It was too dangerous. Her husband would never leave what was *his* behind on that island. While so tempting, returning with her husband now spelled certain catastrophe.

Instead, she decided Jackson's timely departure would give her room to breathe and to plan her vanishing act without a trace. When she returned to Cameron's arms it needed to be forever. Nothing less.

"There is nothing there for you," he said.

She nearly choked on a mouthful of rice.

"I understand," she said with feigned disappointment.

He pushed out his chair. In three steps he stood behind her. He began to rub her shoulders.

She recoiled at his touch.

"I'll shower you with jewels like never before," he promised.

He caressed the back of her neck.

She took a nervous sip of wine.

His fingertips circled around to the front of her neck. He began to trace along an imaginary outline of a necklace.

She stilled a tremor.

His fingers inched toward her breasts.

She grabbed his hand.

"Go find what calls you," she said.

He leaned over her. She held tight to that hand. He kissed her on the side of her cheek. He wanted more. She knew it. With the slightest twist she diverted his hand. She held it against her face and then kissed it.

"The wine is fine," she said, "I'm just feeling bloated."

He retreated and they finished dinner in a polite silence. He mulled over a notepad on what she could only imagine contained the details of his pending trip. Her mind filled with the uncharted vistas of a new life.

That silence grew between them in the last days before his departure. She heard him in the study plotting into the late evenings. One night she pulled open one of the doors and peeked in to find him culling through books on Aztec rituals.

"Greatness never sleeps," he muttered.

She smiled. If nothing else, she still admired his passion. That passion had been so intoxicating when she had been its object. But its shift, perhaps inevitable, had dropped her into a void. She had become secondary. She had begun to feel like nothing more than another old bauble to him. Or maybe that was just her rationalizing what she had done. She truly hoped he would find the bracelet. But she wrestled with whether she genuinely wanted this for him or only in order to ease her exit from the display case of his life.

His words served as an ironic, timely gift. Those simple words highlighted their dwindling relationship. Subtle inequities had long ago surfaced. He rarely opened a door for her anymore. He always entered the room before her. He either dominated social conversations or when not doing so complained them to be trivial. Even when it still had mattered, he rarely retired to bed with her. She would never flourish beside him. She knew it.

His confident passion had once made her too feel alive in so many ways. Now his gaze left her feeling incapable, ornamental, unworthy of his regard. Over time, his small gestures said as much. Around him, she now felt of a lesser kind. And those feelings sprouted the seed of her rationalized transgressions. Her deceit was a mere yearning for light and air and water and wind, for a life, and a craving that needed to be nourished. What she had done on that island wasn't a deceit at all. What she craved didn't exist in her husband's kingdom. Maybe for her it never had. Maybe he had fooled her to believe it ever did. Maybe she had fooled herself. But the secret of eternity wasn't inscribed upon some ancient trinket buried at the bottom of the sea. It was burgeoning inside of her.

And yet hours later, before she went to sleep, she once more checked on him. *Greatness* had collapsed on the sofa in his study. She walked over to him, stared at the black dagger and realized she would never again stroke his thinning hair. Glancing at the open book on his lap she imagined that ceremonial Aztec chants now scored his dreams. She wished him immortality, if only to outlast his father's legacy. She threw a blanket over him. She pulled shut the mahogany door when she left.

§

"Dead?" asked Elia.

"Yes," Cameron said.

"But surely she returned?"

"No. I waited and wrote. Then I wandered all those years hoping that if I didn't find her somehow *Secrets,* like a signal fire, would guide her back to me."

She noticed that his hand clutched the worn, scarlet-jacketed copy of *Secrets.* She felt the hint of a light chain around her neck. She recalled the feeling of its silver links between her fingertips. She reached up and rubbed her neck. Only the memory of that long-lost childhood locket hung there.

His gray-blue eyes sharpened.

"*Secrets of Odysseus* was translated into seven languages. I demanded the Portuguese translation."

"But no more letters?"

"Nothing," he said.

"I don't understand. And all those years—"

"I'm only a man," he said.

The conviction in his eyes sank into melancholia. An awkward hesitation crept into the rhythm of his voice.

"There were others," he confessed, "but this watch was never far."

He rubbed the silver band.

"None of them understood. I suppose I never really gave them the chance. Even when not pressed against my skin that inscription marked me."

She leaned back. For the first time she understood the irony of the book's title. *Secrets of Odysseus* was not about the keeping of secrets. It was the opposite. It was a call to his lover. She pictured copies of the book sitting aloft a bookshelf, or jammed into a discount bin at some used bookstore, or collecting dust on a nightstand, or stuffed into a backpack, each carrying a message, each ready to beckon her back to him. She wondered whether his lover's fingertips had ever touched upon a copy. Had she pondered the title? Had she read the author's name? She imagined the unyielding undertow he described, an undertow that swept aside all other lovers. She started to comprehend the possibility of something more powerful than any poem she had ever read. Tears welled up in her eyes.

"How did she die?" she asked.

He turned his head and stared toward the window. She followed his gaze. The humid breeze lilting through the window dropped into a stultified stillness.

"Killed by the darkness," he said.

CHAPTER 25

How long, dare this memory run
Beyond a rivulet's drop
Returned to the sun.

How deep, dare this memory dive
Below a blue snuffed opaque
Stilled currents, alive.

How high, dare this memory soar
Above a featherless peak
And sight never more.

Zahir, how long, deep and high
Beyond dimension you roamed
'Til now, in her eye.

A luna stood barefoot on the landing just outside the opened front door. Morning sun lit a long flight of pavers that cascaded down to a circular driveway. Clay-potted agapanthus bordered wrought-iron hand railings on either side of the stairway. Puffs of violet petals burst from shoots like exploding pinwheels.

A black sedan's engine idled. Polished steel glistened behind a silver-winged hood ornament. The driver slouched in the shadows behind the steering wheel with his window rolled down. Jackson tossed his leather shoulder bag into the trunk. The driver leaned forward to adjust the side mirror. Aluna recognized the coiled serpent peering out from beneath the short sleeve of the driver's crisp T-shirt. It was Esteban, one of Jackson's divers.

The thud of the slamming trunk startled a crow from beneath an old grumichama tree near the front gate. A twig of purple berries dangled from its beak.

Sweat streaked the back of Jackson's pressed white shirt. He turned and smiled at her. But it was another man she imagined about to embrace her, one who would caress the soft lines of her hand, noting the precise moment they fell from his own. A man who would slip his hand between the buttons on the back of her sundress to clutch her lower back, memorizing the curve of her spine as he pulled her close, a man who would stroke his fingers through her tussled hair, a man who would forever relish one more second of a parting kiss.

Jackson did none of these things.

Aluna had long forgotten whether he ever had. He waved one finger at the driver and trotted up the steps, rolling his sleeves as he brushed past the agapanthus. Stubble framed his square jaw. He hadn't bothered to shave. His restless eyes betrayed an eagerness to depart. He crossed his arms as if to mask his urgency.

"So," he said.

His thin hair frizzled in the humid air.

She felt confident he was blind to the enigma before him. He was somewhere else, she thought, probably already sifting through sand along the bottom of the sea. So when he leaned toward her she had no doubt the ripples of change within her were lost on him.

"I'll be fine," she said.

"Are you sure?" he asked.

She thought she discerned a flicker of genuine concern in his tone. She felt a slight pang of guilt. Maybe she would leave him a note. He hugged her. She relaxed ever so slightly.

"I know it can't be easy without me," he said.

His cheek scratched hers.

In one remark he punctuated with perfection the void between them. *Just go already*, she thought.

Two bleats of the sedan's horn echoed through the courtyard. His eyes darted toward the driveway. His jaw tightened. The sweat from the crease of his elbows felt sticky against her arms.

He kissed her on the mouth. His lips filled with a nonchalant confidence, like he could and would have her again and again, upon his whim. Her tongue recoiled. She fought the urge to deaden her mouth. He clutched her tighter. She embraced only a shadow.

So as not to betray her ambivalence she submitted to his stale breath and that one last brush against her lips. She recalled Cameron waxing poetic on kisses. But her poet had failed to mention this, one of the greatest kisses of all. As awkward as it felt, this last kiss with Jackson tasted of freedom.

Jackson hadn't even reached the bottom of the steps before she wiped that kiss from her lips.

A low cloud of dust coughed up behind the black sedan. It crunched along the cinder driveway and crawled through the front gate. The agapanthus looked to be wilting. She tiptoed down the hot tiles. She stepped barefoot across gray cinders. The jagged stones pinched at her feet. But she collected a tin watering pail cast aside the front fountain and dipped it between clusters of lily pads. A frog plunked through its reflection into the shallow water. She prickled back across the cinders, watered each of the potted flowers and sat down at the top of the steps.

Pouring the remainder of the cool water over her feet, she sat and let them dry in the warmth of the morning sun.

He had contemplated and calculated upon nautical charts. He had consulted atlases and almanacs. And he had ultimately concluded that the reef-to-shelf-to-channel drop-off a mile east of the tiny Caribbean island would buffer even the heaviest of sea swells. He had counted on that gorge to act as a breakwater to protect their diving intervals. All of Jackson's assumptions proved wrong.

The swells that broke around the island reformed to batter across the submerged reef. The depth of the shelf and channel were unable to deflate the sea's fury. Three- to four-meter crests rolled across the dive spot above the wreck. They pitched the fifty-foot yacht back and forth like a toy boat. At times the boat became so precariously tethered to the ocean floor they hoisted anchor and gunned the engines to maintain their position. The nondescript speck on those nautical maps proved to be a whirling frenzy of wind and water.

In the scant quells, diving opportunities lasted at most half a day. For weeks the yacht bobbed like a cork upon unsettled seas. But even in those rare calms, unexpected challenges arose beneath the surface too. The peculiar results from their dives taunted him worse than the unforgiving weather.

Jackson gripped a bottle of Chilean Pisco and hovered over the gridded map. Its curled ends were tacked to the wooden tabletop with rusted pushpins. He had plotted each recovered artifact with a red "x" in order to plan subsequent dives. He marked the location of every goblet and Spanish doubloon and, of course, the obsidian dagger tucked into his belt. The bracelet was down there. He was sure of it. But as the ship rocked on its axis, and with only the bottle of golden brandy to steady him, something in the hodgepodge of red crosses still puzzled him, some encrypted message remained that he alone could decipher.

"Something doesn't fit," he grumbled.

Esteban stared at him.

For weeks now, Jackson had studied the odd pattern, knowing that even after centuries most salvaged relics were found in clusters. Remnants of entire staterooms had been retrieved within an arm's length, even when their wood-beamed walls had long deteriorated. He recalled the story of two wine bottles recovered from an eighteenth-century Spanish wreck off the Florida Keys. One old Rioja, now displayed in the Barcelona Maritime Museum, lay intact thirty meters beneath the sea for over one hundred and fifty years before recovery. The other bottle was tucked right next to it, less than half a meter away, cracked clean at the neck, its cork still plugged into the mouth. Not just time but movement as well often seemed stilled at the bottom of the sea.

The three goblets had been clustered, yet they had recovered a single medallion with nothing else around, and then the Aztec dagger more than ten meters away. The red crosses mocked him. It was as if someone, or something, had already foraged the wreck. He swigged a gulp of Pisco. Tangy pear and hazelnut scratched down his throat. He wiped a trickle across his bearded chin. In the morning they would be able to dive again.

"Fuck it. Tomorrow we go into the channel," he said.

The channel of which he spoke dropped to unknown depths. But Jackson had a hunch. He glared at Esteban.

Esteban shook his head and grimaced. They both had enough dive time under their respective weight belts to know relics seldom settled along channel walls.

"I don't think—" Esteban said.

"I pay you to dive, now get out," Jackson said.

Esteban shrugged and left the cabin.

Jackson drained the bottle, tossed it into the sink and collapsed onto the daybed. The empty bottle rolled back and forth in the metal sink. He snored through the pitch of the sea until just before sunrise.

The next morning visibility was terrible. The water just wouldn't settle. The first fifteen meters of depth was like diving through London fog. But below that level the sea began to quiet. Clarity improved. Jackson's throat felt a little raw. His head was a bit dull, but the steady hum of his breath into the mouthpiece of his regulator centered him. His headlamp shone along a triangular patch of sand. His light cast in and out of the light from Esteban's lamp. He checked the direction on his dive compass when he reached the flag where he had found the dagger. Not even a dull ping emitted from the underwater headphones connected to the metal detector. He reached across his chest. The net pouch was still tied to his vest. It was attached, but empty.

Six body-lengths past that last marker they headed toward the channel, following nothing more than Jackson's hunch into the unknown. A school of elongated pink and blue needlefish shimmered by. It looked like a wall of fluorescent spaghetti. The final stragglers passed and the view cleared. He undulated forward. A faint ping froze his progress. A tingle rippled down his spine. He held out his arm to signal Esteban. They both slowed. Jackson circled the long wand of the metal detector to the left. Nothing. He swept it across the sand to the right. But again the detector fell silent.

It was like searching for a pinhead in a gigantic sandbox. But another half-flutter of his fin forward brought another ping. Jackson inched along the bottom.

And then a flurry of pings filled his headphones. He put down the detector and pushed aside the sand with his hand. He peered through a cloud of settling silt. A metallic loop about the size of his fist was revealed. He gave the loop a gentle tug. The sea floor yielded its hold. The base of a rusted padlock no bigger than his open hand appeared. The cloud of sand fell away. Even with its crustaceous coating Jackson knew the lock to be from the same period as the Spanish wreck. A smile pressed against the rubber mask suctioned to his face. Locks protect precious things.

Destiny felt ever so close.

He removed a weighted yellow marker from his vest and settled it into the sand. He studied the lock under his light. It was about an inch thick. The rusted latch was stuck permanently ajar. It looked to take a skeleton key. He held the lock in one hand while he waved the metal detector in the other in a long circle around the spot. Not another ping. He scanned the seabed. Just past Esteban the ocean floor turned rocky. He swam across that jagged bottom. He swept the metal detector over the rocky outcropping. The bottom dropped away into a dark ravine.

He kicked over that underwater ledge. He held the metal detector in one hand and the lock in the other. But a torrential current wrenched him sideways. He tumbled in an awkward somersault. The metal detector scraped along the rocks. His mouthpiece yanked from his lips. An explosion of bubbles swirled about. The metal detector's headphones yanked from his ears. He grabbed at a crease in the rocky face to steady himself. He swept his arm over his back and down along his side. Where was his fucking regulator? His lungs emptied. The water got colder. He couldn't find his primary regulator.

He unclasped his secondary regulator from his vest and chomped down on the mouthpiece. He fought panic and sucked in a slow breath of air.

Something clutched at his calf. He looked down. Esteban was clawing up the ravine. Their startled eyes met. Esteban released his grasp. Esteban's regulator was still intact. His partner seemed to be breathing okay.

Jackson double-checked his oxygen. He fished his right arm behind his back. His fingertips found the base of the rubber tube to his primary regulator. He traced the tube until he could swing his primary regulator in front of his face. He released a spurt of bubbles. The line cleared before he switched the primary back into his mouth. The metal detector had slipped from his hand but was still tethered to his belt. It twisted in the underwater torrent and banged against the rock.

He forced himself to steady his breath. Gulping air at this depth was deadly. He fought the current that dragged against him. His entire body lurched to the side. He saw Esteban's startled face. Neither dared let go of the rock. They kicked up alongside one another and scaled over the ravine's lip to escape the underwater rapids. In just over a body-length they passed back over the ledge and out of the underwater torrent that had nearly swept them away. The sea floor returned to a near dead calm.

Jackson reeled in the metal detector. The lock, however, was gone. He shined the headlamp into the canyon. The cone of light faded into blue nothingness. He swung the metal detector all about. But all he heard was silence. He again checked his air supply. The dial on his air gauge would soon dip into the red. He pointed to Esteban and then up toward the surface. But before turning back he flashed his headlamp one last time into the canyon. A magnificent green shell rocketed past him. A sea turtle, its carapace larger than his torso, effortlessly rode the surge of the underwater jet stream.

He swam back toward the yacht. The net pouch clipped to his vest was still empty. He passed directly over the yellow flag that now marked only a memory.

Aluna was reading Gabriela Mistral's *Los Sonetos de la Muerta* and longing for her island poet when a knock rapped at her bedroom doorframe. She put down the booklet of poems.

"Come in," she called.

The long face of Doctor Silva peered around the door.

"How are you today?" he asked.

He walked to her bedside. The wooden floorboards beneath the Turkish rug creaked.

"About the same," she sighed with a bit of a pout.

"Let me see about that," he said.

He reached into his black leather satchel. She saw him glance at the booklet of poems. He untangled a stethoscope and propped the pronged ends into his ears. A silver circle of coolness pressed against her belly.

She watched the bristle of his alabaster eyebrows. They looked as wild as those of a wirehaired pointer. But his eyebrows didn't move. She hoped it was a good sign. She had grown up guessing her prognosis from this old man's frosted eyebrows, from chicken pox to tonsillitis to pneumonia. So far her fourth month of pregnancy had been worse than the first three, which prompted no relief from the doctor's orders of mandatory bed rest. She was relieved to see his eyebrows hold firm. She prayed for a reprieve from house arrest.

"Cherry today?" she asked.

His breath had long gone stale, like that of a person whose insides were winding down. But before a doctor he was first a gentleman. She had never suffered anything but a candy-flavored breath from him.

He grinned.

"You're hard to fool."

"So what today then, am I ready?" she pressed.

Over the past months she had unfurled to him the fantastic tale of an island, from every oar stroke of a gap-toothed fishing boy to a market filled with pomegranates, an old woman and a poet, including treks to a mountaintop loft and each clandestine meeting thereafter. Visit after visit, the old doctor had listened so intently she even shared naked swims, underwater caves and sea turtles. But mostly she told him of a man like no other and an unyielding desire to keep a promise to return to him. In due course the old doctor had in turn shared a bit of his tale of a woman like no other, whose picture to this day he tucked into his chest pocket, pressed against his heart.

He understood.

The doctor pondered her question. His face drew serious. He reached into his jacket pocket. But instead of the picture he took out a linen handkerchief. He dabbed the sweat forming along his brow.

"Today I have a different story for you. One I've never told you."

He took a long breath.

"Your mother's pregnancy was hard. Your birth was very complicated, for the both of you. It was by far my most difficult delivery, yet to this day one of my favorite results."

Her eyes moistened at the mention of her deceased mother. He squeezed her hand. His touch quelled her.

"This island of which you've told me sounds magical," he said.

His eyes lit up. But then he got quiet again and his voice grew stern.

"Since I'm old, though, let me tell you something. Your story is anything you want it to be. But this tiny heartbeat pulsing within you has a story too, just waiting to begin. This tiny heartbeat is my patient too. I want you both to live a long time on that island if that's where you choose to go, but you just can't go now. If things got complicated—" he said.

His voice trailed off.

She had the peculiar feeling he was speaking about the woman in the picture.

He stared at her.

"You want this baby. This baby wants a mother. Let's make sure everybody gets what they want."

Doctor Silva stood up. He leaned over and kissed her forehead.

"The island will be there in a few more months," he whispered.

She smelled the sweet scent of his cherry lozenge.

He raised his eyebrows and said, "And any man worth his salt will be there too."

He creaked back out the door and down the staircase.

She lay there in bed deflated. She mulled over what he had said. Maybe the old doctor was right about the island and the man. Maybe they would both be there for a long, long time. But it felt like her future was being dangled right in front of her, yet still just out of reach. She started to hyperventilate.

Her fingers brushed over the booklet next to her. She picked up another, thicker volume. She trembled through its pages. She found the maroon ribbon and perched the book atop her growing belly. She glanced down at the poem, "Cuerpo de mujer."

The cadence of the rhyme calmed her like the ripples of a deep massage. The words soothed her breath. She repeated the four stanzas of Pablo Neruda's poem. She wrought every passionate syllable of its one hundred and forty-four words, until the poem came alive as if each word had pulsed from within her. She continued this way all afternoon, as she had the day before, and the day before that, reading every poem in the volume until she reached to her nightstand to place it on the growing pile next to her bed.

She twisted toward the teetering stack of books on the nightstand. And for the first time she experienced the most peculiar sensation. The feeling took her breath away. It felt like the wings of a butterfly fluttering against the insides of her stomach.

CHAPTER 26

Gazing at midnight's dust perpetual
Seeking constellations conceptual
Beyond hilltops where hearts stop
Beneath dropped lids these dreams crop
Of eyes long distant yet a soul so near
Scattered stars wished upon a fractured mirror
Gazing at midnight's dust perpetual
Seeking constellations conceptual.

"Killed by the darkness."

Cameron's revelation sent pins prickling across Elia's skin. His defeated tone triggered both curiosity and dread. Her mouth felt dry. She forced a swallow and eyed the glass of water on the nightstand but dared not budge, because Cameron had yet to move. He still stared out the window toward the mangrove trees. His blue T-shirt was crimped against the gauze bandage around his broken ribs. The white bedsheet draped over his legs. She felt obliged to honor the stillness in the room. Straddling the three-legged stool, she exhaled as quietly as possible and waited. A wisp of incense rose like a gossamer prayer. What darkness?

He grimaced. Then he turned his head toward her.

"There's one last thing you need to know."

"Tell me everything," she said.

He cradled the watch around his wrist.

"There's a place, part of this island and the sea, yet beyond it all."

His voice regained strength. His eyes, again keen as the Caribbean sky, locked on her. The sun-bleached hair on his forearms stood on end. His cheeks flushed. Two fire-feathered birds with blue bonnets landed upon the windowsill, one right after the other. Their shrill staccato whistles bristled down her spine.

She moved from the stool and knelt beside him.

"Where?" she asked.

He lifted his head from the pillow. He propped himself on his elbows. Planting his hands onto the mattress, he dragged himself back until he rested against the wall. His strength seemed to match his resurrecting countenance.

For the first time since setting foot on the island Elia looked up at him. Even at half-mast, she witnessed a command she had not before seen.

Cameron patted the bed.

"Sit with me," he said.

She got up off the stool and sat upon the edge of the bed. Less than an arm's length separated them.

"Beyond the hilltop hut is a cliff."

"I know it," she said.

She had hiked down that cliff to fetch water for the pomegranate seeds.

"Not like I do," he said.

Chuey leapt onto the windowsill. The two songbirds flew away. The monkey's shining eyes, big as oyster shells, cased the room. Cameron grabbed the last banana on the nightstand and tossed it toward the furry interloper. Chuey snagged the missile midflight. He bobbed up and down like a little prizefighter. Then Chuey hunkered down on the windowsill with his lunch.

"I guess we can trust him," Cameron said.

Elia grinned. Even the mundane now seemed magical.

His voice dropped to a hush.

"Follow the path toward the cliff. There is a steep trail with lots of tight switchbacks. Climb down to the water. At the bottom is a flat landing stone, maybe ten feet wide, that drops off below the surface like a little boat launch. Take about three steps onto that stone. Depending on the tides it may be waist deep. Look to your right and you'll see a U-shaped branch sticking out from the rocks."

Elia nodded. She realized he was describing the same stone upon which she had launched herself, empty wine bottle in hand, into the sea. But another feeling began to rise in her. Cameron's revived tone began to sound almost hypnotic. His voice had the same soothing effect upon her as the whale's song.

"Climb over to that branch," he said.

She felt light enough to fly. His hands reached up. For a second she thought he might embrace her. But he just mimicked clutching the branch.

"Grab hold and pull yourself up and around to the tree trunk. Tied around the base of that trunk is an old canvas bag. Inside the bag are flippers and a mask. Take them back to the landing rock."

He scratched his head.

"Let's see your foot," he said.

Elia paused. Did she hear him right?

"Come on now," he said.

He patted his palm against the bed.

She slipped off her turquoise sandal and pulled one knee to her chest. The top of her foot was tanned caramel, the bottom toughened from wearing nothing but sandals and going barefoot. The worn sheet felt cool against her rough sole. She stared at the bright red polish and teeny yellow flecks she had painted on each toenail. Days ago a grinning young island girl had playfully tied a rainbow bracelet around Elia's ankle. Charmed by the girl's smiling innocence, Elia had worn it ever since. The two of them were now bonded by a giggling wink every time they passed one another along the promenade.

With her brightly adorned foot displayed beneath the eye of the poet she felt like a silly schoolgirl.

"Do you have socks with you?"

"Back in my room," she said.

She wished she had them on now.

"Take your thickest pair to help snug the flippers. They'll be loose, but should stay on."

He looked again at her foot.

"Hibiscus?" he asked.

"Yes," she said. She felt herself blush.

His eyes fixed on her.

"Magnificent," he whispered.

Elia stared at him, unable to lower her gaze. The warmth of that one comment filled her. By his tone she knew it was not her toes or feet, nor the colors of the exotic island flower, that he had complimented. It was she with her sun-streaked chestnut hair, coconut tan and even the playfulness of the anklet. Elia felt a wave of confidence. His words meant more than she could have anticipated. His comment surpassed the approval of her professors and bordered upon a smile from the boy from Professor Weitzel's class. Wait, where did the boy from class come into all of this? But she wished he could see her now. For the first time she could remember Elia *felt* magnificent, lovelier than any poem.

"Swim out to the right of the landing rock, I'm guessing about a dozen strokes for you. Go at about eleven o'clock. That's when the light's best."

"For what?" she asked.

He didn't reply. He had fallen back under his spell, absorbed into the map he was laying out before her.

"You'll be in about ten feet of water. There's an underwater ledge where the bottom drops from sight. Dive down a couple of times. Let your lungs get used to the depth. Just beneath that ledge you'll find a tunnel. How long can you hold your breath?"

"Long enough," she said.

But she really had no idea. Cliffs and rocks and fins and masks and underwater tunnels, her thoughts were starting to spin.

If only to catch her breath, she asked, "And you?"

"Longer than I thought. Remember, dive around eleven o'clock. You will see a speck of light at the end of the tunnel. Surface and catch your breath. Then gulp the deepest breath you can and hold it. Let your legs and the fins do most of the work. Stay calm but don't hesitate. Follow the light."

Elia had no doubt she'd do it. She had to. He lifted his arms like he was spanning the width of the tunnel.

"Watch out for sea urchins on the rock. When the sand rubs against your belly claw into it," he whispered.

"Dig into the sand?" she asked.

She imagined herself underwater and short of breath.

"It's a secret cave," he said, "and sacred."

"A secret, sacred cave," she said.

His trance broke. He looked at her. "You'll know once inside."

"What?" she asked.

"You'll know," he said.

Then he whispered again, "Longer than I thought."

Chuey let out a skittering whoop and tossed the empty banana peel out the window. Isabella eclipsed the doorway and jangled into the room. She carried a plate of calaloo bammies and chimed, "What you two talkin' 'bout?"

Cameron grinned.

"Just a little island magic," he said.

She slapped the plate down on the nightstand and frowned at Elia. Elia shrugged her shoulders. She couldn't help but smile.

"Yep, just a little island magic," Elia said.

Isabella planted one hand on her hip. She stroked the raven strands of her charm with the other. She stared at the silver watch around Cameron's wrist and then looked back at Elia. She shook her head.

"Well, I ain't no *toutoulbay*. Seems lots of juju floating 'round right here in this room," Isabella said and chuckled.

She has no idea, Elia thought. Just a little *island magic* had already set off an eddy swirling inside her. Yet something in the way Isabella stroked her charm calmed her. Elia realized her fingertips mimicked those of the big woman, only it was a lock of her own sun-streaked hair curled between her fingers.

You'll know.

Cameron's words from that morning ricocheted inside her, bewitching Elia as she tossed and turned that night. Tomorrow was filled with promises of underwater passages, sacred caves and *you'll know*. Plus, for the first time she could remember, a man had stared into her eyes and she had dared to hold that gaze. And not just any man, but a poet, and he had declared her magnificent.

Kicking off the twisted sheet, she walked barefoot to her window and gazed at the sky. A velvet blanket of sparkling sequins flickered at her. She traced along Ursa Major, the Great Bear constellation thought to date back to an oral tradition thirteen thousand years old, well before even the first written word. She thought she could even make out Cetus, named after the sea monster of Greek mythology and tying back to the

Hebrew word for "great fish." She blinked to be sure. But Elia believed she saw Cetus, the whale constellation.

"Thank you," she whispered, uncertain which celestial body had guided her to this island.

She crawled back into bed, a magnificent, grateful speck within the universe, and listened to the waves hiss against the shore until sleep kissed her good night.

CHAPTER 27

Pearl-tipped waves crest
but even
blue thunder
pools silent
to yearn,
Ebb flow abreast
the wonder
a promise
the tide will
return.

Plunked on the wet sand like a conch shell after high tide, the gap-toothed boy sat cross-legged in a warm drizzle. His bare shoulders glistened beneath a slick of black hair. With the frayed end of his rope belt he brushed away a few granules grating down his shorts, but he was otherwise impervious to the sand caked to his legs and feet. A bamboo pole dangled over the bay's dimpled surface. The fishing line swished back and forth in the restless waters near the jagged outcropping. He had it weighted at the end with a rubbery clam impaled over a rusted hook. Taut then slack, then taut and slack again, the wisp flailed in a dull rhythm that only he, the lone fisherman, witnessed.

Dead slack.

He straightened, slipped the line between his finger and thumb, and waited for the slightest tug, curious whether an underwater bandit had struck. Nothing. He planted the rod in the sand. He stood up and hand-over-hand hauled in the line. The filament grazed over his palms, already callused from an apprenticeship with the sea. With his last yank the bait popped into the air. His copper face fell into a frown. He pondered the latest riddle from his mentor, the sea. Apparently Spanish mackerel avoided the shallows in this chop.

"*Ven a mi, bonitos,*" he whispered.

He flung his line toward open water.

Beyond the arc of his cast, swaths of steel brushstrokes plummeted from slate clouds. The storm swept toward him. Drizzle began to feel like pellets against his skin. But just as it looked as if the sky and sea would melt into one another, a distant beam of sunlight pierced the dull canopy. He squinted. His keen eye detected a silver spark against the faint horizon.

That flash reminded him of the gilded trim from the ivory yacht that had anchored in the bay months ago. For a simple young boy of the sea such majesty was hard to forget. He had never before, nor since, witnessed such floating grandeur. Now his every gaze across the water was tempered by the thought of whether the boat might reappear, because even more spectacular than that vessel was the smile of the woman who had climbed down its ladder. He had rowed the auburn-haired stranger ashore in his wooden boat.

He slipped a hand into his pocket. He felt one of the two green bills she had pressed into his palm. The other had sustained him for months.

The rolling swell sounded a familiar thumping. No more than a stone's throw to his left his tethered skiff knocked against the dock. He studied the ropes. Both were wrapped tight. He was confident his knots would hold against anything.

Beyond the dock a light, not unlike the specter of that solitary ray of sun, shone from a cottage window. The man from the hilltop hut seemed to be hiding inside that cottage. Young Paco wondered why. His gut told him it had something to do with the woman from that ivory boat. He had followed the woman up the hill. He had seen the woman kiss that man, and return day after day to do the same before she disappeared.

He turned back toward the sea. He squinted hard for that ripple of light on the horizon. But he couldn't find it again. The lone sunbeam had withdrawn back into the heavens, swallowed by the dark clouds. The storm would rule the remainder of the day.

Standing in a full rain, Paco contemplated the sea that had fed him yesterday. It looked like it might kill him today if given the chance. The same water that had dripped from his oars as he rowed the woman to her island lover had also sustained the yacht that carried her away. The great water seemed to connect his entire universe, that man and woman, his rowboat, the yacht, the bamboo fishing pole he had nearly forgotten was still in his hand, the phantom Spanish mackerel, and his young, soaked self.

The tide splashed across his feet. He pulled in his line. He slid the morsel of clam off the hook and tossed the bait into the water.

Rain splattered against fogged glass. Jackson rubbed the window with the back of his fist and stared outside. The bronze-ringed portal framed a nightmarish seascape. Torrents swept across roiling waves. The scene resembled a sandstorm pulverizing desert dunes. Visibility was dropping by the hour. So was his mood. Diving wasn't an option. The stench of his stale, Pisco-laced breath against the portal glass only irritated him all the more.

A burst of sunlight sliced through the deluge. It swept across the waves like a searchlight and engulfed the boat. For a second he dared imagine that Huitzilopochtli, the ancient Aztec sun god, had illuminated the sea just for him. He peered through the glass in search of a crack in the looming clouds. But nearly as quick as the sunbeam appeared it was gone.

"Esteban!" he yelled.

The boat pitched. The cabin door flung open. Esteban's sculpted frame filled the doorway. A ribbed white tank top clung to his sweaty chest. The eyes of his serpent tattoo seethed from his bicep.

Jackson lurched toward the wooden table. He hovered over the dive map. Esteban, a lean four inches taller, joined him. Both men held onto the table to steady themselves against the rolling waves. Jackson pressed the obsidian dagger atop the map. He scratched the bulbous-eyed figure crouching along its handle.

"Get me another bottle," he said.

Esteban raised his dark eyebrows.

Jackson scowled.

"Now," he said.

"Aye, aye, *El Capitáo*," Esteban said.

But any deference had drained from his voice.

Esteban bent down over the teak liquor cabinet. He pulled open the door. Two squat bottles of Pisco Mistral rolled out, both empty.

"*Nada*," Esteban sighed.

"In the pantry," Jackson said as if Esteban should have known better.

"*Dois!*" Jackson shouted.

Esteban mock saluted and ducked out the cabin. He pulled the door shut behind him. Jackson heard Esteban speaking in a hushed voice to someone outside the cabin. But he couldn't make out what they were talking about. The only word he caught was "*maluco*." Jackson knew that word all too well. Before they were married, Aluna had been the first to translate "*maluco*" for him. To him, in any language *crazy* felt like a compliment.

"Just bring me my fucking Pisco," he muttered.

His thumb pressed the blade into the crimson "x" on the map. That spot marked where he had discovered the Spanish lock. He felt close. He dragged the blade across the map toward the channel where the lock had been swept from his hand by the underwater current. The Aztec bracelet was no doubt lighter than the Spanish lock, even more capable of being swept away. He traced along the channel. He circled the hair-thin markings charting the depth at the channel's floor: one hundred meters. He scratched his patchy beard.

"Fuck!" he yelled as he thrust the dagger down into the map, stabbing it to the table.

He glanced up. Esteban had already opened the cabin door. Esteban walked to the table. He set down a bottle of amber liquor next to the dagger.

"I said *dois*," Jackson grumbled.

Esteban looked him in the eye. He just shook his head and walked out. Jackson cracked the seal on the bottle and took a swig. He cursed after Esteban and yanked the dagger out of the table. The tip of the five-hundred-year-old blade had fractured, leaving a serrated edge. It just pissed him off even more.

The next weeks on the *Atlaua* were long and dull. Long days slipped into meaningless nights with little to plot on the slashed map. On the rare days that the rains quelled enough to dive their yields became mundane. Some days no more than a single Spanish coin was scraped from the sea bottom. Other days not even that was recovered. No bracelet. Not even a hint. Time crawled without significance beyond its passage. Communication between Jackson and Esteban and the others dropped. As the quest for the ancient bracelet slipped away further, so did the boat's captain.

Jackson isolated himself in his cabin. He embarked upon solo dives into the murky depths of the bottle. There he explored a sea of numbed dreams filled with endless treasures parading just out of reach. Eventually, his days mirrored his sodden nights. He could no longer distinguish whether it was his dreams or reality that eluded him. Any hope of recovering the bracelet diminished. So did his delusions of immortality. Those delusions were eventually replaced by immortality's harsh antithesis. He was adrift in uncharted territory, laden by his own mortality and yearning comfort. He missed Aluna.

He staggered along the deck reeking of brandy, his speech reduced to mumbles, spiked by Portuguese slurs at his crew. Esteban barely acknowledged his presence anymore. Plus, not only Esteban but the others as well had become more vociferous during their infrequent crew meetings. In their last gathering Jackson went so far as to accuse Esteban of sabotaging the scuba tanks. Esteban waved him off, not even bothering to respond.

One groggy morning Jackson slouched atop the captain's bridge. He squinted over the water. The sunrise was visible for the first time in weeks. But the rare light just taunted him, blinding him like an interrogator's lamp. Finally even he realized that the shipwreck had been picked bare. So had his liquor cabinet, along with the crew's waning patience. Clutching tight a half-full bottle of Pisco in one hand, the dagger loose in the other, he watched as Esteban uncapped a bottle of Chilean brandy on the deck below.

Esteban lifted it up to toast him, took a swig, and then passed the bottle amongst the crew. Each crewmate followed suit until the last handed the bottle back to Esteban. Esteban craned his head up toward the bridge. He made sure *el capitão* was watching and then stretched his tattooed arm over the water. He poured the rest of the bottle into the sea. The streaming liquor drained like liquid gold. The others stood alongside Esteban and collectively stared up toward the bridge, each with his arms folded.

A scaly head craned up from the water. Its jade hump of a shell rolled up and then out of sight. Jackson rubbed his eyes. But as fast as the sea turtle had surfaced it was gone, if he had really even seen it at all.

Esteban's stare locked on Jackson. Within Esteban's deliberate nod was an unequivocal ultimatum.

Jackson could not deny that Esteban and the others were right. It was time to go home. But this was still *his* boat. *El capitáo* swiveled around and flipped a switch. The motor rumbled awake. He looked back. Esteban saluted him. Churning vibrations trembled the boat's skeleton. The crew scattered to prepare for departure. A rusty chain groaned. The boat swiveled. The anchor hoisted from the sea bottom. The chain recoiled like a python until the anchor clanged on board. Two of the crew lugged it into a dank corner of the stern.

In minutes they were underway. The ship cut a foamy swath across the sea, which now seemed bluer than ever. Soon even their trail was erased by waves washing toward the horizon. Any hint of the tiny island drifted from sight. It became nothing more than a mirage subjected to memory. Jackson had never even set foot upon that piece of land.

He swigged a gulp of Pisco. He heard a gravelly voice whisper over his shoulder, "*Like the mist in the sun.*" It sounded like his late grandfather's voice. He twisted around. There was nobody there. All that was behind him were whitecaps cresting across an endless sea.

§

During the three new moons of her husband's absence, the frequency of Doctor Silva's bedside visits grew in proportion to Aluna's expanding belly. She faithfully submitted to the doctor's lozenge-scented advice. It was difficult for her to stay put. But she spent her days mostly bedridden, tucked within volumes of verse that helped soften the confines of her bedroom.

"What do you have today?" she asked.

"Let me see," he said.

With a serious face he pushed up the reading glasses teetering over his drooping nose. He fished into his old leather medical bag and handed her a well-worn paperback.

"*The Essential Rumi*," he said.

"Essential?" she asked.

"That's what it says," he said.

He brought out his stethoscope.

"Then I must have it."

This is how it had gone between the two of them for months. The old doctor shuttled books to her from his office, then from his home and ultimately from São Paulo's *Biblioteca Central*. Tucked within his old leather satchel, his stethoscope brushed against the likes of Luís de Camões, António Dias Cardoso, Gabriela Mistral, Pablo Neruda, Cervantes, Kahlil Gibran, and eventually Wilde and Shakespeare. Last week it was Dickinson. Today Rumi. Only after presenting his latest offering did he press the stethoscope against her flesh.

His visits lengthened. Their bond strengthened. Aluna welcomed her elderly confidant's companionship. His explanations of the kneading sensations against her bladder were reassuring. His grandfatherly smile calmed her. His long fingers held her stomach while the baby kicked.

One day, cemented within that trust, he pointed at the stack of books on her nightstand. He raised his wiry eyebrows.

"How is it that you can read all this?"

She brushed a strand of auburn hair behind her ear and she scrunched up her brow.

"What do you mean?"

"Well, isn't it torture?" he asked.

She gazed at the stack of books on the nightstand as she pondered his question. Within that leaning tower, which had already displaced a previous pillar, were thousands of words. Each page had been flipped by so many the edges felt soft as butter against her fingertips.

Her eyes met his.

"Not in the least," she said.

Not a hint of doubt.

She thought for a moment.

"I've yet to read anything that surpasses what lies within my heart."

She motioned toward the stack of great works.

"This wellspring flowed long before me. It will continue long after I'm gone. My small and great miracle is that it moves in me now," she said.

She placed a hand on her stomach.

"Oooh," she moaned.

She felt the baby shift.

"Okay, maybe I don't feel so sacred all the time. It must be a boy," she said.

Doctor Silva grinned. He leaned over and kissed her other hand.

"I'll return in three days," he said.

"Take this," she said. She slid a silver key off the nightstand and pressed it into his weathered palm. "I've given the maid the weekend off."

He stared at the key.

"To the castle?" he asked.

She smiled up at him.

"You've been a prince."

The antiquated prince straightened up tall as his old bones would allow. He tapped his leather heels together. He placed the key against his heart.

"And you, my queen," he said.

He looked at his watch.

"*Tenho que ir agora*," he said to her.

Then he promised with a wink, "*Ate logo.*"

CHAPTER 28

Between
specter and shadow
lies softness of light
where shades of a day
kissed beacons good night.
Between
memory and myth
one tear shed the muse
an emerald at dusk
light dared not refuse.

Elia's sandals kicked up the sand and broken shells embedded between the worn cobble along the esplanade. Two barefoot boys slapped past her. They ran so fast she wondered whether the soles of their bare feet might be leather. The boys wore only billowy swim trunks, one pair lime green and the other taffy orange. Like two bronze stick figures they careened across the beach toward the sea. Their feet skimmed across the surface until the water swallowed them, whoops and all.

She watched for a few long seconds. Then two wet mops of black hair popped up from the water like corks. Their giggles rippled across the bay. Elia felt a shiver of anticipation. She wondered how long she could hold her own breath. She would soon find out.

Only a few short paddles from the boys a fisherman pulled a wooden lobster trap from the bay. His rowboat teetered back and forth. The boys swam toward him. Their arms splashed like little waterwheels. Paco thrust a spiny lobster into the air like a trophy. Its claws snapped at the air. The morning sun glinted off his gold tooth as he waved the lobster at her. A mud-feathered pelican loitered at the end of the dock. It craned its orange bill. It looked to be contemplating whether it was possible to gulp the lobster, or maybe even one of the boys, down its gullet.

Elia smiled. She removed her white baseball cap and waved back at Paco. She wondered if he had any idea where she was going. She wondered if anybody knew, other than the recuperating poet in the back of Paco's *cantina*. She flipped on the cap and pulled her loose ponytail through the back. The feeling of her hair between her fingers reminded her of Isabella stroking that charm of hers. Now a bit anxious, Elia wished she had her own little charm. She could use a little juju this morning.

She peeked into her sackcloth bag. Thick gray socks were balled up next to a bottle of water. She wondered whether the socks would be enough to snug the diving fins to her feet. What if the fins weren't even there? Her stomach began to feel a bit queasy.

A bright-eyed mongrel trotted up alongside her. *Pot hounds*, that's what Isabella called the island strays. She had seen this pot hound before. It seemed to be invisibly tethered to Fatty's disheveled clinic, no doubt a regular benefactor of a treat or two from the good island doctor. Fatty called the mutt his *El Salvadoran street dog*. He had cackled like a chicken when he told her this a few days ago. She could hear Fatty snoring inside.

She knelt down on one knee and rubbed its little head.

"Are you from El Salvador?"

The brown, black, white and tan freckled fur-ball smelled like corn chips. The pup's tail whipped back and forth like a metronome gone wild. It licked clean her hibiscus-painted toenails. Elia's stomach calmed.

She smelled a waft of calaloo bammies. The scent seemed to lilt from an open window. She stood up. The pup scampered toward the window and then got distracted by a young boy raking a straw broom along a square patch of reddish dirt. He shook the broom at the pup and it loped off into an alley.

The young boy caught Elia's gaze. He puffed out his chest.

"*Warri?*" the boy asked.

She saw the fishnet sack of nickernuts and the pitted game board sitting atop a cane chair. But the elderly pomegranate woman, crowned by a flowered bandanna beneath her sun hat, shushed the boy. He deflated back into his morning chore. The empty square apparently couldn't make its daily transformation into the morning market until the boy was done sweeping.

Elia pointed at the boy and winked.

"Champion," she said.

His shoulders squared. He swept faster.

The pomegranate woman nodded at Elia. The woman reminded Elia of a gypsy fortune-teller. The old gypsy gummed a smile. Elia wondered whether the old woman knew of her mission. But by the glint in the old woman's eyes Elia figured somehow she must. Elia grinned. Everything and everyone on the island seemed more than just familiar, something much more, something that Elia had only imagined for a long, long time.

Elia's thoughts hastened as she scaled the hillside path. Maybe she *should* have told somebody. Cameron knew where she was going. But had he told anyone? What if something happened? The air was like a hot blanket. The headband of her baseball cap was sweaty. The sea would cool her down. She unscrewed the cap of her water bottle and rationed a sip.

No, she shouldn't tell anyone. It was a secret, *the poet's secret*. But just the same she was dying to tell somebody. After all, wasn't that why she had come to this island? Only weeks ago, she had declared in front of Professor Weitzel and her classmates, "I'm going to find him." Now here she was. But the one person she really wanted to share the secret with was the boy from class. Yet all semester she had taken such great pains to avoid his stare. Why had she avoided those eyes? She was *magnificent*. The poet had said so. She was thinking way too much.

A jeweled hummingbird flitted past her face. The bird hovered next to a blossoming star jasmine. It tucked its needled beak into a white flower. Elia stopped and caught her breath. The scent was intoxicating, but the hummingbird's slick back was even more spectacular, feathered in an effervescent teal sheen. And the sunlight seemed different, so radiant it created bursts of halos. The bird's coloring looked not just vibrant but surreal. The jasmine leaves looked greener than any green she could recall. The flower was ivory perfection.

She had climbed this path before, but never at mid-morning. It was the same path but different light. It was the same Elia but *in* a different light, variations on a theme. Images of Monet's *Haystacks* flashed to mind. The paintings of hay piles in different seasons, times and weather portraying stunning variances of light. Depending on the light, even the mundane was magnificent.

"Go at eleven o'clock," Cameron had said, "that's when the light is best."

It was getting close. The sun arced higher. The light would soon be right. She anticipated anything but the mundane, but just what she might find in that secret cave she had no idea.

"You'll know," was what he had said.

At the crest of the hill, Elia spotted the bamboo hut. Still barren, even the hut seemed to resonate. It emitted a particular sanctity beyond the glow of morning sunlight. The leaning hut, her destination days earlier, now felt like a bridge to an even greater pilgrimage. She knelt down over the three alabaster stones nestled in the dirt along the hut's wall. They lay exactly as she had left them. She reached into her bag. She removed the water bottle. She took one gulp and then soaked the ground above the buried pomegranate seeds with the last of her water.

Elia wondered whether the seeds would one day bear fruit. Would the pomegranate seeds she planted nourish another? Maybe *she* was a seed. The tiniest and greatest destinies intersect and connect. She wiped the sweat from the back of her neck. It seemed even hotter.

She walked over to the cliff and gazed across the ocean vista. Not even the eurhythmic push and pull of the waves slowed her adrenaline. Her stomach fluttered. She wondered what leaping off the edge might feel like. She kicked off her sandals and rooted her feet into the dirt. She left her sandals behind. She climbed barefoot down the steep trail.

As she descended Elia heard Cameron's voice inside her head. "Listen to the whale's song," and then "longer than I thought" and "you'll know." She imagined herself scaling down one of his poems, verse by verse, each rock or branch another word.

And then other poems began to fill her head. Poems percolated up from the farthest recesses of memory. Long-forgotten sonnets surfaced. Even lyrics Elia couldn't place came to mind.

Never, never again?
Not on nights filled with quivering stars,
or during dawn's maiden brightness,
or afternoons of sacrifice?[1]

She felt her skin starting to burn. She looked to the sea. The blue beckoned with such cool promise. Streaks of teal spanned across the water like fingers ready to soothe her. She slipped, fell onto her buttocks and skidded down. Her shoulder bag snagged on a branch, breaking her fall. The back of her thigh was scraped, but not bleeding.

She stood up and rubbed her leg.

The landing stone was right there. She dropped her bag, tiptoed across the rock and soothed her bare feet in the lapping tide. She splashed water onto her face and rubbed it across her neck and shoulders. The seawater tingled against her skin.

To her right she saw the U-shaped branch jutting from the rocks. It looked just as Cameron had described. She crept along the rock, wary that even a slight misstep threatened to snap an ankle. She reached up, grasped the branch and pulled herself alongside the tree's trunk. The weathered canvas bag was nestled against the tree's base. The rope had disintegrated.

She squatted down and opened the bag. She was relieved to find an old diving mask and rubber fins inside. Both smelled of stale brine. The rusted metallic ring around the mask's faceplate bore a greenish patina. The blue and black fins had a grayish saltwater film. But otherwise both the mask and fins looked intact. Looping the fin straps and mask around her wrist, she negotiated the rocks to the landing stone. She retrieved the balled-up gray socks from her shoulder bag and slipped off her baseball cap. Next off came her halter and shorts, beneath

---

1 From "To See Him Again" by Gabriela Mistral.

which she wore a black bikini. She tightened the bikini strings and pulled on the socks.

She grinned at the thought of herself in a black bikini and thick sweat socks. She pulled the flippers over the socks. The fins were loose, but felt snug enough to stay on in the water. The mask's black strap tugged at her hair as she pulled it onto her forehead. She waddled into the water, careful not to slip again on the landing stone.

The plunge felt so good. It soothed her baking body.

Even Elia's casual kicks of the fins bobbed her shoulders well above the surface. She spit into the inside of the mask. She rubbed her saliva around to coat the lens from fogging.

Then she pulled the mask over her face. She pressed it tight. She took a deep breath and duck dove down into a brand new world.

"*Itztlacoliuhqui.*"

Jackson repeated the name over and over again. He liked the way it rolled from his tongue. *El capitáo* had rarely left his cabin since the liquor disappeared. He entrusted Esteban to guide them down the South American coastline and back to Sáo Paulo. That was three days ago. Three days surrounded by a sprawl of history books, maps and artifacts, three days to sulk over the bracelet and the secret of immortality that had slipped from his grasp.

A flurry of knocks startled him.

"What is it?" he growled.

"*Com licenca, como vai?*" Esteban asked through the cabin door.

"*Itztlacoliuhqui,*" said Jackson.

"*Náo compreendo,*" Esteban said.

Silence.

And then in English, Esteban said, "We'll be there tomorrow."

Esteban's footsteps drifted down the corridor.

Itztlacoliuhqui.

Jackson leered at the book open on the table. A colored sketch depicted a hand-forged headdress adorned with raven feathers. Fiery eyes scorched from a rubescent face. He stared at *Itztlacoliuhqui,* the tattoo-chested warrior, more feared than revered, the Aztec knife god.

Jackson's finger slipped from the page. He leaned back in his chair. The page turned itself. Another colored sketch appeared. This one depicted birds and butterflies that swooned about a woman draped in magnificent silks. Flowers and feathers rained down upon her. The caption beneath the picture said *Xochiquetzal.* She was the Aztec goddess of love and fertility. He gawked at her voluptuous figure. He marveled at her face. The eyes were the greenest green he had ever seen. He thought of Aluna. So were hers.

A tear trailed down his bearded cheek as he contemplated the one gift he could never give his wife.

Aluna stirred with a late morning dream.

An angular man and dark woman with flowing hair clutched one another. A haze surrounded them. They stood upon a sandy beach on a tropical island. She recognized the beach. A fishing boy had rowed her ashore there nearly eight months earlier. The murky vision was cast in rusted sepia like an old photograph.

Even through the mist she recognized the curve of the man's shoulders. She had clutched him in her arms before. It was her lover. She was certain of it even though she couldn't discern his face. The fog lifted. Two faces began to reveal themselves. His eyes dazzled like beacons, alive and passionate. They were the eyes of the man she loved. His arms cradled the woman. Yet the woman's face was still buried against his bare chest.

Aluna felt her chest pressed against Cameron. She stared at the woman. A green teardrop, like an emerald at dusk, trickled down the woman's cheek.

She felt Cameron's lips against her own. Then he was upon her like a lion. She welcomed him again and again. He relented. He became gentle and protective once more. Fingertips caressed every curve of her cheek and chin. His fingers traced down her neck. His touch felt like a dream within a dream. She felt his fingertips pressing into the dimples in her lower back, pulling himself into her, slow and steady, the most perfect, welcomed reprise.

She felt him just as if he were right there on top of her in her bed.

She roused from the dream impassioned with the thought of Cameron inside her. She felt the wetness between her legs. She felt the weight of her stomach and the kick of their love deep inside. Stars spotted her vision. She began to feel a bit dizzy. The stars vanished. She glimpsed something else. She rubbed her eyes. And for the shortest but most brilliant moment she thought she saw flowers and feathers raining down upon her, and swooning birds and butterflies.

CHAPTER 29

Within that last breath
laced rapture's memoir
drifting, like a wisp
into the ether.

Daggers of sunlight pierced the surface and dispersed around Elia. She had never swum in water so clear. Her silhouette crept along the rocky bottom just meters below the surface. She fluttered forward one fin at a time. With each kick her fluid shadow twisted. Then she undulated like a dolphin with her thighs pressed together. Gliding through the water with such ease was liberating. She felt natural, fluid and confident. She could do this. Her lungs were full. The surface was so close. Her next breath was just an easy kick or two away.

She dove deeper, arms by her side. The cool tingle of water against her skin subsided into a feeling of streamlined sleekness. Yellow and black angelfish drifted just out of reach.

She kicked toward a glimmer that shone from the side of the submerged reef. Silvery shells mirrored a beacon of refracted sunlight through the blue. A solitary ray reflected toward the sea cap. That glimmer beckoned like an evening star. Everything felt connected. Elia grinned.

But her lungs began to tighten.

Beyond the reef's ledge turquoise blended into a sapphire abyss. She peeked past the drop-off and suddenly felt like an insignificant speck in the infinite blue. An eel slithered around the rocky ledge. It nearly poked right into her mask. The eel startled and disappeared along the rock. She thrust to the surface and gasped.

She bobbed there at the surface to replenish her lungs. She pushed the mask up onto her forehead and rubbed her eyes. A mouthful of seawater slipped past her lips while she treaded there. The saltwater puckered her tongue. Two yellow-billed seagulls swooped past. The tips of their wings skimmed the water until they landed onshore. They glared at her as if gauging her resolve. She could go back to the *cantina*. Maybe she *should* have told someone.

A black gannet torpedoed from the sky into the water with barely a splash. She watched for what seemed an eternity. The seabird finally surfaced and shook its sleek feathers. A bulge wiggled down its slender craw. Cameron's words returned to her. *You'll know.*

She tugged down the mask, pressed it against her face and dipped beneath the water. The ledge was directly below her, only about two body-lengths down. She lifted her head, gulped one big breath and dove. Her dolphin kicks were now more confident and smooth.

The reef proved easier to reach this second time. Tight-lipped mollusks were tucked into crevasses along the rock. Silver-dollar sea flowers lazed in the current. A purple starfish clung to the pitted rock, surrounded by a regiment of black-spiked sea urchins.

In another surge of her hips the rock face rounded into an oblong opening. It was just as Cameron had described. Her lungs were still fine, but now her sinuses ached. She clamped her nostrils and blew hard. Her ears popped to relieve some of the pressure. Inverted, she swirled around in a scramble of bubbles and stared into the hole. A faint, greenish light glowed in the distance. She rubbed the face of the mask.

Her chest felt ready to implode. She kicked back up and into daylight and refilled her lungs. She pulled back the mask. The seagulls were gone. So was any doubt. That dim green glow had cemented her resolve. And her resolve confirmed another feeling that had been brewing inside.

Trust.

She felt like she was about to trust Cameron with her life. Maybe that trust had sprung from the simple sharing of his secret. But he asked nothing of her, not even that she come back. Sure, she knew she would. Still even more so she trusted that this whole crazy adventure was now *her* story. She wasn't looking for him anymore. She sculled there about to submerge and a remarkable sense of purpose overcame her.

Stay calm. Keep your wits.

She was about to dive farther on a single breath than ever before. She trusted in the poet's pledge. And she trusted herself too. Something sacred was at the end of that tunnel. A cave-full of air might be sacred enough. She took three long breaths, each deeper than the prior. On the last breath she filled her lungs, inverted and kicked hard, pulling the water aside to speed her descent.

She dove to the ledge. Without hesitating she pulled into the opening. In the next instant she was cramped by rock on all sides. The walls were too narrow to turn back now. The light inside of that tunnel was dim as dusk, except for that faint glow at its end. Within those confines she battled against flashes of claustrophobia. She stretched her arms in front, avoiding the spiked urchins. Her fingers felt along the rocky bottom. *Concentrate on the light.* Her lungs emptied. *Trust.* Her shoulder nicked against something. Was that a rock or an urchin? She didn't dare check. What if there was another eel down here? Time slowed. Her heartbeat quickened. *Stay calm.* Her lungs crunched.

That meager glow beckoned with such simple promise.

All she craved was another breath.

Her fingers dipped into a soft pocket of sand. She felt more rock, then another soft pocket. The dusky water turned greenish blue. Light spread. Lungs depleted. Empty. She kicked hard. Fingers raked sand.

She rolled a shoulder, clawed deeper, and craned her head to see the glassy underside of the water's surface. With one final lunge she burst through the surface and sucked in a glorious breath of hot, humid, brackish air. She ripped the mask off her head and rolled onto her back. Sprawled on the cavern floor she gasped for air. But she was alive and tingling all over.

Two portals stared from the cave ceiling. Both shafts blazed with overhead sun. *Go at eleven o'clock. That's when the light is best.* Now she understood. The two cockeyed ducts warmed the cave like a sauna. Light reflected off the inlet and shimmered against the walls. She rolled her head on a pillow of sand. The cave looked about half the size of her cottage room. It smelled of stale brine and clamshells.

Elia sat up. She eased a rubber strap over her socked heel and removed a fin. She rolled off the soggy sock and set it aside, then rubbed her cramped foot. She took off the other fin and sock. Her bottom planted into the sand.

She scratched her head where the mask had tugged her hair. *You'll know.*

Okay. What?

She *felt* incredible warmth and stillness. The tide sulked near her painted toes. The cave seemed a contented hush. Small shells littered its floor. She shouted "Hello." A scarce echo of "lo" faded to nothing. Sharp sunlight contrasted against the dark rock. Her vision began to adjust. She discerned slight movements and squinted so she could better see. A scattering of sand crabs scurried along the walls, perhaps startled by the thunderclap of her shout.

Her ears attuned to the silence. She began to detect the muted percussion of their claws scraping across the stone. While the shells camouflaged into the black rock, her ears picked up a faint cadence within the cave: the clicks and clacks of those tiny crabs against the hiss of the tide. Even within such apparent silence a rhythm remained. She just had to listen close.

She pushed her palms into the sand and stood up. The sunlit portals were just beyond reach. She gazed up at the portal directly over her head. A watermelon could plug it. Her hands dropped to her waist. She wondered how many had ever peered down the hole into the secret cave. She imagined that even fewer had ever peered up through that hole from inside the cave.

A speckled crab rappelled down the shaft. She watched as it traversed a ridge in the ceiling. Burnt orange splotched its coffee-brown shell. She became mesmerized by the crustacean's dexterity. It defied gravity and disappeared into a crack.

"Where did you go?" she whispered.

She traced along the crack. The cave's rear wall sloped from the sand like the inside of a pup tent. The crack splintered up a slant into that back wall and grew wider just above her shoulders. She squinted into the shadowy recess.

The crack widened into a natural shelf.

She inched forward and crouched beneath the crag. She leaned backward like she was about to begin a limbo dance. Just as the crown of her forehead grazed the rock she glimpsed something above the lip of that narrow crevice.

It looked like a little half-moon.

She grabbed the lip with her left hand and reached into the chasm. Her palm patted against the cold, slick stone. A flurry of pricks scuttled across her fingers. She flicked them off. *Ugh*, were there poisonous crabs? She fished around until she felt something soft. She looped a finger into what felt like a strap and gave it a tug.

Metal scraped across stone. A cylinder the length of her forearm tumbled out. The tube nearly struck her on the head. She swerved and the canister swung to her side. She let go of the rock and fell back onto the sand, nearly landing atop her discovery.

The jadish-gray container was the color of moss-covered cement. Its dinged and dented exterior looked battle worn, like an old army canteen. A cracked, leather strap looped through one buckled clip at its bottom. Another clip forged onto the lid. The leather reminded Elia of the back of Paco's weathered hand.

"What have we got here?" she asked herself.

She knelt over it.

It resembled one of those containers looped over the architecture students' shoulders on campus back in Columbus, only shorter. Images of blueprints and diagrams and *treasure maps* filled her mind. After all, she was sitting in a secret cave on a remote island. A red rubber washer sealed the gap between the container and its lid. Flecks of green speckled the red washer.

She rubbed her palms against the cool tin like it was a genie's oil lamp. Oh, for three wishes. She had imagined this as a child, always certain of that first wish. A muffled thud sounded when she flicked the tin with a finger. She shook the tube. She heard something shift inside. It wasn't a sloshing or clinking. It sounded more like something sliding back and forth.

She glanced up to the sunlit portal and then over her shoulder at the water. Nobody was watching. She unscrewed the cap. The lid made a metallic grinding noise, like it had been sealed for centuries. She pointed the canister away from her face. She grimaced when she opened it, but nothing flew out. She tilted the tube back and peeked inside. She rotated the canister like a kaleidoscope. Instead of brilliant shapes and colors, though, she glimpsed the swirled edges of scrolled paper. The smell of onion wafted from the tin.

The tube was nearly stuffed full.

She tilted the canister upside down, but the scrolls didn't slide out. She shook the tube. Several tips of paper slid past the opened mouth. She guided them out and into the light of the cave.

She unfurled the pages.

Upon the first yellowed sheet, scrawled in squirrely-printed handwriting, were words she recognized.

She knew the words by heart, because that's where she carried them.

You'll know.

Tears fell as she read the first line:

Stop the bells from ringing

Just before the word *ringing* was hand-printed another word. But that word was crossed out with a flattened "x." She brought the paper closer to her face. The redacted word was *clanging*.

"Stop the bells from clanging," she whispered.

She closed her eyes. Church bell towers rose above pastoral hills. Heavy knotted ropes swayed in the wind.

Ringing, she thought.

Ringing was better. *Clanging* was too harsh, much too noisy. It almost overpowered the *stopping*. And that was what mattered, the stopping, the silence, the requiem. That was the whole point.

She wiped a tear:

Hush the infant's cry

Above the word *Hush* was written, *Quiet*. Not even a question. She loved everything about the word *hush*, and always had. Even its appearance, with the tidy balance of an "h" on either end, like two idyllic breaths pacifying the "us" in between. It was a perfect word, and the perfect choice. Mothers soothed their infants in church pews, cooing "hush, my darling, hush." These choices mattered. Every choice did.

Lovers lower your gaze for one moment

After "*moment,*" in parenthesis was written "*of respite.*" Again it was the right choice, for she knew well what was about to be revealed. She read the last line of the stanza aloud:

I am among you no more.

And though she had read this verse so many times before, and could easily recite it from memory, an uncontrollable tremor overtook her. Within that cave she felt the poet's loss like never before. She imagined Cameron swimming into the cave with a canister of poems to his muse looped over one shoulder.

She wiped away a tear before it dare fall upon the parchment. But as she looked down she noticed watermarks had already discolored the paper. Dried droplets clustered beneath the words she just read, "*I am among you no more.*" Gray circles bled from the ink strokes, as if the letters themselves had wept.

And it dawned upon her what she held.

Not just original drafts of the poems that had become *Secrets of Odysseus,* but something much more. Within her hands she cradled the dried tears of the poet himself, the seeping heart and soul of another.

Elia clutched the papers to her chest. She took a quivering breath and her own tears finally broke the near perfect hush within that cave.

CHAPTER 30

Dusk's fading mirror languished
beyond the dread of death
Daylight's last vestige vanquished
within one lover's breath.

"*Vamos!*" Esteban yelled.

He rushed Jackson down the pier.

Gray clouds choked overhead. Jackson glanced back toward the yacht. Two crewmates coiled lines. A third hosed down the deck. His sea legs wobbled toward the waiting sedan. The pitch of the waves was still inside him.

"*Itztlacoliuhqui*," Jackson mumbled into the serpent eyes tattooed upon Esteban's bicep.

"*Prazer em conhece-lo.*" Esteban shrugged.

He guided Jackson into the backseat content to let *el capitáo* call him whatever name he wanted. Esteban jumped into the front seat and slammed his door. The clouds burst into a downpour.

Jackson scratched his beard. He leaned his head against the car window and gaped at the sky.

"*Tlaloc*," he whispered.

He envisioned the Aztec god smashing a clay pot full of rain.

The deluge drummed against the dark sedan. Rain splattered everywhere. The car lurched. Jackson's clench on the obsidian tightened. He was exhausted. He stunk. His shirt, once pressed and white, was now a rumpled, ashen gray. He wanted a drink. He needed a bath, a shave and about a week of sleep.

The thought of seeing Aluna eased his grip.

His knee pressed into the pocket on the back of the driver's seat. Empty. Leaning over, he fished into the back pocket of the passenger front seat. His fingertips grazed against dimpled pewter. He grabbed the nickel-sized neck. Flask in hand, he slouched back into the leather upholstery, unscrewed the cap and took a swig.

The sweet, familiar burn laced down his throat.

He caught Esteban's glance in the rearview mirror.

"*Maluco*," Jackson said.

"*Sim, muito maluco*," Esteban said and shook his head.

Jackson's thumb brushed across the initials embossed on the flask. He traced up the peak of the "J," descended down the valley of the "U," and circumnavigated the "G" before flying from its ledge. He had always envisioned his monogram to be a symbolic bas-relief depicting his life: the adventures of the great Jackson Ulysses Gray.

But he was running on fumes. He needed a spark. The sweet surprise on Aluna's face would help. He took another swallow of brandy. He pictured himself falling asleep upon her breast, but only after taking all of her for himself. His chapped lips curled into a smile. It would be good to be home.

Aluna shut the bathroom door. She waddled back into bed. Amidst the driving rain that pelted her window she thought she heard what sounded like a key turning in the front lock downstairs. She glanced at the clock on her nightstand. It was just shy of noon. Outside it looked closer to midnight. A bolt of lightning severed the gloom. A horrific thunderclap sounded like the trunk of a mighty oak cracking. *That was close.* A tremor shook the house. The shuffle of slow, deliberate footsteps downstairs brought a smile of relief. She could use a visitor.

Which book would Doctor Silva bring today?

The right panel of her bedroom window flung open. Rain sprayed across the tower of books on her nightstand and onto the Turkish rug. She rolled out of bed. Her feet planted on the wet rug. She adjusted her loose white blouse and black cotton skirt. Her stomach had grown big with the baby inside. Nothing felt comfortable anymore. Wind buffeted the glass. She forced the window shut. *No need to ever worry about replacing these old locks*, she thought. Her bags were packed. She gazed down over the front yard.

The circular driveway was empty.

She wished the stubborn old doctor would drive in this weather. His office was five blocks away. She hoped he had at least remembered an umbrella. She stared at the phone on her nightstand and realized it hadn't rung all morning. He usually called first. The receiver felt cold against her ear. The line was dead. She set the receiver back into its cradle. The storm must have knocked it out.

She peered back out her bedroom window. One of the potted agapanthus was overflowing. Muddy rings formed around the pot, only to be sucked away into rivulets that cascaded down the red tile steps toward the garden. Streams gushed along the edge of the driveway and escaped beneath the dripping black spearheads of the wrought-iron gate. A curb drain had already flooded onto the cobblestone street.

She heard the familiar creak at the bottom of the wooden staircase. Yet the images of turbulent water had captivated her.

The rainwater overwhelmed everything in its path. But the water seemed incapable of escaping its own torrent. Urgent, impatient, moving, but somehow still trapped. She knew that feeling. She felt an urge to climb out the window and into the storm. She wanted to feel the rain pound against her flesh. She wanted to let the torrent carry her away.

The window began to fog.

She pressed her palm against the cool windowpane. She lifted her hand from the glass. She gazed at the storm through the outline of her own handprint. A memory of a dream recurred. Two figures enveloped in fog on a beach. She envisioned Cameron and the dream woman she believed to be herself standing in the garden below.

Cameron stared toward the window. She could see him through her rain-beaded palm print. A sense of longing filled his eyes. Aluna felt a familiar tug in her pelvis, and then a harsh kick. The dream woman turned and looked toward the window. Aluna's breath hastened. Her handprint fogged. Rain slapped against the glass. Wind rattled the window frame.

Life pulsed every which way with each escalating breath. She imagined an island finch fluttering beneath a tarp-covered market. She saw an old pomegranate woman's grin. She recalled Cameron's eyes the first time she saw him. The leaf of a banana tree thumped against the window. She pictured entangled bodies a thousand miles away, and what seemed a thousand years ago. In the next kick it all felt so immediate.

The glass knob of her bedroom door squeaked. Through the fogged window she detected a shadow near the front gate. She rubbed the window to clear the haze. The vision of her dream vanished. The wrought-iron gate to the flooded driveway swung open. An old man struggled at the gate with an umbrella. Doctor Silva looked up toward her window.

The bedroom door opened.

She hugged her belly. She looked over her shoulder and turned.

A soggy, bearded apparition stared at her. His eyes filled with disbelief. Jackson's mouth dropped. Everything slowed.

His face flushed red. Another flash of lightning obliterated any doubt. The chasm between husband and wife filled with an undeniable truth. She felt a thunderclap in her stomach.

He stared at her, dumbfounded.

"I'm sorry," she said.

She grasped the windowsill.

"I gave you everything," he said.

She glanced down at her belly before returning his gaze.

"All I ever wanted was a man," she said.

"What?" he bellowed.

"A man with *me*, not a thousand leagues beneath the sea."

"It's my *life*," he said.

She felt another kick inside. Guilt transformed to defiance.

"And this is mine," she said.

She straightened up, filled with an immortality Jackson could never spawn. She knew it, and she knew that he did too. She felt empowered. It was he who was cornered by his own emptiness.

"I should have told you," she said.

And her voice grew strong, "But I'm in love."

Jackson's chest began to heave.

"So am I," he stammered.

She glimpsed toward her suitcase beside the armoire. He tracked her furtive glance like a hunter.

His eyes simmered.

He slammed the door shut.

"You fucking whore!"

Froth spat from his lips.

He reached beneath his shirt and into his belt.

"You've been drinking!" she shouted.

"Not enough," he said.

He lunged toward her and his arm arced overhead.

She froze, unsure whether it was better to run for it or to jump from the window.

A dark flash gleamed.

She twisted away too late. A sharp pang punched into her chest. He grabbed her like he might devour her. Their faces were only inches apart. His eyes were furious, confused and primal. His breath stunk of brandy. Drool slathered across his beard. He was someone else, something else, an animal she didn't know.

A fire scorched through her chest. The wind knocked out of her. Her ribs ached. With him still clutching her she stumbled back and grasped the nightstand. Books tumbled to the floor. She thrust a knee into his groin and bellowed, "No!"

He wailed and fell backwards, but his fist tugged her chest with him.

Blood splotched his shirt.

She saw the dripping black edge of the jagged blade and glanced down. Her blouse had ripped to the side. She saw a gash in her chest. Blood seeped from the wound faster than her thumping heart. She couldn't breathe and started to tremble. And then she felt it. The horror ripped through her.

She tried to scream, but nothing came out.

Her knees buckled. She fell toward the bed. She couldn't pull herself up. Where was her strength? He towered over her. He raised the dagger above his head. The bare skin of her stomach fully exposed.

"No," she begged.

But he lunged toward her again.

The bedroom door almost tore from its hinges. Doctor Silva's crooked frame crouched in the doorway. Jackson's arm swept down. A shot screamed out. Jackson's arms flailed like he had been smacked between the shoulders with a plank. He pivoted toward the doorway. The doctor's fingers were wrapped around a *pistola.*

Doctor Silva squeezed a second time. Jackson's head flung backward. The bloodied dagger dropped to the carpet. Jackson staggered a step toward Doctor Silva. He took one long, foul-throated gasp and collapsed.

Aluna slumped onto the rug. The dagger lay between the two of them. Blood-smeared books cast alongside her on the floor. Doctor Silva knelt down. His hands crossed over her wound. She couldn't feel them. Her chest burned and then felt like ice. Her limbs were cold. She stared into his eyes. The rusty taste of blood gurgled up in her throat.

"*Bosta*, I went back for my umbrella," Doctor Silva said.

It was the first time she had ever heard him curse.

He straightened her onto her back. He propped a book beneath her head.

Tears streaked down his cheeks.

"I brought you Thornton Wilder," he said.

He ripped her blouse, wrapped it into a ball and pressed it against her chest.

"Have you read *The Bridge of San Luis Rey?*" he asked.

She wanted to tell him she hadn't, but she couldn't.

With one hand holding the makeshift bandage in place, he pulled the phone from the nightstand.

"*Foda se*," he muttered.

He banged the phone against its cradle.

He raised it again and listened.

The receiver dropped from his ear to the floor.

Her eyes darted toward the old writing desk and then the rain-splattered window and then the rug's abstract motif. Her vision blurred. Ram's horn and warped figures with arms akimbo danced beside her head. The old doctor steadied her face in his hand. But it was Cameron's caress she felt on her cheek. Doctor Silva's gaze didn't flinch. A tear pooled on the inside of his glasses.

She longed for the scent of his cherry lozenge breath. The old man's eyebrows froze. She raised her right hand up against his. She clasped her left hand against her convulsing belly.

My baby, she mouthed.

She needed him to promise that her baby would be okay, but he didn't. *Tell Cameron °til the end of time,'* she thought, but she couldn't even breathe the words.

She clutched his hand and murmured, "I'm dying—"

Doctor Silva bent closer to her.

"I've got you," he said.

Tears coursed from his old eyes.

"In," she whispered.

Aluna winced. And then she mouthed something to the old doctor. But not another sound passed from her lips.

CHAPTER 31

While the shaman
> *strung silken seeds luminescent beads*
>> *into fables mystique atop towers oblique*
>>> *vaunting oracles of bliss,*

Wept the bard who
> *spun a kingdom's tome one treasured poem*
>> *crumbled spires composed beneath cobwebs exposed*
>>> *the muse who beckoned his kiss.*

Elia's tears fell like an overdue summer rain. Her sobs echoed within the muggy cave. Her knees anchored into the sand and her sweaty thighs collapsed back upon her calves. Bits of broken shells prickled her shins. She cradled her forehead. Her fingertips pinned back her damp hair as she huddled over Cameron's drafts. And she began to rock back and forth.

But somewhere amidst that squall a deep drought ended.

A notion began to take hold, at first imperceptible but eventually undeniable. She no longer was crying from sadness. Something else was driving those tears. She was crying because she no longer felt so alone. And as she realized this, her tears quelled. She wiped her face and opened her eyes.

The canister was right beside her on the sand. She still clutched Cameron's poems in her hand, but her grip had eased. Her tears now spotted the backsides of those original pages.

And somehow that seemed all right. From that back bedroom at Paco's *cantina* Cameron had guided her to this cave. But that was all. The rest he had entrusted to her. They had done this *together*. No, she didn't feel alone in that cave at all anymore.

She gazed toward the ledge from which she had pulled the canister. The scouting crab was nowhere in sight. She was tempted to try to capture the colorful crustacean and carry it away with her. That way, when she retold *her* story and doubting eyes began to roll, she could pull out her speckled accomplice and explain that *this was the crab that I watched climb through that portal into the secret cave* ...

Visions of Isabella stroking the braided black strands of her voodoo charm rushed to mind. The warmth she felt encompassed not just Cameron, but the speckled crab too. It included Isabella and even enveloped Isabella's not-so-old-man-of-the-sea, Paco. That warm feeling swelled inside her. It blanketed the stoned, nickernut-playing crawdad of an island doc, Fatty. And it spread across the old pomegranate woman with the toothless smile, and even the laconic, island-hopping pilot Falcon. That warmth felt big as the sea, certainly big enough to encompass the blue whale that had swum alongside the seaplane's shadow on her flight to the island.

Listen close to the whale's song.

The siren seemed everywhere. It was embodied in everything. It surrounded her. The hair on her forearms pricked up. The whole island had become as much a part of her as the goose bumps that rippled her flesh. Within the lightness of gossamer in a breeze the universe of books she had called home for so long was supplanted by a feeling of real, living warmth all around her. And that warmth was inside her too.

She sighed a long, whispery exhale.

Half a heartbeat later she heard a ...

Puuuuuuhhhhfft.

The sound of a tiny hot-air balloon blast filled the cave.

She twisted so quickly she nearly toppled.

Peeking from the water was a scaly green head twice the size of her fist. Deep-set, black opals stared at her. A glistening dome of jade armor crested from the water. Elia froze, unsure whether she should back away. The giant sea turtle glided toward her. Ripples cascaded off its magnificent shell, which grew larger and larger as it swam closer. The sound of the phantom's deep exhale had startled her. But the sight of its serene, prehistoric majesty brought her calm.

The creature's front flippers clawed into the sand. It pulled its massive shell ashore. Sand caked to its flippers. The right flipper had a large, crusted-over gouge in it. But the apparent wound didn't seem to hamper its slow and steady progress at all. Elia gasped. The carapace was nearly as long as her legs. Much like the sand caked to the sea turtle's flippers, sand and broken bits of shells were still embedded into her shins. But she didn't brush them off.

The sea turtle craned its head toward Elia like an inquisitive dog. Elia stared back at the camouflaged spelunker. She wondered what the sea turtle could be thinking. And she wondered which of the two might have traveled farther only to bump into one another in this maybe not-so-secret cave. The turtle's Zen-like gaze was so steady. Only its shell rose slightly with each laboring breath.

Elia mustered a dry swallow.

The sea turtle scuttled within a flipper of the canister. A divot tracked behind it into the sand. Elia gathered the rest of Cameron's poems from the sand. But the turtle showed no interest in her movements. Instead it just lumbered toward a shaded corner along the far side of the cave.

The sea turtle passed so close to her. Its shell shimmered in the sunlight pouring through the overhead fissures. Fans of emerald, aquamarine and teal fused together within each plate of its glossy, quilted shell. Elia marveled at the sight. She recalled once reading a *National Geographic* article about centuries of sea turtle slaughter triggered by such lovely, ornate shells. That article had transposed glossy pictures of shells like the one within a finger's reach of her against horrific images of devastating butchery. Haunting photos of severed heads and flippers and gutted carcasses filled that article. But only now did Elia truly comprehend the loss of such living beauty.

The sea turtle's flippers began to cleave into the moist sand. Elia smiled. She realized the turtle had arrived at the brightest time of day as well even though it still had claimed the shadiest spot in the cave. She wondered whether the sea turtle had also been lured by the same faint glow at the end of the underwater tunnel. *Go at eleven o'clock. That's when the light is best.* Maybe Cameron wasn't the only one who knew this secret. Maybe it was more innate than any person could imagine, some primal setting buried deep within all creatures. Maybe Nature metered her most precious magic in such basic beats as light and dark.

The sea turtle dug deeper. Burrowing down, the turtle fanned sand to either side of the hole. A horseshoe-shaped mound formed around half its great bulk. The turtle looked to easily weigh as much as a man. Then just as abruptly as the sea turtle had started to dig, it halted, pivoted a half turn and teetered at the edge of the pit. Its rear, paddle-like limbs, shorter and flatter than the front flippers, and an even shorter spade of a tail slid into the hole.

Elia set down Cameron's poems. She crept nearer.

The turtle didn't even turn its head. The spaded tail flexed upward. Elia slinked closer. She kept low to the sand. The tail dropped and then lifted. It moved like a slow, mechanical lever. Elia peeked over the crest of the horseshoe-shaped levee. She stared into the gully. Inside was a small heap of what looked like oblong, rubbery Ping-Pong balls. That *National Geographic* article had mentioned the other reason the gentle sea creatures had teetered upon extinction: the fervent belief by so many cultures that sea turtle eggs were an aphrodisiac. But to Elia the sea turtle's eggs looked like a mound of slick papier-mâché miracles waiting to happen. She could not fathom desecrating a single one.

The sea turtle continued its birthing ritual, seeming to be frozen in a trance. Only the lift of its tail, its slow, steady breaths and the deposit of its precious cargo into the sandy pit continued. She counted the eggs as they tumbled out: ten, twenty, and thirty. There were more underneath already covered by others. She guessed there might be fifty in the clutch.

All this time the new mother turtle remained oblivious to her. Elia couldn't resist. She reached her hand just above the shell. And with the next deep inhale the turtle's massive shield lifted. Elia held her breath. Her fingertips grazed the cool shell. Her fingertips remained on the shell as it sunk again with a quiet puff. The turtle didn't seem to notice. For sacrosanct seconds, maybe as much as even a minute, Elia felt every laboring breath. She thought she even felt the faint quiver of each life-giving push.

Elia lifted her hand and stared at it. It was the strangest sensation. Even with her hand raised, she not only heard but also continued to feel the turtle's breath ripple within her fingertips.

A low, guttural groan echoed within the cave. The sea turtle began to shift. Flippers shuffled. It fanned sand over the eggs. Elia peeked into the nest of eggs. She wondered how long before the hatchlings wriggled from the incubated sandpit to trek out toward the sea. Each tiny egg filled with such possibilities.

And out of all of her own life's many possibilities one face came to mind in that cave. Maybe it was the face of her Tristan, her Romeo, perhaps even her own poet. There was only one way to find out. But when so many weeks ago her classmates had mocked her quest, his steady, soothing voice had defied them all. She envisioned his unkempt black hair that always made him look like he had just rolled from bed. She saw his angular nose notched with a slight crook at the bridge, almost like a prizefighter's. She noted the pallor of his cheeks, covered in a haze of stubble, betraying a preference for the nocturnal. And she longed to gaze into his deep-set hazel eyes.

She glanced back at the nest.

One solitary egg had tumbled from the pile into the corner of the pit. It was separated from the others by the length of her palm. It nestled against a ridge of sand that formed a halo. The sea turtle continued to shovel sand over the brood. Soon the lone egg would be covered, but all alone, separated from its slumbering siblings.

For some reason the plight of that particular solitary egg tugged at her. She scooped two fingers into the sand and prodded it toward the rest. That felt better. Sometimes just a little nudge is all it takes.

Careful to not even graze the others, she pulled back her hand. Her knuckles glanced against the sand that had backstopped the stray egg. The edge of a tarnished, muddy gray ridge unearthed. It looked like a fragment of a shell or maybe even an old, corroded can of some sort. The sea turtle's strokes swept closer. Sand flicked against her hand. The entire nest would soon be smothered.

She couldn't resist, just one more touch.

A burst of sand covered the ridge. She brushed it away. A dark arc, about the size of her wrist, protruded from the sand. That buried object had for just a moment cradled that lonesome egg. The puffing sea turtle pushed another heap of sand. The sides of the nest began to collapse.

It was now or never.

Elia grasped the object between her fingertips. Another push of sand buried the nest. Elia rolled back away from the nest. The sea turtle, seemingly exhausted, roosted upon the buried nest, now just a mound of sand. Its flippers, underbelly and the ridge of its shell were all covered with sand. So was Elia's sweaty skin. Sunlight crept onto the buried nest.

Elia stared at her hand.

Looped around her fingers was a rough cuff of metal. A corroded patina of black and gray with hints of silver and tinges of green coated the hefty bracelet. It felt weighty as iron. She traced along the forged surface that was a bit over two knuckles wide. She brushed away grains of sand embedded into its grooves. The cuff formed a near complete circle, with a gap just wide enough to slip over her wrist.

She had never seen anything like it. It looked older than old, like it was from another time and place, another world.

Hints of silver and tinges of green highlighted protruding ridges along its surface. Mystified by its simple, antiquated form, Elia rotated it. On one end a rough circle had four squiggled lines shooting out from its circumference. One of those lines pointed toward a crescent shape. Elia had relished the shape of a crescent moon ever since Sister Rita Magdalena had dubbed Elia her little "moonchild." Elia's fingertips rubbed across the face of the crescent. She could hear Sister Rita Magdalena's reassuring voice. She recalled how Sister Rita had told her the story of how Elia had dropped from a starlit sky. Sister Rita's explanation was that the heavens couldn't bear not sharing young Elia with the earth below.

Rotating the bracelet Elia found what looked like a silhouette of a swallow in flight, and then a rudimentary fish surrounded by wavy lines. It was everywhere again. Elia felt encompassed by *the whale's song.*

The turtle puffed.

A raised, beaded design ran along each edge of the bracelet. It looked like little interconnected seeds. Except at one spot right on top the beaded protrusions crossed over the face to the other side in an "x" pattern. At that intersected cross, sand clumped around what looked like another metallic symbol of some sort. But as Elia rubbed away the last stubborn flecks she realized it wasn't metal at all. A dark, odd-shaped stone was melded into the center of the bracelet. About the size of a quarter, it looked like an inverted spade from a deck of playing cards.

The stone was almost black, but ringed by a brownish green patina around its edge. She scratched her fingernail against the surface. A thick coat of grime chipped off beneath her fingernail. A dull hint of green appeared. She held the bracelet directly into the sunlight, which had continued to shift to now envelop her, the sea turtle and its buried nest. The green was different than the flat, corroded patina ringing the stone. The dark shade of green matched the deepest hue of the turtle's shell, but the revealed speck of stone was more glassy and translucent.

"Whoa," she muttered.

The grayish black beads running along the bracelet's edge were coated in the same soot. Several were missing. She rubbed her fingernail against one of the tiny beads. A fleck of grime scraped free, revealing a similar, translucent nick of green. She counted more tiny beads than buried turtle eggs, plus the one large stone with that scrape of translucent green set atop them all. The pattern reminded Elia of the mother sea turtle hovering over her brood beneath the sand. She swallowed.

She slipped the cuff onto her wrist and looked at the sea turtle.

"Can I keep it?" she asked.

The turtle didn't object.

Elia turned her wrist. She raised her arm to watch it slide down her forearm. Then she pushed it to hang down over the back of her hand. She conjured up images of pirates and hidden booty.

The poems were scattered across the sand next to the mask and flippers. With the bracelet dangling from her wrist she collected the loose pages. Each page curled up into a little scroll. Elia wondered about the treasures that can lie buried within a soul, and for how long. But then she thought about how long she had lived immersed in the words of others. The needle of her compass spun toward something else now, something not stacked upon any bookshelf or buried on some mythical shore.

She scrolled the poems back into the canister. She recalled that night at the Village Poet. Whatever had tugged her away from her studies that night to stumble upon the poet had led her here as well. She gazed into the impenetrable depth of the old sea turtle's eyes. It all seemed so implausible, yet so perfect.

The turtle didn't even blink.

With a deep sigh, the sea turtle shuffled off its sandy throne toward the water. It submerged without even a final glance back. Elia was stunned at how quickly it melted beneath the surface. She wanted time to move even slower. The sea turtle left behind barely a ripple. That unheralded departure saddened her at first. But then it occurred to her that perhaps it wasn't so callous. Maybe the mother turtle had simply done all she could. Maybe, that's what we all do. Soon it would be time for her hatchlings to do their part. She pictured their little flippers flinging through the sand toward the open sea.

She slid the bracelet up her forearm and wedged it against her flesh. The afternoon was slipping away. She was careful to make sure the ends of the pages didn't stick out and screwed the lid back onto the canister. The rubber seal looked watertight.

She pictured herself presenting the original drafts to Professor Weitzel and Dean Baltutis as the rest of the university's literature department watched. She imagined the frenzied response that would follow. The original poems could fetch thousands, if not more. They might foster scholarly review and debate, and perhaps even spike sales of *Secrets of Odysseus*. Perhaps the originals would end up preserved behind tempered glass in some university museum. All this seemed destined to assure the highest honors on her thesis.

It was all right there in her hand.

She grinned, flicked the canister with her finger and rechecked the seal on that lid.

Elia rocketed through the underwater tunnel like a torpedo. No sea turtles were in sight. Perhaps the mother lurked somewhere beyond the tunnel's end. Perhaps it patiently waited for the day the hatchlings would make their debut into the deep blue just like the moon in a night sky, seemingly out of reach, but always watching.

It should have been easier to stay calm. She knew the tunnel. She was now confident of her lungs. But it was nearly impossible. The open water couldn't welcome her fast enough. Clearing the end of the tunnel, she shimmied up between sun streaks that danced down from the surface. She burst into daylight and gulped in a breath of salty air.

Her arms spun through the sea toward shore. She kicked hard. She could barely feel her body. She couldn't wait to tell Cameron about the canister, of which of course he knew, but also about the sea turtle and the eggs and the bracelet clasped around her forearm. She checked to make sure the bracelet was still there. This was really happening. But her compass was spinning from some frenzied magnetic vortex. And that vortex wasn't emanating from Cameron or the canister or the sea turtle or the bracelet.

It came from somewhere else, somewhere deep and unfathomed.

She wanted to scream, cry, collapse and explode all at once, ever since she had placed the canister back upon the rocky shelf in the cave. She hadn't stopped shaking since. She couldn't.

The markings were scrawled like a pictograph upon the low, sloped cave ceiling just above that rock shelf. They had been there all along. But she hadn't seen them when she initially fished out the canister. Even though her hand had pressed right over them. Her own hand had covered the etched stone while she kept her balance, blocking them from her view.

Only when she had leaned back to replace the canister into the crevice did she face the jagged letters scratched into stone. Five letters of a word she repeated as she swam ashore. Five letters of a word she knew. Five letters she would never have seen had she not placed the poet's canister back into its secret nook.

Every decision counted.

She had one last question for Cameron.

But even more so, she had something to tell him.

CHAPTER 32

In this last
of last night skies
colors fade
like comets
from view.

But emeralds
of the sea
awaited
the last of me
at last with you.

Doctor Silva brushed back a wisp of brown hair from Aluna's forehead. His thumb traced along the fallen arch of her brow and he caressed each eyelid shut. He lifted the blood-soaked blouse from her wound. The blood had tapered to a trickle. He pressed up to his feet and staggered around Jackson's body. The smell of burnt sulfur hung in the doorway where the *pistola* had fallen from his hand after the second shot.

His medical bag had scattered down the staircase. He stooped over. His arthritic fingers grabbed the bag and fumbled out his stethoscope. Syringes, suture kit and bandages spilled across the steps. They were all worthless to him now. The book he had brought for her, *The Bridge of San Luis Rey,* splayed open upon the landing.

His head began to spin. He nearly toppled down those steps. He had to move faster, but his balance was playing tricks with his old body. He grabbed onto the banister to steady himself. Then he crouched down and crawled back to the top of the stairwell, where he was able to pull back to his feet. He reeled into the bedroom and knelt down beside Aluna.

He pressed the stethoscope against her stomach. He squinted through the tears running down his face. The rainstorm still cursed against the window. He held his breath, clenched shut his eyes and tried to will the storm into silence.

He waited for any sign. Deep in that black pool of nothingness he thought he heard the faintest thump.

He dared not breathe.

And then he heard another.

He ripped the stethoscope from his ears and thrust his hand into his leather satchel. He scavenged into every worn corner and inside pocket. Where was it?

"*Não!*"

He dumped the bag onto the Turkish rug. He sifted through splints, gauze, antiseptics, a blood pressure cuff and pill bottles. Nowhere! He hadn't seen it on the staircase. Where was his scalpel?

Sheets of rain pelted against the window.

And then he saw it, just beyond his reach.

"*Claro que sim,*" he whispered.

It had been there all along.

He stretched across the rug, right between the bodies of Jackson and Aluna. His fingers grasped the cool handle. Lightning flashed. The whole bedroom shook. He picked it off the carpet. Another bolt exploded. It felt like he himself had been struck. The window flung open. Rain spewed across blood-spattered bodies and books and the blade in his hand.

He sucked in a deep breath as he crouched over Aluna. He wiped his eyes on his jacket sleeve. His vision cleared. He pressed the tip of that blade against Aluna's skin. The jagged edge touched her belly, well below the fatal gash. He hesitated for an instant in an effort to halt the room from spinning.

And with the steady hand of a surgeon, Doctor Silva did what he was trained to do. He did what he had done before, but not in many, many years. And never like this. He sliced a long incision from her navel downward. And in one deep stroke the obsidian dagger carved through the horror in that room to reveal the most incredible light he had ever seen.

Later that night, Doctor Silva sat alone in his study, still numb from the ordeal. He sipped a tumbler of Scotch, no ice, beside a river-rock fireplace. The rain had finally stopped. He had explained to the *Policia* all he cared to reveal about the events of that morning. An officer had returned his stray scalpel. It was found downstairs beside the staircase. Doctor Silva had dropped the obsidian dagger on the Turkish rug, right where he had found it, but only after he had first draped Aluna's body with a bedsheet.

Now he just wanted to forget.

He melted deeper into the worn leather chair. Its tufts split at the seams. He began to drift off. An extra pour of Scotch swirled around inside him. He cut himself a bargain. For just this one night he would forget it all. All, that is, except for those innocent eyes. He wouldn't forget them. He didn't want to. He clung to those little eyes like a life raft.

He slipped one hand into his chest pocket. He pulled out his wallet and slid out the sepia-toned photograph. The vintage portrait, its edges faded into a cloudy oval, had been pressed against his heart through it all. He gazed at the woman's dark skin and hair. He studied the silver butterfly broach above her heart. It had been his gift to her on her twenty-fifth birthday. And he stared at the full lips that forever pouted from beneath the slight turn in her nose. But it was the woman's eyes that dominated her face. Those eyes had remained forever young. They had never got the chance to grow old and blurry alongside his.

He closed his old eyes. He imagined that somewhere on some island one man would remember Aluna's eyes that way, forever captured in a moment in time. He pressed the picture against his heart and wondered how Aluna's lover would venerate her.

Tucked beneath a quilted lap blanket, he nestled the back of his head into buckskin long stained yellow from the oils of one man's life. And even later that very night, as the embers lost their glow, the final sleep came to relieve him of his burden. The old doctor succumbed once and for all to his forever.

Frenzied colors whirled past Elia. Blues and browns and greens. Images of water and sky and rock and sand and leaves barely registered. She dashed past the yellowish brown bamboo hut and down the hillside's path, a blurred green gauntlet with splashes of orange and red, burgeoning cape honeysuckle and hibiscus. Her sandals slipped on the loose dirt. She kicked them off and carried them to run faster. Halter and shorts clung to her damp bikini. Her baseball cap was long gone.

Outside the *cantina* she wiped the sweat from her face. She adjusted her halter and righted her twisted shorts. She slipped her dusted hibiscus-red toenails beneath the straps of her sandals and ran her fingers through her hair just once. Clasping the cuff bracelet, she took a deep breath and plunged into the *cantina*. It was empty, except for a remnant still life at one table: plate, mango, cheese and Paco's ivory-handled buck knife.

Walking down that hallway felt like swimming through the underwater tunnel. Except now she could breathe, but she had to remind herself to do so. Walking through that doorway was like emerging into that cave. The hair on her arms prickled up.

Isabella was standing alongside Cameron's bed with her back to the doorway. The bulk of her dark arms, orange sundress and floppy straw hat eclipsed Cameron. Paco leaned against the windowsill. His wiry brown frame was covered in a ripped, sea-blue tank top and baggy, tan cargo shorts. Chuey hunkered down by Paco's side. The little monkey held a nickernut in his hairy little hand. No incense was burning. Not a single candle was lit. Paco flashed a big, gold-toothed smile at the sight of Elia. He glanced to Isabella.

"Come on, momma bird, time for a bath," Paco said.

"What? You look like you seen a *jumbie*," Isabella said.

And then she turned around to face Elia.

"*Mama yo!*"

Isabella's jaw dropped. For once, she was speechless. She glanced back at Cameron, who sat up in bed. He raised his eyebrows at Isabella and shrugged his shoulders.

"Go on, Bella," Cameron whispered.

Elia felt Cameron's eyes upon her.

Paco's arm swept around Isabella. They stepped toward the doorway. But Isabella slipped from his grasp and took Elia's hand into her own. Isabella smothered Elia in a brawny, hot hug. The big woman smelled of sweet coconut. Isabella finally let go of her, but cradled Elia's face in her bear-sized paws. Yet Isabella's palms felt soft against her cheeks. Isabella gazed at Elia like she was looking for something.

"Come on, Boo," Paco said.

Paco tugged Isabella toward the door.

But before letting go, Isabella pressed her lips against Elia's forehead. She inhaled a long breath. Elia felt like a nuzzled cub. Paco grinned. He pulled Isabella, who was still holding that deep breath of Elia, away and out the door.

"Tonight I'll sizzle up some lobster *buljol* and *pholourie*," Paco said.

He winked at Elia.

"I thought they'd never leave," Cameron said.

His cheeks were flushed. His eyes were bright sapphires. He patted the mattress. She sat down and took his hand in hers. He grazed his thumb across the bracelet clasped on her wrist.

"I found it buried in the sand," she said.

"Stunning," he whispered.

He seemed more enamored with her skin.

"There was this speckled sand crab and a canister and a sea turtle," Elia said.

Cameron's eyes lit up.

"Really?" he said.

"Just stashed away in some cave?" she said.

She shook her head at him.

"Not just any cave," he said.

But for the first time she raised her hand to shush him. Her eyes, which for the last half hour had witnessed nothing but blurs, settled into his deep blue.

"When I was little there was a nun, Sister Rita. She was older than old, with deep-set wrinkles creased into her face and brittle red hair. She used to call me her little *moonchild*."

Elia pictured Sister Rita's sweet smile. She recalled how Sister Rita's eyes danced. How her nose crinkled up whenever she spoke Elia's name. It was like the old nun was just another schoolgirl in the play yard sharing secrets. Elia felt a tingle in her throat. She sniffled back a tear. Her fingers traced over the ridges of Cameron's knuckles. His hand felt strong.

"One day I heard Sister Rita was sick. One of the other nuns told me Sister Rita would soon be going to heaven. So I snuck into her room, because I knew someone up in heaven. I was nine."

Her grip on Cameron's hand tightened.

"So I asked Sister Rita to take a message to heaven. I asked her to tell my mother that I missed her."

Elia felt tears coming. She squeezed Cameron's hand harder. It felt rock solid. He didn't budge. She glanced at their hands.

"She promised me she would. But I wasn't so sure. What if she couldn't find her? There's supposed to be lots of angels up there. And that's when Sister Rita told me why she called me *moonchild*."

Elia felt like she was kicking toward the surface.

"That's when she told me my mother's name."

Tears streamed down her face.

"Sister Rita's next word was the last word she ever spoke to me before she went off to heaven. And that word is scrawled upon that cave ceiling," she said.

Elia nearly burst within her whisper.

"Aluna."

The hand that she prayed had scratched those five letters into the stone ceiling pulled her close.

"She made me promise to never speak her name," he said.

But Cameron finally broke his vow.

"Aluna," he whispered.

"My mother," Elia said.

She collapsed onto his quaking chest.

"My love," Cameron said.

He squeezed her tight in his arms. They wept beyond control. She was shaking so hard she thought she might collapse. But he held onto her throughout. She could feel him shaking just as hard. Which just made her hold onto him even tighter.

Finally she was able to find her breath again.

"How long have you known?" Elia asked.

"Since now," he said.

Tears covered his face.

"Everything before was just a dream," he said.

She melted into him and pressed her ear against his chest.

"Am I really?" she asked.

"Yes," he said.

He rocked her back and forth.

"My poem," he said.

They held onto one another for what seemed like forever. His hug felt strong and reassuring and safe. His chest, even with those broken ribs, felt like armor. She had fantasized for so long what such a hug might feel like. It felt even better.

She wiped her face.

"Why didn't you look for me?"

"She promised to come back. So I waited and wrote down every last memory. *Secrets* was meant to guide her back home. But when she didn't return I went looking for her. I scoured the earth."

His fingers stroked through her hair.

"Months ago I was at the *Museu Histórico Nacional* in Rio. A placard in one of the exhibits detailed where some artifacts had been found and the date when they were found. When I read it I nearly keeled over."

He pointed toward the bay.

"Right out there in some old shipwreck, twenty years ago, a couple of miles past where Bella and Paco are swimming right now. The docent had to pry me off the glass. I told her that I was on the island back then. She pointed at a dagger in the display case. It was five hundred years old. And then she told me how the treasure hunter had lost his mind and killed his wife with it. I collapsed right then and there. I made her tell me everything, but she *never* said anything about a child."

She pulled away to look at him.

"Never," he swore.

"Killed?" she asked.

She went numb.

"Yes," he said.

He pulled her back to his chest. She felt his heart racing.

"*Secrets* was my plea for her to return. But she was already gone."

Elia cuddled beneath his arm. She closed her eyes. A most incredible calm overtook her.

"Here I am," she whispered.

"Elia."

She stood up and stepped down the narrow aisle. She deliberately brushed past her favorite classmate and toward the blackboard at the front of the classroom. Elia had purposefully sat right behind him. She wondered how he might react, what he might say. But most of all, she wanted to know what he smelled like. Clean. As disheveled as he looked, he still smelled fresh. That straggled black hair curling over his collar was freshly washed, just not combed. What did he taste like? She wanted to know that too. She longed to know so many things.

Each of the other master's candidates had presented their start-of-the-semester updates at the front of the cramped seminar room. It reminded Elia of *what I did on my summer vacation* reports, except layered with references to Goethe, Faulkner, Cervantes, Dostoyevsky and the other untouchable gods of Literature. But she had remarkable trouble trying to pay attention. Only upon hearing her name called by Professor Weitzel and taking her cue did she find her palms again gripping into the worn grooves of the mahogany lectern.

She brushed strands of auburn hair from her face. The ends were now bleached golden from the Caribbean sun and sea. She gazed out across her classmates and toward Professor Weitzel. They all looked the same, but different. A few faces were reddened from the sun. Others still looked ghostly white, like they had been chained inside a dungeon the entire summer. The beatnik had shaved off his goatee. Perhaps he had finally run out of Kerouac.

"So, tell us, Ms. Aloundra, have you unearthed the ghost poet? Have you found the reticent Cameron Beck?" Professor Weitzel asked from the back of the classroom.

Images of Cameron and Isabella and Paco and sand crabs and sea turtles and pomegranate seeds swirled about. "Yes," she said.

In her periphery she saw the boy sit up. She still did not look directly at him, but by a flash of white she could tell he was smiling. To a person, her other classmates quieted. Even the carnival-barker jokester and reformed beatnik leaned forward in their chairs. Professor Weitzel pushed his glasses onto his forehead.

"Really? And the muse as well, I take it?" the professor asked.

She clasped the bracelet on her wrist and drifted back to that back room in Paco's island *cantina*. She smelled the fresh catch in the market, the star jasmine outside the hilltop loft and the musty brine of that hidden cave. She felt Isabella's arms around her. Afternoon sunlight streamed through the window. Its glimmer against her bracelet reminded her of Paco's gold-toothed grin.

But mostly Elia felt the embrace of a poet who was no longer a ghost. He was alive and breathing, having jumped off the page into her life.

She looked up. The entire classroom locked on her.

"Please?" she said.

"I imagine you've quite a tale to tell. So what is your thesis? For whom was *Secrets of Odysseus* written?"

She envisioned an orphan kneeling before a cross, that little girl with one question. Her heart, that for so long had seemed so empty, could hardly contain itself.

Her shoulders straightened.

"For whom was it written?" she repeated.

"Yes, please tell us," the professor said.

Elia traced her finger along the bracelet. She felt the large stone embedded in the middle, at the point where all the jeweled beads interconnected. After it had been polished, the grimy emerald that had looked so much like an inverted spade looked a bit more like a heart, at least to her. That's where the beads, surrounded by the sun and the moon and the sea and the birds, intersected—in the heart. Maybe, that's where everything did.

Elia looked up.

In a voice as light as a speck of dust she whispered, "Me."

"Excuse me?" asked the professor.

She smiled and stared directly at the boy. For the first time ever she met his longing gaze. And she did not look away. She smiled at him like she had never smiled at anyone ever before and said, "It was written for me."

ABOUT THE AUTHOR

Kenneth Zak was born in Parma, Ohio in 1962 and resides in San Diego, California. The original manuscript of *The Poet's Secret* was selected a Golden Heart® Finalist in romantic suspense by the Romance Writers of America. The poem "Two Bits" from *The Poet's Secret* previously appeared in Kelp Magazine. His short fiction "A Promise" appeared in *A Year in Ink*, San Diego Writers, Ink Anthology, Volume 4, and his short story "Thea" appeared in *A Year in Ink*, San Diego Writers, Ink Anthology, Volume 8.

The Poet's Secret is his debut novel.

For more information, please visit www.kennethzak.com

ABOUT THE WATER

It's always been about the water: pools, puddles, rain, lakes, rivers and oceans. Seventy percent of the earth's surface is covered by water. Over sixty percent of the human body is water. Much of the water in the universe is a byproduct of star formation. Water is elemental. Water is all-powerful. But like most elemental things water is too often taken for granted. So for every copy of *The Poet's Secret* sold, in addition to Penju Publishing's 1% for the Planet commitment to conservation causes, the author shall donate $1 to The Surfrider Foundation, an organization dedicated to preserving the earth's oceans, waves and beaches.

KENNETH ZAK

ACKNOWLEDGMENTS

My deepest gratitude extends to all who have supported me along this long, serpentine path.

Endless love and thanks to my mother Rita and late father Clayton, and to my son Cooper for asking the right question at just the right time.

Thank you to everyone at Penju Publishing and particularly to my creative gurus Bill Livingston and Randy Gibbs, and, of course, the lovely Gaelle. A heartfelt thank you to Kyona, my Executive Everything, who embodies a lifetime of intentions.

Thank you to author, muse and provocateur Judy Reeves, and to each and every one of the Wednesday night sorcerers who sat around that table and shared their souls.

Thanks to my Sano Surf Club brothers for keeping me afloat all these years. The first rule of Surf Club is you ONLY talk about Surf Club. Here's to our next waves.

Thank you to my many editors, and particularly Jill Patchin and my copyeditor Lisa Wolff.

Thank you to the Romance Writers of America for accepting me into your fold, and a special thank you to the Unsinkables, those awe-inspiring sisters of mine. I am so grateful to be your brother.

Thank you to everyone at San Diego Writers, Ink for years of nurturing so many writers.

Thanks to The Ohio State University, its faculty, student body, alumni and particularly my ageless water polo teammates. You are all Undisputed Champions, Go Bucks.

Thanks for the efforts of everyone associated with 1% for the Planet and The Surfrider Foundation for your dedication to our sustainable blue.

Lastly, I bow to the poets of Avdou, who provided me a candlelit sanctuary during one magical Cretan summer and forever after, and to the literary luminaries in whose inspired light I humbly scribble.